HOLDING SUPERMAN'S HAND

HOLDING SUPERMAN'S HAND

UNDER THE BAR LIGHTS

Amy Katherine

atmosphere press

© 2022 Amy Katherine

Published by Atmosphere Press

Cover design by Kevin Stone

No part of this book may be reproduced without permission from the author except in brief quotations and in reviews. This is a work of fiction, and any resemblance to real places, persons, or events is entirely coincidental.

Atmospherepress.com

"In the end, only three things matter: how much you loved, how gently you lived, and how gracefully you let go of things not meant for you." —*Buddha*

"The mind is everything. What you think you become." —*Buddha*

"It's not just in your head anymore. We have made this real for both of us." —*Matt*

CHAPTER ONE

"The Kiss"

I knew he was behind me. Not that he made a sound as we traversed the wet street in tandem on our way to the car park. After a heavy summer rain, the briny smell of warm cement gave a comforting aroma to the late-night air—a happy smell. Silent though we walked, I knew he was there, catching up to me. The strong invisible rope between us, a bond forged in both trauma and the accompanying resilience of the last two months since we had met, was the only hint he was there at all. And suddenly, he was in my ear as well as in my head.

"You are in such a hurry tonight," he breathed. "So fast. You have exams coming up, right? Going to get some study time in before you go to sleep?" Matt panted as he slowed, his pace matching mine.

"Yes," I managed, tugging at my hairband, holding back my long blond hair. Talking to him still made me incredibly nervous, and I had to concentrate on making my voice come out evenly. He spoke on easily and naturally, his tone full of confidence and affection...affection for me, it seemed tonight from the compliments. That same voice that used to fill me with both irritation and disdain had become something else. Something else entirely. Something that kept him on my mind long after we left the bar on Sixth Street in Austin, Texas, where we both worked into the early morning.

We managed to volley a light conversation back and forth, mostly about exams and the new work schedule that JR, the bar manager, had just posted. Spending time with him like this, as he walked me to my car each night, oddly made me feel refreshed and renewed like I had just woken up. My senses were more heightened and aware; I both dreaded and loved this part of my day. I felt giddy exuberance, as if I had just gotten out of a steaming morning shower, coffee in hand, not that I dared show it. In reality, I had spent much of the morning and afternoon in grueling double time summer classes before hitting the gym hard and eventually rolling into work at ten in the evening. I should feel anything but refreshed at this hour. The glow of the bars' sparse lights and the buzzing incandescent lighting of the late-night pizza venues gave the illusion of midmorning. The bars had closed to Austin revelers at two, but after restocking the liquor shelves and beer fridges, cleaning, counting, and divvying up the enormous piles of money, it was now quickly approaching four a.m.

We made our way past the strip's darkening bars and turned the corner of Seventh Street and Trinity, when suddenly laughter like screeching seagulls startled me. I instinctively leaned in, grabbing his arm. Pleased that I had turned to him to protect me from the unexpected and execrable female horde, a slow smile formed in the corners of his mouth.

"A tiring bunch of loud drunk girls always scares me too." His smile was genuine and accompanied by twinkling piercing brown eyes. Eyes that I had only recently begun to notice. Eyes I didn't dare meet. We continued to walk, only a few blocks from the car now. And then it would be over. I could go home and dream about him.

"You can do this," I whispered so softly it was inaudible

even to myself. Shyly, I moved my hand from his bicep in a half-hearted but fractionally genuine attempt to let go. This rather tepid attempt was met with his other hand tenderly pressing my fingers back to their rightful place on his arm. I wasn't sure what to do in response to this. This embrace was new territory for us. My legs were still walking down the sidewalk, but I could no longer feel them, nor the rest of my body for that matter. My body was buzzing softly all over like a window screen repeatedly attacked by a gentle breeze, never getting a break from the windy onslaught. My trembling fingertips were somehow uproariously communicating their joyful elation to the rest of me. He felt good.

I tried to keep up with the conversation, school, his family's ranch in Wimberly. I suddenly felt like I had been turned into a cloud. A shapeless mass of condensation, floating freely, and somehow, he was the only tether to my barely visible form, guiding me from floating forever lost into a dark oblivion. I often felt like that with him. The warmth emulating from his strong bicep seemed to be somehow flowing into my body, filling me with an almost intolerable heat. I could feel my face burning.

His familiar blue flannel shirt loosely covering his torso made little effort to hide his incredible stature. Working together three to four nights a week for weeks on end, I had noticed. Every girl had. But it was something altogether benumbing to touch his brawny form. His bicep and forearm were so hard it was like they were made of something inhuman. I looked down at my wet Converse and smiled weakly. His comfortable, conversational banter was silencing the shaky voice inside that wanted to scream at this new sensation and unexpected intimacy of his hold.

Since we had first met in the months before the incident that had created a silent and irreparable bond between us, he had attempted to get to know me—asking me out to get three a.m. pancakes at Kerbey Lane or Magnolia Café with a slew of other staff in tow. These friendly group breakfast date attempts were appealing and nonthreatening enough.

However, I had been warned vehemently by my best friend Kate before getting the job. I was a good girl, and she had reminded me, lecturing me relentlessly while simultaneously being nonspecific about the threat. The teddy bear sitting on my bed in the dorm, a gift from my maternal grandmother a few Christmases back, was an analogy for where I was in life at the moment. I was a good girl, actually— that kind of a good girl. And good girls, take heed.

At the start of my job in late May, my desire to make new friends, not just with Matt, who had seemed to dislike me immediately, but the entire staff at the Azure Bar, had made it tempting. I could never be convinced, though. Night after night, I had turned him down. All of them. Even the girls who wanted to socialize outside of work at the university gym or on the campus green known as the South Mall. I was genuinely busy with summer school, overwhelmed by the course load, and wanted to keep my good reputation as a nice person and hard worker, one that had been established the first week I began at Azure. I had found and returned a rather prodigious envelope containing a barback's entire backpay for several months. Bartenders, barbacks, and the bouncers like Matt, it was almost an entirely cash business for us. Henry, the chain-smoking wiry barback, had been out of town attending a funeral, and his envelope had been swept off the old desk in the basement and fallen behind a box, where I had just placed my backpack the second day on the job. His job requirement was the worst, running giant tubs of ice to the coolers on both floors of the bar all night, as well as constant crates of beer. Henry was not the only person who noticed my altruistic deed and was impressed.

"You stand out around here," Matt had said the following week, removing his hat and running his fingers through his wavy dark brown hair, making me suddenly feel young and insecure. Quickly judging my face, he added, "It's a good thing," uttering the first nice words he had ever spoken to me. "Henry looks young, but he's actually super old like me," He paused to shake sawdust off his shirt and continued. "He has a two-year-old daughter to support. And a lot of people would not have returned a thousand dollars in cash. You are sweet, Amy," he added with a chuckle. Wow, he was actually speaking nicely to me for once.

"Old?" I asked, "and what is that approximately, mid-forties?" I had worked to keep my face inquisitive and serious. Matt had frowned.

"No, we are both twenty-eight. That's not old, really," he said, a pained look on his face. "Just old for Sixth Street. For this job, I mean." I smiled cynically. "I'm in graduate school for finance," he added reluctantly, clearly feeling the need to defend himself. I smiled again and admitted that I was only joking. His face remained severe and slightly hurt, but his soft brown eyes twinkled at me to say that all was forgiven. And to say that he was proud of me for joking around and stepping out of my comfort zone for seemingly the first time since we had met.

The more I turned down attempts to meet up after work while maintaining I was busy with school and declaring I didn't have a boyfriend or other social plans, the more curious I made the staff. At seventeen, I was not just the youngest staff member, I was an illegal hire for a bar. Johnny Ray kept me off the books on a cash-only basis with no time card. I was "training" with the other bartenders, especially Jason, for an extended time. Specifically, until November when I would finally be eighteen. Bartending was fun, and I immediately became good at it, loving the speed, cadence, and focus needed to work fast in crowds and exchange light banter with regulars when it was slow. I was a cocktail waitress on occasion when required. And wherever I worked—main bar, upstairs bar, or waitressing—my Herculean shadow was leaning on a wall nearby, arms crossed over his chest.

Suddenly, I stopped walking, still in cloud-la la land, attached to my tether that had apparently stopped short. He had asked me a question and was waiting on my response, somewhat amused at my inability to pay him any attention.

"What?" I managed apologetically. I looked him in the eyes now, an attempt, I hoped, at showing I was sorry for not giving him any attentiveness. Had I been daydreaming about my crush while ignoring him in his very presence? Wow. I must really be exhausted. "I'm so sorry, Matt, it's been a long day and a longer night. I am super tired."

"It's okay." He smiled reassuringly and replaced my hand, linking my arm in his to cross another street. He had been talking about pancakes apparently and which ones were his favorite from Kerbey Lane. An attempt to ask me out again? Not sure, I hadn't been listening, which I now regretted even more. I was thinking of taking him up on it. But not tonight. I was genuinely tired, and honestly, my nerves had taken over any space that hunger might have occupied. When would I stop feeling like this around him? I stole a quick glance. Paul Bunyan, I mussed to myself, smiling. I bet he could eat a thousand pancakes right now. Guessing correctly as to the question, I told him I loved the banana macadamia ones best. But quickly added that the buckwheat ones had a special place in my heart. He stopped, turning to me, his face serious and only his eyes full of fun and laughter. He didn't want to be talking about pancakes right now. And suddenly, I didn't either. Instantly, I felt like a desirable nubile woman with how he was looking at me, not at all like the frightened girl in a ponytail, wearing wet canvas shoes. His gaze scared me. It was like looking into the future and seeing what would become. It was seeing how he jostled his foot nervously under the table while keeping his voice kind and steady in deep conversation. In a look, I could see the thoughtful husband he would be, the way he twirled his pencil when he was reading in focused concentration, the sort of protective patient father he would become, one arm behind himself balancing the toddler on his shoulder. His soft brown eyes were like magical orbs telling me secrets of the future. Our future. It was too much for shy me, though I wanted this silent telepathic conversation so badly to continue. I had to break away.

I stepped off the sidewalk and into the street and felt his hand on my back. Not gentle and kind but steadying me at first, then assertive. I was instinctively not afraid of him, but I was confused as to what was happening. I couldn't imagine what he was doing, but I managed not to scream. The fist on my back grabbed my shirt deftly and twisted it, gleaning a better grip as he thrust me forward, directing my feet from behind. Then I felt it. Like a bomb had gone off. There was confusion at first, and then I was aware of dull noises that turned into loud thuds and then screams as partygoers ran for cover. A Bronco near us screeched as it overcorrected a turn in our direction. My first thought was a shooter.

"Matt." I was able to at least say his name. My heart was beating out of its chest as we quickened our pace down Brazos Street. I repeated it, my voice somehow replacing "help me" with his name. "Matt," I called out again. "Matthew." This time, it was barely a whisper escaping my lips. Now his name had morphed into an umbrella word meant to communicate that I was scared but that I trusted him, that I was confused, and possibly going to become angry. "Matt!" I called a fourth time, this time more assertively. Still no response. He was focused on something I couldn't see—those seconds with him guiding me and not speaking felt like an eternity.

I realized we were running now. I was wet. He was holding my hand, pulling me along Seventh Street. Streams of water were dripping down my temples and collecting to fall together in droplets off my chin. Something rammed into my shoulder, knocking me off balance as two strong arms reached to steady me. My shoulder hurt but not severely. More like unpleasantly irritating, very much like the entire situation itself. Where was this water come from? I could feel the water soaking my shirt, creating suction to my skin. I tugged at it unsuccessfully. My second thought was maybe we were being hit by a famous Texas summer storm. Sudden and strong.

Mid-run, I managed to turn and face him, never breaking stride, and uttered something to the effect of, "I am scared. What's happening? Answer me." In that exact moment, inertia still with us, I heard him laughing as he scooped me up in his strong arms, my legs wrapped around his waist, my head laying on his shoulder. My beating heart found his. We had never been so close as we were now. I was so frightened, and I felt like crying. I was weary-tired and suddenly ravenously hungry. And though I was not scared of him, I was truly scared. Scared of something unseen in the night. He ran us over across the street, over the sidewalk, and into the safety of a building enclave.

Between the two giant marble pillars, we took refuge. He had pushed me up the concrete ledge and into the aperture first, with his massive body joining mine seconds later. We had just enough space to both stand and for him to lean in closer and whisper in my ear.

"It's okay." He smiled, breathing hard. "You look so scared." My hair was dripping wet, and I was honestly completely petrified at this point.

"What?" My squinting eyes were angry but pleading with him to behave himself and to tell me what he knew, and I did not. He leaned back on the pillar behind him and looked up at the high ceilings of the awning that supported the bank building in which we had found refuge. I was beginning to relax, sensing his ease. "What? What is this? Matthew, tell me this moment!" I was stern-sounding and irritated enough for him to notice and find it funny. He threw back his barrel chest and laughed so heartily that all the irritation was instantly replaced with wonder. I felt amused curiosity at how a man who physically looked exactly like Superman could sound just like Santa Claus. "You laugh like Santa," I chortled. I was trying to be insulting, but oddly he took this as a compliment.

"Thank you." He dismissed my words, pulling me backward onto his knee to whisper in my ear. "Water balloons, sweetheart." I couldn't see his face, but I could tell he was smiling by how he formed his words through his teeth. "Scared me too, to be honest. We are okay, though, aren't we?"

"Oh, my goodness, of all strange things." I looked out to the street and saw blue, green, and red spheres pelting down at cars, people, trees, anything and everything that moved. "Where?" He pointed his finger straight upwards.

"The roof." That did explain the screaming and the water. I laughed then, relief flooding over my body, images of a shooter leaving my worried mind. I flipped my head down and twisted the water from my long blond hair like a towel. "You look like you just got out of the shower," he said admiringly.

"Out of the shower with my jeans and shirt on, like every night," I added, instantly wishing I hadn't attempted a joke. I always felt so shy around him. He smiled, seeing my fear had dissipated entirely now. Shifting my eyes from him to the graffiti on the wall, I shivered slightly, and he reached out intrinsically to touch my forearm.

"Amy, you are cold." It was not a question; rather something he would decide for me. He looked around, lightly patting down his shirt and undershirt, both ranged from damp to soaking. "Come to me." He opened his inviting arms. "Just to get warm. I'm cold too."

"I am not that cold. I will be okay, I think." This would be too much.

"You think? Not good enough for me." He lunged at me then, using his foot propped up on the back pillar to push himself towards me. Arms open, he caught me and spun me around before I could protest. Slowly, we fell backward together to the marble, where we stayed. He leaned back on his pillar, his massive arms wrapped around mine, my back to his chest. "Feels better?"

"Yes," I admitted, too embarrassed by the embrace to talk further. His chest was as hard as his arms. "You're bumpy," I murmured. We were both distracted by a group of men running from incoming balloon fire.

"What was that?" He hadn't heard me. Good. It was a weird thing to say to someone. I tried again.

"When we renovate this place, can we put in a fireplace?" He looked down at me, smiling broadly, his bright white teeth gleaming in the soft light. "Are you so comfortable with me now that you are telling dumb jokes?" I smiled shyly. I wasn't sure what to say to this. He leaned down to reach my ear. His soft, warm breath brought instant goosebumps springing up on my arms. He pulled my hair away from my neck and rested his hand there momentarily. "Tell me something else dumb." His huge hands dropped down to my waist and then rose slowly to reach my rib cage, ready to attack. I didn't care.

"Matt," I whispered back to him, laughing. His fingertips dug into my ribs softly but firmly, sending all of my nerve endings on fire with tortuous tickles. Our home became an echo of screams, and more bad jokes, followed by howling laughter and more screams. Panting and happy, I half-turned the side of my face to him, against his chest, looking outside and trying to catch my breath. "You have a nice laugh." I smiled happily, breathing hard and looking up at him. His hand reached out, touching the side of my face, and I stepped back. Suddenly embarrassed by my compliment and our intimacy within the nook, I blurted out, "So can we leave?" Not that I actually wanted this night ever to end.

"No. The police will be here any minute. We better stay here." Just as he spoke, a man carrying a pizza was lobbed with yellow and pink spheres, sending his pizza box flying.

"Oh no. Poor guy," I whispered. He was shaking his fists and cursing at the pranksters above us. Oh wow, that was graphic. Matt covered my ears.

"Don't listen." He smiled. I pulled away from his chest, where I had been recovering from my tickle session, and stood up in my allotted space that seemed unfairly small in comparison.

"No. We should go," I said sleepily. "We could be stuck here all night." He shook his head slowly.

"We could. Let's stay. Honestly, I could not have planned this better if I would have tried. I think you know by now—well maybe you do; I've been trying to get a moment to talk with you. We never get that. You usually get better parking." I smiled. It was a far walk tonight.

"Okay, fine." I relented, feeling my pulse race and my heartbeat quicken and hoping it was not visible through my clothing. "Tell me whatever you need to. I'm here. Maybe forever," I blushed. "I'm listening."

"I feel," he began, as a water balloon exploded directly outside, splashing our pants. I squealed, and he leaned forward and grabbed both of my wrists in a gesture of both earnestness and grave seriousness. "Listen to me. What happened to you a month ago. It was horrible. And you are such a good, kind person. Honestly, it's been killing me. I want you to know how sorry—"

"Please," I suddenly felt like I had lost my voice. I didn't want this. There was a lump in my throat. Why was he bringing this up now while we were having so much fun? My guard was so down—I didn't want to do this.

"Let me finish. Please, Amy." His tone was caring but parental and stern. He needed his say. "I want you to know that none of that was your fault. I found out from Charlie that he made you a sugar shot, and it wasn't alcohol you took with those guys. You were just doing your job. I thought you disobeyed me, and to be honest, I was angry at first. Not that you deserved any of that, of what happened, regardless. But you didn't disobey me, did you?" I shook my head. I hadn't.

"And to be clear... it would not be your fault even if you had."

"I know. Please don't. We don't need to discuss anything." I looked down, tugging on a hangnail. I couldn't meet his eyes again. It had taken me almost three weeks to look at him after the fight. I didn't want to go back to that place where I would be behind the bar, totally aware that he was behind me restocking, but I couldn't dare myself to look at him. I sighed, remembering every fiber of my being, stressed until he was out of sight around the bend of the stairwell. He had behaved so naturally, and I had shamefully avoided him for weeks. The staff knew, I was sure of it. There were witnesses at the bar, and people talk. The girls on staff had been extra kind and sweet to me. Amber had even knitted me a hideous yellow scarf, but I was sure it was a genuine and thoughtful gesture. I had worn it a few times out of gratitude before putting it away. But in the back of the cab that night, a seatbelt over both of us, only he had seen me crying, almost whimpering in his arms, and only I had seen and attempted to wipe the blood streaming from his temple with my sleeve. That was for us alone. "You don't need to say anything," I reassured. "But to be honest, I do," I paused, finding the strength to push through this awkward moment, "Actually, I need to say something to you, Matthew." I was stalling.

The memory of his cut and blooded knuckles was a searing image in my mind weeks on, and now I couldn't shake it. It was like he had been hitting a brick wall for ten minutes. "Well..." I couldn't find the right words. He let me finish, his body language eager to hear what I had to say. "Matt." He waited patiently without prompting me, unwilling to put words in my mouth. "You were so brave and kind to me. I never thanked you properly for what you did. I thought I would die, and you took care of everything and gave me the confidence that I wasn't."

"I would never have let that happen to you."

I nodded, certain it was true or at least he believed it. "Still,

I was so scared, and I appreciate you. All that you did." I forced myself to look up at him. He looked serious. Very unlike Santa in any way now. "Thank you, Matt." I squeezed his hand, feeling better that I had finally said something that needed saying after nearly a month.

"We went through something very hard together. I imagine that was difficult for you being so young...and pretty." His hand reached out and grazed my jawbone. The sexual tension between us was pulled taut, and something inside me began to hurt. Hurt. Hurt.

"Oh no. Matt, how are your ribs anyway? I heard from Charlie that—" I stopped, not wanting to say it.

"Well." He popped the brim of his hat up, flicking it with a snapping sound. "Four cracked ribs, three on the left side, and one right." He smiled proudly like they were a privilege as he lightly touched over his chest. "Hurts when I lift heavy, but I'll be just fine. I'm on the mend." He started to speak, but I interrupted him.

"Don't. It's a part of us now, I get that, but I don't think we need to talk about it all the time."

"Well, I agree. We don't need to talk about it all the time. The thing is, we never did talk about it, Amy. Also, you are a girl. And you are acting weird. So, I wanted to make sure that you are okay." He paused to drop his hat to the floor and run his hands through his wavy brown hair in light exasperation. It was wet. So apparently, he had gotten hit as much as me. It wasn't as noticeable until now, seeing his hair. It had all happened so fast.

I was suddenly even more grateful he was with me. I wouldn't have known what to do alone. Maybe hide behind that white Chevy truck like the unfortunate couple still getting pelted outside. Their random screams were distracting. I hoped they were okay. Why hadn't they moved yet? They didn't have a Matt with them, I concluded.

"Amy, look at me, please," He waited for my deep blue-green eyes to meet his. "Hey," he almost whispered. "I know you are tired. Last thing I need to say. It won't happen again. Statistically, it won't. But also, I won't allow it. I'll be there faster next time, should there be any trouble, and..." He paused, choosing his words carefully, trying not to scare me. "I won't take my eyes off you again." He paused and leaned in closer to me and added. "I should have killed them. I could have. I might regret that until the day I die." I shook my head at him.

"No."

"Yes. I mean, it would have been a hassle if I had. We would be better off with no news and less police. Less paperwork." He tried to make light of the verbal boulder of what he had just said. I stared at the wall past him, stunned that anyone would say something like this, and my face showed it. He didn't apologize for himself. I had no response, so I just shook my head, my wet hair dripping. My eyes burned, and I wiped a stream of water from my face. Where was the water coming from now? I wasn't sure. Maybe I was crying.

"No, Matt." He pulled my face close to his, so our foreheads were touching. I looked at my shoes. I felt him nodding "yes." Silently arguing about something we both knew was overkill and ridiculous. He kissed my forehead sweetly, and when he pulled away, I could see the reflection of police lights on his handsome face: red and blue flashes of color on his cheek and in his hair.

"Amy." His eyes were studying me carefully.

"Hum?" I wanted to collapse in his arms in an emotional, physical fit of fatigue. But I also wanted to stay with him, in this nook in the bank building crevice, as long as possible, building us and showing my maturity and my strength. What little of it there was left. All the things in my heart and in my head were becoming manifest here in the nook.

Then he said it. Words I secretly ached to hear. Words I

suspected to be true for both of us for some time now: "Amy, I am falling so hard for you." He shifted his stance and momentarily closed his eyes. "I think about you all the time. You are always on my mind morning and night." He opened his eyes and found mine. "You are beautiful. Smart, innocent, kind. All the things that are void in this industry. In the world, really. All the things I have wanted to find in someone." At least it was said. It wasn't love. Not yet anyway. But it was close, and I was just as smitten. This Herculean man, smart and handsome, had said that I was beautiful. His words baffled me, and yet they burned like a brand on my heart, searing their emotional meaning to me. He had shown himself so many times now. I knew his heart, his character. I smiled, reassuring him that his words were well received.

"I feel the same. I had all these things in my head. I thought it was just me. I like you too," I said incredulously, dazed by my own confidence.

"It's not just in your head anymore. We have made this real for both of us." He smiled back at me but instantly took me off guard. "May I kiss you? I would really like to kiss you." I had waited for this moment for so long! Everything seemed to be happening so fast. All of my childhood dreams about boys and love had all led me to a water balloon fight in an Austin, Texas, bank building at what was quickly approaching five a.m. on a warm July morning in 1999.

I nodded, brushing the blond flyaways from my face, and closed my eyes. I smiled, and then, trembling, I opened my mouth, waiting for my kiss. The seconds flew by in my head fast and then slow. Nothing. He didn't kiss me. I closed my mouth, opened my eyes, and found him looking at me with a curious and amused look on his face. He smiled, his eyes locked on mine, but he didn't say anything, which made it feel copiously worse inside my girl brain. Did he suddenly just not find me as attractive as he had literally declared seconds earlier? Could boys be as fickle as girls in this way? His low voice startled me.

"Amy." What? I couldn't talk out loud. But I was starting to love the sound of his voice saying my name. "Has anyone ever kissed you before?"

"Yes," I answered flatly. Why was he asking me this? He was ruining this. I thought I wanted him to kiss me, but now I felt uneasy.

"On the mouth?" he asked, smiling widely, his eyes searching mine.

"Well. No," I admitted. His face showed total awe and some disbelief, so I quickly added, "On the cheek only. Religious community. Strict parents. Is it very obvious?" Clearly, it was. This was horrible. I dropped my eyes to the ground, completely embarrassed. "I guess I don't know what to do," I admitted looking past him to the marble wall finding comfort in its chalky plainness.

"No, it's okay." He was holding my hand now, his thumb rubbing circles on the back of it. "So, the first thing is, I'm not a dentist, so you don't need to open your mouth like that." He laughed. I could feel the heat flash in my cheeks and flood across my chest like lava.

"Oh, okay," I whispered. He smiled, touching my jawbone tenderly with his thumb, heartening my bruised soul.

"Well, I am a little surprised because you are so beautiful. But I am so happy..." His hand lightly touched over his heart. "I am so honored that it is me who gets to teach you." He spoke slowly and carefully, like he was speaking to a child afraid of something. And I knew that he meant every word. "Honestly, it's okay, Amy. I'm so happy."

"Great." I was feeling relieved that my inexperience was not so wholly unattractive that all bets were off. "So, what should I do?"

"Just stand there and look exactly like that." He was on me like an ocean wave crashing into my body. His lips were gentle and soft. His hand was already behind my head, so his force didn't bump me into the marble pillar. I could feel the back of his hand getting lightly crushed behind my head, but he didn't seem to notice. He was both gentle and forceful, and he tasted like peppermint. There is nothing I had ever experienced before that could have prepared me for this kiss. There were no words now for what he was saying to me. But he told me everything I needed to know. My body felt limp in his arms, his hands now on both sides of my face supported me and changed the angle when we needed it. At times he seemed unaware of where to put his hands. They moved from my shoulders to my collarbone and even his pockets. I loved this new language, but he wasn't telling me everything tonight. I closed my eyes. I could hear myself making little noises like the sound you make when you pick up heavy groceries, only slower and in a whisper. He opened his eyes and smiled, pulling me to him again. I was beginning to understand the dynamics of our unfamiliar language when suddenly I pulled away, gasping.

"Matt."

"Oh no, sweetheart. Are you okay?"

"I can't breathe. I think maybe you are going to kill me," I panted. He lightly touched the tip of my nose with his finger like he was disciplining an infant.

"Breathe through your nose, silly." He laughed, giving me a second for air before invading my mouth again. I smiled, leaning back, the force of his kiss rocking me backward and his hand cradling me just in time. I was making soft sounds again, unfamiliar to myself, and the only known consonants to our new language.

"Mmmm." I stopped when I heard myself, unsure if it was him or me. What was I doing? I sounded like I was trying to repeatedly say the letter *M* in a thousand different ways. Matt looked up.

"The cute sounds?" he guessed. "I like it."

"What are you doing to me?" He smiled at my question.

Then he leaned into me again to taste my mouth and caress my arms. His tongue probing, then retreating to slowly and softly kiss my lips, and finally pulled back from me completely.

"Amy. Amy. Amy. Amy." He was shaking his head slowly, looking down at the marble below our shoes. Oh no, was this good or bad? "You taste so good. That was so nice. Thank you. So, how was it? Did you enjoy your first real kiss?" Greatly relieved that he liked it too, I whispered back to him.

"I did," I murmured, falling back on the cold pink pillar breathless.

"Describe kissing to me then." His handsome brown eyes locked on mine, fascinated by what I might say as a proper review.

"Well...it felt like our bodies were embracing but floating in an ocean." He smiled, eyes twinkling in the low light of the streetlamp near us. "Your turn. My turn. The ocean waves pulling us to and fro. Your turn. My turn. And somehow, we swallowed that ocean so that all we knew, or ever had known, was the cadence of the waves inside us. All I could think about was you. Not the water balloons or the world..." I trailed off, looking outside to the quiet, empty street—no signs of hooligans or a police presence now. I turned back to him, a broad satisfied smile growing on his face. "Lots of times it was your turn, your turn, your turn. But I was glad about that. I don't know what I'm doing, and I liked how the way that you were kissing me gave me little tingles all over my body."

"Really?" His voice was delighted and two octaves higher than usual.

"Yes. And they would fade and then come back again suddenly. Again and again." I reached out and ran my nails lightly down his giant forearm to his wrist. "It was like this. All over me."

He shook his head and then smiled, pulling me in closely for a hug. We stayed motionless for some time; the pinkening sky gave a holiday glow to our hair and skin. He touched my head lightly.

"I like this too. You are very sapient."

"Sapient?"

"It means smart. Never mind then, babe." We both howled with laughter as we stepped out into the soft light. "Your first kiss. My best kiss." I looked up at him disbelieving. "I mean it. Promise." He nodded truthfully, his eyes twinkling. "So, where did you park again?" I smiled, taking his outstretched arm, and walked into the soft glow of morning.

"Hatred does not cease by hatred, but only by love; this is the eternal rule." —*Buddha*

"Early us was not good us." —*Amy*

CHAPTER TWO

"They Call Him the Haymaker"

He watched me pull away from the curb and head back towards west campus; then, he turned back at a brisk jog towards the bar. Pulling into my parking spot in the adjacent garage to my dorm off Pearl Street, I checked myself in the rearview. Pretty good actually, my left eye had some mascara smears; otherwise, I looked normal. Thank goodness.

The security guards' judgmental looks were not a great welcome home as I walked through the silent lobby heading to the elevator. They were usually so friendly. Maybe not morning people, I surmised sleepily.

I unlocked my room quietly and tiptoed to the shower, kicking my jeans off my ankle with the help of my other foot. "Matt," I whispered his name to the friendly hot water running over my hair and face. My aching body was so tired. Wrapped only in my towel, I fell onto my comforter, not even bothering to get underneath it. A minute of heavenly deep sleep passed. My phone rang, and my roommate stirred on the other side of the room. I lunged for it in a feeble attempt to silence the sound.

"You got home." It was a statement.

"Umm," I mumbled.

"I miss you. Go back to sleep," he said and hung up.

"Umm," I spoke into the empty receiver. I laid the phone down on the floor, my arm flung over the side of the bed, and resumed my sleeping.

Moments later, I could hear my roommate waking up for Friday summer school classes, and apparently, she had to put my phone back on the receiver to silence the intolerable honking.

"Sorry, Kate," I murmured into my pillow.

At 1:00, I woke up and made coffee. I had one class starting at 2:00, and then I needed to go to weigh-in and drill practice. I wanted to stay at home longer in case he called, but reluctantly I left at 1:45, cutting across the mall to get to the English lit building in central campus.

It was the late nineties, and plenty of my friends had pagers or cell phones, but I didn't feel the need yet. I had a phone in my room, which was the only time I had to talk anyways, I argued. If I was out, I was busy.

The day was balmy, and a soft breeze flitted easily through the leaves as I walked. A heavy gust picked up my long hair, where it hung at my waist, and scattered it in my face, momentarily blinding me. I checked my wrist. No hairband. Shoot. The UT clock tower chimed, signifying my imminent tardiness, and I rushed on. Pigeons scattered at my passing around the student union, and I paused long enough to empty my granola crumbs on the grass for them.

My class passed by slowly. I tried not to think about him. The professor was discussing Bronte's *Jane Eyre*, and though it was a good read and lively discussion was ensuing, I was a cloud with no tether. I drifted in and out of the conversation, easily coming back time and again to the cold marble and warm arms under the awning.

At four, the discussion groups finally dispersed, and I caught sight of my friend, Stephanie. We walked together under the blaring Texas sun towards the stadium gym. I took out my water bottle and took a long sip. Looking at me disparagingly, she tapped it out of my hand, where it landed on the floor.

"After." She reminded.

I smiled, tossing it in the recycle bin. We walked down the long corridor towards the changing rooms, eventually getting in line.

"Emerson. Amy Emerson." I walked up to the assistant coach and shyly dropped my robe. "107," she said without looking up, still briskly typing on the laptop on her lap. I nodded and retrieved my garment. I took a shower, changed into my sports gear, and headed to the stadium.

Outside, some girls were already stretching. Some cordial waves and a few friendly greetings, and the head coach came out of the office onto the field track. She walked past me and smiled. I was glad she was our coach. I had liked her immediately when I had met her last month. Safety and positivity seemed to be her main focuses.

"Okay, some of us are up, and some of us are down. You know who you are. You know what you have to do. You are all precious and amazing! Proud to be here with you. Let's get to WORK. Go!" She blew the whistle hanging from her lanyard, and we started on the first lap around the stadium track. Workouts and drills were my new bread and butter now. And despite the time they took, it was fun.

Stephanie met my pace. "Hey, listen, thanks for your copies of *Wuthering Heights* and *The Tempest*. I saw them by my locker with a note, and I knew straight away you had responded to my ad I posted at the student union bulletin board."

"Well, I read them fast and enjoyed them both. I included my notes." I smiled. "Not cheating. Just my opinions and some highlights. How did you know it was me?"

"You put a ribbon around them with a hand-painted note. Honestly, I didn't expect anyone to respond. But a letter, smoked almonds, and ribbon—I only know one person that nice."

"Geez." I smiled. "You're welcome, of course, no big deal. Glad you got them."

"What's different about you, though? You seem distracted. Your mom?"

"No. Actually, she's good and I'm great. Good news. I had my first..." I paused, not wanting to sound weird to my new friend. "I kissed someone last night. Someone I think I really like."

"Really! Oh, do tell," she panted.

"Well, we work together. Known each other for a bit." My sides were cramping.

"Is it that guy? From the university gym, we sometimes see."

"Yes! Him!"

"Is he nice, though?" She seemed concerned. "He's cute. Total gym rat, huh? He seemed like he was in a bad mood last time."

"He was in a bad mood. He often is. But..." It was hard to explain Matt. "He's a solid, really good guy, I think. He carries the weight of the world on his shoulders."

"He can probably hold it too. Hard yards, that guy." She smiled her braids swishing. "Is he a good kisser?"

"Oh, my goodness." I paused, making the assumption. "Yes!"

"Did y'all like each other right away...a love or lust at first sight sort of thing?"

We were on mile two—three more to go. Then weight training. Done. I could finally go home and rest before going to work.

"No, actually. We disliked each other from the first moment we met," I frowned and looked over at her. "Early us was not good us." I laughed, thinking it over. "He hated me right away."

She smiled, then giggled. "That's hilarious. I don't believe it. If he is a grouchy dude, he is probably just like that to everyone. Who would dislike you, Amy? You are so giving, agreeable, and freaking nice."

"Thanks, friend." I smiled and stopped at the water station. We both downed twelve ounces, tossed the cups in the can, and continued our run. "Sadly, no, we didn't like each other when we met in early May."

"Go on." The main coach had gone inside, and we could keep an even ten-minute relaxing mile now. It was refreshing, and we could talk.

"So, growing up, my dad had money issues. He sometimes poorly invested, day traded. We would be high, then low. That sort of thing. He's the salt of the earth, best dad in the world, but financially it can be good, or it can be hard." She nodded, taking in this new information about me. "Everything's okay. I love my parents with my whole heart, but it makes me a little unstable when it comes to university." She nodded. "And with summer school classes being what they are and with this taking so much time…" I looked at her desperately, and she giggled. "I honestly don't know if I can keep this scholarship. Like anyone, I need to maintain my health and a 2.0, and there are so many meets for drills, it's just tough to keep up with the studying. I am having a hard time being everywhere at once."

"Me too! Go on about the boy," she prompted.

I laughed, out of breath. "Well, so the secretary at my dorm, she's friends with the manager of a bar downtown named JR, and she asked on my behalf if I could go interview. And as you now know, I bartend at Azure. I figured I could save some money quickly and not wreck my course load. Just my sleep schedule," I laughed. "It's nonexistent."

She grinned. "It is hard to picture you in a bar, Amy."

"Ah, well, I don't have time for shift work at a coffee shop. My only availability is midnight."

"Ah, so true. And it's so funny you actually know the

secretary at your dorm. Amy, no more backstory."

"Okay, well, she's super sweet." I breathed. She smiled at me as we jogged on. "So, the first night, JR had explained on the phone how things would go. That I was too young to be technically hired, but that my birthday was only six months away and that he could pay me in cash and keep me as a trainee."

"Isn't it all a cash business downtown anyways?"

"Yes, but like waitstaff apparently, there are these time-cards, and you earn like three dollars an hour that must be officially reported, taxes paid on it, that sort of thing."

"Ahh. Okay."

"JR had gone over some things with me over the phone but apparently ran out of time to inform Matt, who was checking ID at the door. JR is his uncle and loves Matt. Matt runs security, is an assistant manager. Essentially everything."

"Right."

"So, as I walk in the first night, he grabs my arm and says 'ID' to me. Thinking this was a security issue only and JR had told him about my situation, I reached into my pocket and fished out my driver's license.

"He looks at it with this rude disbelieving look on his face and says, 'This is a bar, not an ice cream store. They sell candy and ice cream that way.' He pointed his finger judgmentally towards Fourth Street.

"'Oh, hi.' I responded shyly. 'You must be Matt.' He looked at me rather quizzically then.

"'What is this?' he demanded.

"'I'm the new hire. Maybe JR said something to you?'

"'He did not.' He slowly handed me back my ID. 'Why would he hire a little kid?'

"'Excuse me. I am an adult. I go to the university. And I think—' He cut me off.

"'You are not an adult, legally or otherwise. Your little brain has not stopped growing yet.'

"My eyes had popped at this insolent remark. Such a meanie. 'Why are you so rude?'

"'Because you are so young. There has been some sort of mistake, and you need to leave.'

"'I won't.'

"'You will.' He stepped closer to me.

"'I will scream.' I moved farther back. He stopped in his tracks, his eyes blazing.

"'I am not going to hurt you. I am going to remove you. Put you outside where you belong.'

"'Like some alley cat.'

"He paused at my odd remark. 'Okay,' he said flatly."

Stephanie burst out laughing, then coughing, from the exertion of our run. "Big guy did not say that stuff to you, Amy. You are making this up." She was gasping for air, completely entertained by my sob story on the subject of love.

"This is exactly as it happened. May was a crazy month with training, moving into the dorm, and meeting this guy." I looked at her laughing. "It gets worse."

"What? And now you guys like each other two months later? You are too forgiving."

"Maybe I am. We do. I think we really do."

"Go on. We have three miles left."

"So, he takes me by the hand and pulls me towards the back of the bar. My legs stiffen, and my Keds slide along the smooth floorboards like a child being pulled away from the zoo. Like I was skating."

"Haha!" She laughed at my description.

"'Where are you taking me?' I asked, worried. He didn't speak. Across the length of the bar, we paraded in front of what would be my new friends, the now horrified staff. Down the steps he dragged me, through the narrow corridor, to the office door. Bang bang bang. I had never heard someone knock on a door so hard. My ears rang. Not waiting for a response or an invitation, he opened the door with such force, it slammed backward then tried to close on us as we entered. His hand shielded my face from it as it returned the assault. Seated at his desk, JR looked up.

"'I found this,' he nodded at me, 'and we need to talk about it.'"

"What! So rude!" Stephanie said, repeating "this," her eyes enormous.

"I know, right." I stopped momentarily to retie my trainers.

"Go on."

"So, JR goes on to explain to him that the bar earnings numbers are down. He spoke about how they needed to work on their PR, the bar image, the brand. That he had hired a college cheerleader and that night, when needed, I would change into uniform and do back handsprings down the length of the downstairs bar."

"'What?' He looked at his uncle in disbelief. 'No, man. No way.'

"'Why not?' JR challenged.

"'She's too young to work here.'

"'She doesn't technically work here. She is in training for six months. I will move her around with different bartenders. Pay her in cash only. That's the way around it. That's how I see it.'

"'It seems...' Matt looked for the right word. 'Inappropriate. Fucking inappropriate.'

"'Hey,' I looked up in horror, struggling to escape the grip he had on my hand.

"'Don't move.' He didn't even look at me, and I stopped moving.

"'Don't speak like a boy in front of me,' I warned him. He looked down at me.

"'I am a man, and that's how I speak. Bars are adult places where adult people drink alcohol, curse, and generally attempt to fuck each other figuratively or literally.'

"I opened my mouth, stunned. 'Don't say that.' My voice was soft but shrill. Mortified, I closed my eyes in silent prayer that he would magically turn nice or into a pumpkin, hoping they didn't notice my bright reddening face. I wanted this job to be a friendly and lucrative situation for everyone. I prayed things would work out. This was not going well.

"'JR.' Matt was stern.

"'My mind is made up. We need this. She needs the money. It's good for everyone. The staff too. We don't want to lay anyone off this fall, and we need to be the hot bar again.' He nodded towards me. 'We can be proactive about that. Little things here and there.'

"Matt looked down at me.

"'Little Thing…don't you have a scholarship? Cheerleader?'

"'Yes. I might lose it. I'm struggling with my classes, and I need to maintain my GPA. Doing well now, but it's so much to manage with drills and meets. Obviously, school must come first.'

"'Taking this on will not help you. Only hurt you. Welcome to the night. We don't sleep.'

"He turned back to his uncle. 'Fuck you, JR.'

"JR smiled and opened his laptop. Matt dragged me to the door and pushed me through it gently but forcefully, slamming it behind him. Back on the main floor, I turned to Matt as he released his grip on my hand.

"'Listen, I need this. I will be good. I will obey any and all the rules of the bar. I won't be a problem for you.'

"'You are already a problem for me. We need rules for this situation. For you.'

"'Okay, no problem. I will listen to you. Proceed.'

"'Rule one. Even the British don't think you're old enough to drink. So, you will not drink here. Everyone else who works here, even the beer delivery guys, are all over twenty-one. Sometimes, there are situations after hours at someone's house or with staff and regulars taking shots before closing, but not you. No one can buy you a drink either. The law doesn't care about who pays.'

"'I don't drink. I have never actually had a drink before. Except...' He waited, somewhat surprised. 'I had Chambord about four months ago. It's a French raspberry liqueur, and it was drizzled on a grapefruit. At La Zona Rosa's Café, or wait, maybe it was Maybree's. I don't remember. It must have been a misunderstanding with the waitstaff. I didn't know Chambord was alcohol when I ordered it.'

"'Okay, enough talking. You fucking stress me out. Listen.' I cringed. 'Rule two, you do what I say. No one is too high-ranking or female enough to be exempt from restocking glasses or wiping down bottles during downtime.'

"'Okay. I am a really hard worker. No problem here, either.'

"'Three...I will always—' A voice behind the bar interrupted us.

"'Matt, fire in the well.'

"'Damn.' He looked over at Henry. 'That could be three, actually.' I looked up and noticed the bar had grown more crowded.

"'What does it mean?' I followed him, trying to memorize rule three.

"'Don't scoop ice with a fucking glass. Use a metal mixer only. It breaks, and legally I've got to poor all this ice out in the back alley and replace it. Every piece.'

"'Oh no! That must be so irritating! Especially when it is packed in here.'

"'Yes,' he said, straining as he lifted the full ice container out of the well. It must have been a hundred pounds empty. 'It is irritating, as you expressly stated, so don't do it.'

"'Okay. Can I help you with it now?'

"'No. Get out of the way.' He made his way behind the bar, the enormous container in his hands. 'Behind!' He was speaking to James now, letting the bartender know not to step back. Like a culinary kitchen, I noted, dodging another bartender to comply with Matt's instructions.

"In Matt's fifteen-minute absence, I was passed around from person to person, meeting most of the staff and finding them all to be stupendously friendly, competent, and affably good-natured."

"Are you sure this is the same guy you kissed last night? What changed?" Steph was loving my story. This was complicated.

"Real life. Odd circumstances. I feel a bond with him. Like we have been to war together, or we were in a train wreck but survived. The only survivors. It is weird, I guess. But something has definitely changed." I hoped this vague answer would work for her. I wasn't ready to talk about it.

"That's not helpful." She smiled. "You said he got even ruder this first night you met. I want to hear more before we go to the floor for drill." She looked at her watch. Two miles left.

"Okay, so I stayed with James most of the evening. I learned the downstairs floor work and was introduced to regulars. I learned what to do when we are slammed, even made some drinks my first night, and what to do when it's slow—the side work.

"Then I went upstairs to train with Amber. She showed me the upstairs bar. We went over the liquors—top shelf, craft liquors, and premium, where each is located, and how to count your pours without looking like a toddler learning to count to three. By this time, I had looked up long enough to see Matt standing against the back wall, scowling, eyes locked on me. He wore an expression of both boredom and irritation, holding most of it in his glowering gaze. Upon eye contact, he came over, walked behind the bar, and whispered in Amber's ear. And without addressing me at all, he left and walked downstairs.

"Approximately thirty minutes later, JR came up, kissed

my hand, and whispered in my ear. And three short minutes later, I was changed into orange and white and walking with him downstairs. He reassured me they had wiped down the bar, no spills, no glasses, and then whispered in my ear the execution of how it should be done. I nodded and shook hands with the barback and exited with him through the back alley. We walked around the bar, the one next to ours, Crew Brew, turned the corner, and reappeared on the main strip. Talking incessantly, we walked to the front doors of Azure, where Matt was checking IDs, flashlight in hand. He nodded at Henry, meanwhile glaring at me. As I passed him, he grabbed my arm.

"'What's under this?' He pulled the hem of my orange skirt.

"'Bloomers.'

"'And what's that?'

"'Girl athletic underwear that you are supposed to and allowed to see, man.' Henry spoke up for me, already my friend.

"'I am supposed to catch you at the end of the bar. Where do I...how do I do that?'

"'What do you mean?'

"'Handholds. Where?'

"'Not my ears.' I squinted at him, and he smiled slightly. 'I will pop up high and fall body stiff, hands up, just grab. But remember, I am going down the bar length, back again, and then once more towards you and then off. One, two, three.' He didn't respond. Some frat boy's ID was getting all of his attention.

"We walked into the dense crowd. He called Richard over to the door to replace him and reluctantly followed us, ten feet behind, disappearing into the mass of revelers. I came to the front of the bar as instructed. Def Leppard's 'Pour Some Sugar on Me' was rocking from the speakers. James met me at the bar where some regulars and I took a shot and slammed our glasses back down ceremoniously on the bar top. Matt looked at Henry.

"'Hers is grenadine and orange juice. No alcohol.' Henry ducked his head down, cupping his hands to light a cigarette.

"Matt watched as a regular named Sammy lifted me onto the mahogany bar. Def Leppard stopped mid-word to play 'The Eyes of Texas,' our official alma mater tune and unofficial fight song. I looked out towards the crowd, to which a good two hundred excited football fans began cheering at my sight. I lunged forward and leaped into the air, arms and legs spread in a quintessential air split. My feet hit their mark on the bar as I turned and jumped backward, landing on my hands then onto my feet, in a perfect back handspring. Then another. I was approaching the back of the bar. Then another. The screams were deafening. The crowd was pressing closer to the bar, singing along. I reached the end of the bar and jumped in the air doing a backflip. I landed with my arms outstretched, forming the Longhorn sign with both hands, facing the crowd. Some girls near the bar had their hands to the ceiling singing along and a cigarette brushed my leg. It felt like a bee sting, and I instinctively reached for my ankle, my smile hollow. The music blared, 'The Eyes of Texas are upon you, all the livelong day. The Eyes of Texas are upon you, you cannot get away.' The crowd merrily sang along.

"My eyes found Matt near the mirror on the back wall. He was scanning the excitable crowd, arms crossed against his broad chest, an unpleasant look on his face. I repositioned myself and did two perfect front handsprings, landing where I had begun. A man in a polo shirt and wearing a Longhorn hat put his hand on my calf. 'Go, Horns,' he screamed, looking up at me. I looked across to where Matt was. He was halfway through the crowd, moving faster than anyone else in the room, but the density closer to the bar was thick, making moving slow. I swatted the man's hand like brushing away a mosquito and resumed my tumbling. The song was nearly finished. One back handspring, two back handsprings, three back handsprings—I looked, and just in time, he was there. I popped in the air high, my legs straight, toes pointed, and my arms above my head. He caught me, hands at my waist and sliding down, his arms wrapped around me.

"Repositioning me with one arm, we moved through the crowd towards the staircase. A rotund man with a sizable brown beard, wearing an orange collared shirt, rubbed the back of my thigh as Matt carried me upstairs.

"'For good luck,' he said as we passed him. 'For the season. For the team. Hook 'em Horns!'

"Matt shot him a dirty look. 'Don't touch,' he said, brusquely, pushing him out of the way. 'Don't fucking come upstairs either,' he added, and turning, jogged us up the steps.

"The playlist had resumed. Rick Astley's astonishing deep voice was playing, 'Never Gonna Give You Up.' The downstairs bar was now congested with partygoers, and more people were flooding in through the front door filter where Richard was checking IDs, his flashlight gleaming as he nodded people inside. Upstairs was calmer, the pool tables were full, and most of the seats were taken at the tables, but the standing space directly before the bar remained moderately uncrowded. Matt didn't say anything to me. But he was looking at me from the corner of his eyes as he talked with Ben, the upstairs bartender on shift.

"'Watch the beer fridge up here; I need to replace the rubber seal, so it's closing properly. Keep an eye on your pours as well. Make 'em tighter; you're coming close to doubles sometimes. Oh, and help me keep an eye on the kiddo. Keep her behind the bar. No cocktail training tonight, I don't care what JR has said about it.'

"'Actually, he wanted her to train only cocktail tonight.'

"'I just fucking told you no waitressing. Understand?' Ben nodded.

"'Okay, sure thing, Haymaker.'

"'Don't call me that.' Matt's glare was now focused directly on Ben.

"A man in his mid-thirties walked over with a younger friend. They asked for my autograph. Matt watched, arms crossed, eyebrows raised. 'Change out of that damn thing.' His hand gestured up and down, referring to my outfit.

"'Oh, my uniform?' I asked, putting the pen down and handing them their signed drink coaster. 'Okay.' I grabbed my bag of clothes from under the bar and went towards the restroom.

"Don't you hate that?" Stephanie laughed. "Like we're movie stars, happened to me last week. And I wanted to remind them that all I did was a flip. I have a seven-year-old niece who can do the same." We both laughed.

"It's more than that, and you know it." I breathed, making my point with my gasps.

"Half a mile left." She ushered me on with my story. "What was the rude thing? I'm loving the story but fast forward to the good part, the rude part. I love how rude this guy is. Not convinced he is the one for you, of all people." We laughed again, panting from our run.

"Okay, so after the first night, I said goodnight to JR an hour after closing, and I left the bar. I remember feeling lucky that I did not have to see Matt; he was busy on the phone downstairs. So, the NEXT night," I emphasized my words. "I walk in the second day on the job, on time at ten o'clock, and he's at the door. When he sees me, he goes ballistic."

"What? Oh no. Why?" Her eyes were wide with curiosity. "It seemed like the first night had gone well," she smirked.

"Wait, so I walk through the door like everything is fine, and I even nod to him respectfully as I pass him. He is glaring. So, I am chatting with Amber; you would love her by the way, when he picks me up from behind so unexpectedly that I screamed. He throws me over his shoulder like...like I don't know what."

"Free weights on leg day," Stephanie interjected, rolling

her eyes. I grinned, acknowledging.

"And he takes me downstairs to the empty office, seats me roughly on a barstool, and slams the door closed. He folds his arms and glares at me for like thirty seconds without a word."

"What? Why?" Her face scrunched up as we turned the soft curve on our last lap.

"Yes, it was awful. I felt like I was in trouble with my dad. I mean to say if my dad was mean. He's not, so I don't know what it was like." I cannot imagine what I could have possibly done wrong, especially to warrant this behavior.

"So, I said to him, 'Matt, have I done something wrong?' He rips off his baseball cap and tosses it across the room, runs his hands in his hair in exasperation, then shakes his head but will not speak. So, I said, 'I want to be mature about whatever it is that is bothering you. Please tell me, we will discuss it, and then we can both get back to work.'

"'You. That's it. Just you.'

"'That's a good start...so the problem is me. Can you elaborate, or...?'

"'You,' he went on, 'left the bar at three a.m., alone, and walked to your car. You walked six blocks alone, and I know this because you apparently parked behind Amber.'

"'Oh, that's right. I did, she's super nice, she and I—'

"'This is one of the fucking bar rules. You broke this rule.'

"'No one told me, Matt. I am sorry. Johnny Ray didn't, and neither did you; I would have probably done something different had I known.'

"'Probably? You mean definitely. You need to obey. Didn't we discuss rules downstairs yesterday?' I could tell he was struggling to recall last night. He looked like he had not slept well.

"'No, we were interrupted...glass in the ice well. Remember?'

"'Oh, that's right.' His tone was softer. 'Well, that is a huge rule for me. So bars, downtown, east side, west side establishments too, this is dangerous adult stuff. YOU do not walk to your car alone. Ever. Especially after you do cartwheels. Two patrons came knocking on the front door around 3:15, looking for you. And I didn't know where the fuck you went.'

"I tried to ignore his language. 'Cartwheels? What? Are you referring to stunts or tumbling? It is just that I have been doing that for years. Walking to my car. And I am good at it.' I smiled, trying a peace offering.

"'When did you learn to drive?'

"'Sixteen.'

"'So not years. Maybe a year then...' he mocked, a rather blank look on his face. 'Well, if you want to work here, you don't. One of us will walk you to your car. One of the guys, just pick one. Doesn't matter who.' He paused, remembering something. 'Actually, better make it me.' He turned and slammed the door, leaving me alone on the stool."

"What a jerk. A jerk you actually like now! And you see him tonight. Are you sure you like him?" Stephanie and I had stopped running and were stretching at the hydration station near the thirty yard line.

I smiled happily. "Oh, yes. Yes, I do."

"I closed my mouth and spoke to you in a hundred silent ways." —*Rumi*

"Tonight has been awful. I need to go someplace with you." —*Amy*

CHAPTER THREE

"Finding Our Way"

I was ravenously hungry after our long run and workout. I said goodbye to Stephanie, who was staying to sauna and get a sports massage. Stopping briefly at a cafe on west campus, I picked up my to-go order and raced back home. On a college campus in July, the happy buzz of a breezy Friday afternoon put a bounce in my stride. Setting my keys on my table by the tiny twin bed, I looked around the apartment for my roommate. Kate was in the bathroom dressing, so I spoke into the door.

"Kate, I brought you a Buddha bowl from your favorite place. It's on the table, okay?"

"You are so awesome, Amy. Thanks. Did you get the tahini sauce?"

"I did! I got that one for myself, to go with my grilled chicken and sweet potato bowl. It's so yummy."

"Great, I will be out in a minute."

"'Kay." I was looking at my phone.

Three missed calls; no messages, though. My mind picked daisy petals. He called me. He didn't call me. He called me. He didn't call me. My phone rang. He called me! I picked up my phone cursorily, nearly spilling my food. It was my sister. I smiled into the receiver, feeling like a kid. I looked over at the light brown teddy bear in the center of my bed, moving him aside so I could eat and talk. Some changes would need to be made. But not tonight. I kissed him on the nose and tucked him in on the far side of the bed, the blanket covering him so only two fuzzy ears, shiny black eyes, and his nose popped out. Happily laughing and talking to my sister, an augmented sense of real joy and gratitude filled my heart. I had so many happy things to mull over. It was a wonderful feeling. And hearing my voice laughing on the phone, I began to understand why Stephanie had mentioned a marked change in me. I felt it now. Newly aware of myself and my own sense of joy, satisfied by both the conversation and meal, I said goodbye to my sister Laurel, refrigerated my leftovers, and went to take a shower.

The warm water felt like fingertips on my skin. "Matt, what will it be like tonight?" I bent my head down, letting the hot water run down my neck and shoulders. "Is this still real for you the way it is for me?" I said a prayer in gratitude for all the good that God had recently worked into my life. The water ran down my sore back and legs. "God, how grateful I am that You are a creative and dynamic God. I feel Your mindful holy presence in my life, and I love You. I want to pray for Stephanie. She has a physics test next week, and she is apprehensive about it. I pray that she finds the time and energy to put in the work needed and feels proud of the result. I want to pray for the—" There was a knock on the door. It was Kate.

"Amy, what are you doing?" Odd question, I was clearly in the shower.

"I am showering and praying." I just said it. "I'm sorry, was it out loud?" I couldn't remember if it was out loud or in my head. I laughed, embarrassed at my private thoughts revealed. "I will say it in my head now. Enjoy your dinner," I called out. "Sorry."

"No, no. It's only that...Matt...here."

I almost slipped; my pineapple body wash was making the tub slippery and my sudden jerky movement of surprise was creating the perfect injury-storm. All I could think about was me being naked. And he was not—a door between us. The sudden realization that I had not brought clothes or a towel into the bathroom made me suddenly feel qualmish. "What?" Maybe I didn't hear her right. I turned off the water as she spoke again.

"Oh no," She clarified, "No, he was here in the living room, but I said you were in the shower, so he left."

"Did he say anything else?" I was getting cold without the water on, but I wanted to hear every word.

"He left you a ticket."

"What? Kate, you are not making sense. I'm coming out. Warning. I don't have a towel." She opened the door slightly and slipped a violet-colored terrycloth towel through the door. "Thanks." I was wrapped in it and out the door in a flash, hair dripping. She smiled. On seeing her, a new horror flooded my mind.

"Oh no! He didn't see my room did he...our bedroom?"

"He did. He left something on your bed."

"Oh, noooooo!" My eyes flashed to Mr. Fuzzy. Two brown furry ears and adorable eyes were still highly visible peeking out of my comforter. I guess he saw him. "Shoot." On my bed were two dozen beautiful white roses. I jumped on the bed, breathing in their fragrant smell. Their soft petals were brushing my skin as I breathed in every one of them, not wanting to miss one. "You said something about a ticket?"

"Yes, in the white envelope."

"Where?" I spun around.

"On the table by your keys. You like this guy?"

"I think so...depending on what he left." I joked weakly.

"He left you a parking ticket."

"What in the world?" Mr. Bossy and Mr. Safety had gone too far. I was pretty sure his job description did not give him the authority to give people parking tickets. I thought back, not that I had parked illegally that I could tell. I opened the letter. Inside was a plastic pre-paid annual parking ticket for the closest garage near our bar off Trinity, a map of how to get there, and a note in all caps: "I will only give up longer walks with you in exchange for pancakes. Matt."

"He has impeccable handwriting," Kate cooed. "Type A handwriting."

"Oh, you have no idea. Type AAA." It was almost six in the evening, and I looked over at Kate. She had already changed into her pajamas. "Big plans tonight?" I smiled at her attempt at a grumpy face. "I shouldn't tease. I have to stay in and study all Sunday long. Saturday I have a practice game, and I have to work. It's too much. Sunday is going to hurt. I wish I could do the same and stay with you tonight. I am getting behind again. Every day I am inching up or slipping down in something." I looked around our room. "Kate, he left me two dozen roses. Let's split them up and have twin pretty study desks for the weekend."

She smiled gratefully. "No. no. I won't take your flowers!"

"Let's have pretty desks. Please." I walked into the common area and towards the kitchenette. I opened some drawers under the sink, and found vases and handed her a bouquet.

"You are so sweet."

"You too. I will try to be quiet coming in tonight." She smiled.

"Goodnight." She looked at me kindly. "I will keep the light low."

"No, no. I have a mask." I slipped the silk mask over my eyes and instantly fell asleep. I woke up three hours later, feeling better but craving more. Then I thought of Matt and went to the kitchen to make coffee.

"Want some?" Kate was taking a study break and had already made a pot.

"Yes, please. This French press is so good."

"Right! It is. And It is implausibly easy to use. I don't know why we were so afraid of it for so long. I think it was in the box for a month."

We drank coffee, and I looked at my watch. Time to get ready. "Kate, can we listen to music?"

"Yes! I am just going over an outline, and it's been quiet for hours."

"Country? Or NPR?"

"Great. Either one."

I flipped on the radio on the wall and found a local station. "Kate, do I snore? I'm just curious."

"No, no; you talk, though. Not that I understand much of anything you say. A few weeks ago, I heard you say his name." I looked up in surprise. Geez.

In the shower, while sleeping... "It's weird being best friends as young kids and now living together, all the things we never knew over the years."

We giggled, and I went into the bathroom to ready myself. After blow-drying my hair and applying my eye makeup, I went searching for my backpack, stuffing in my uniform, Chapstick, mints, pineapple lotion, wallet, keys, little plastic parking pass, and my map. "Bye, Kate. Night, dear."

"Have fun!" She smiled thoughtfully as I softly closed the door to our dorm.

Parking was easier than I could have imagined. I found my allocated spot on the second floor and descended the spiraled stairwell steps as I thought about him. Some moths were circling the buzzing florescent lighting above me, social and excited. I smiled to myself, feeling giddy. I'm relating to moths now. I rolled my eyes to the boring cement walls that formed the stairwell. I made my way across the street, passing restaurants and bars; their doors opening and closing were giving hints about the music and revelry inside.

From across the street, I could already see him—his

enormous familiar shape standing at the bar entry, checking IDs. I wondered when he got on shift. There was so much I didn't know about him. So much he didn't know about me. On seeing him, I began to feel my heartbeat quicken its pace. Something in my stomach tightened, like riding on a merry-go-round, the colors spinning. I reached into my backpack, grabbed my water bottle, and took a slow sip, trying to settle the internal summersaults. Matt's eyes shot up, somehow sensing my arrival, and he smiled. From the direction I had approached the bar, I reached Charlie first. He put his flashlight in his back pocket to hug me.

"Hi, honey." He hugged me, leaning in to smell my neck. "You smell good. Edible even. Have a great night."

Matt handed the IDs to a couple walking in, his eyes fixed on me.

"Hi." His soft brown eyes did the smiling for him.

"Hi." Suddenly shy, I took another sip of water, trying to calm my trembling body. Little sips.

"Did you park in the garage okay?"

I smiled, replacing the lid, trying my best at normalcy.

"I did, and thank you for adding in the highlighted map, I found it easily. Thank you so much. I don't know what to say."

"Pancakes with me after work."

"Yes, to pancakes with you." I smiled, my face in his chest as we hugged. I looked straight up, remembering last night's water balloons and kiss, suddenly feeling at ease. "I am so happy to see you. Is it okay to say that?" I smiled, and he laughed, a sense of relief coming over his face.

"Yes, it is. I am happy to see you too, sweetheart." I turned to go inside, and he pulled me back to speak in my ear. "I am jealous of your water bottle."

I walked into the bar a few feet, thinking, then turned back and smiled over my shoulder.

Checking in the basement with JR, I realized I would be working downstairs again. Okay, busier pace, less time to daydream. Time to work. Okay, coffee, don't fail me now. I tucked a clean towel in the back of my faded black jeans. Fingers in the air were trying to get my attention, eye contact, and I leaned in for the order. Mixed drinks—go. Log it into the computer, make the change, tip in the jar next. The work was fast-paced, and the customers were thirsty tonight. I spoke to a few regulars, remembering their drinks and setting up their tabs.

An hour into my shift, I could hear the crowd in front of my station start to grow louder above the music. The bar chatter mixed with the music turned to yells. I looked up, adjusting my Azure tank and straining to see through the swell. The crowd was moving away from the center of the floor, like fish responding to an oceanic predator.

"What's happening?" I looked over towards Jasmine.

"I can't see. Wait. Fight. Get Matt or Richard."

"Where? At the door?" Being on the end of the bar, I dashed out towards the crowd and immediately heard a loud whistle cut through the noise. I looked up. Matt was upstairs and pointed at me to go back behind the bar, then he disappeared, returning moments later on the downstairs level.

The sound of drinks spilling and girls screaming fought to suppress the music. A girl in a red shirt shrieked as she was knocked backward into the crowd. The two students exchanging blows seemed completely unaware of any social dissension they were causing. Matt grabbed the biggest one by the back of the forearm and swiftly wrenched his arm up from behind, rendering him prisoner to the pain ripping through his shoulder.

"Okay, okay."

"Not okay. Back alley."

Richard had already grabbed the second undergrad, guiding him by the shoulders as he pushed him to the back exit. In their absence, the enlivened patrons began cheering wildly as the party ensued. Poor Matt. I hoped he would be okay. It had ended fast enough. I hadn't seen him get into too many fights yet, but I had heard stories, mainly from Amber. Allowing a brawl to happen in a bar is illegal. They get subdued and thrown out quickly, but sometimes things are not finished, so the back alley had become a place to resolve these problems fast before the cops came, if they came at all.

I looked down at my icy shaker and added a small splash of almond liquor to the simple syrup, a long pour of vanilla vodka, Malibu, pineapple juice: wedding cake martini and a Long Island Iced Tea. I put the drinks on the bar for a man with green eyes and ran the credit card. Next up, six Shiner Bocks for a couple heading to a table. Cash. Make the change. Beer on the bar. Change in hand—tip in the jar. Go. I found my pace. Even though I still had four months until November, I was nearly done with the actual training portion.

Where was Matt? I felt like I hadn't seen him all night.

Around midnight, JR found me and whispered in my ear. I nodded and followed him upstairs to where I spotted Jenn from my team. She was dressed in her uniform. She had been at dinner nearby with a friend and had come to see me. JR had asked me to make whatever they wanted and put it on the bar comp tab. She shot two lemon drops while her friend had a rum and diet coke.

"Amy, we can get in trouble for this. I know you don't drink, but we can't be in our uniforms around alcohol." I hadn't considered this.

"Oh no, what should we do?"

"Let's just do it real quick. A few back handsprings, and then we will be off. Okay?"

"Okay." I felt uneasy suddenly. I hadn't meant to break the rules; the university, and the cheer program in particular, had always been so nice to me. My pals drank and talked to James while I changed into uniform, and then, arm in arm, we walked with Henry out the back alley to re-enter the bar from the front. To my surprise, Matt was in the back alley talking to a crying girl with pretty long brown hair. He looked tired. "Matt," I called to him; Henry wasn't stopping, dragging us farther out into the night.

He smiled when he first saw me, but his smile faded a split second later when Henry moved, and he saw my uniform. Jenn put her arm around Henry while I dragged my feet trying to speak.

"I told him not tonight. It's a wild crowd." He caught up to me, putting his hands over my ears as he talked to Henry. Henry responded, to which Matt recovered my ears with his hands. "Fucking do what I say...and not..." He pressed tighter, muffling himself. I looked up. He finished speaking and looked down at me, kissing the top of my head.

"Be careful. I will be inside in a minute."

"Is she okay?" I asked, looking over towards the sobbing girl in the alley.

"Yes. I had to call the cops. Her boyfriend was the one who started the fight. They arrested him. When we first came outside, I thought it was over. We were just going to let them go, but they continued out here. He pulled a gun on Richard as we were leaving. I got it away from him. Very aggressive, wouldn't stop coming at us, no matter how many times we put him down. Messy situation. Likely drugs, completely out of control. I was waiting for her cab, but I will find someone else to wait with her." I was getting pulled into the outside crowd.

This was terrible. Poor Richard. "So sorry, Matt. Miss you," I called back to him. I felt like I hadn't seen him in days, not mere hours.

"Me too, Amy." And he was gone before we were around the bend.

Outside in the night air, it was crowded and smoky. Some people near us were running around laughing, throwing bottle caps at each other. We made our way through the crowd to the long line at the front door. Azure was getting slammed. Richard motioned the line aside to let us in.

"I'm glad you are okay," I said to him. He shrugged his shoulders.

"It's Texas. It happens sometimes. Not a lot, actually. And never to me before."

I heard a brunette in a black baseball cap call out, "Bitches," as we ducked under his arm, bypassing the line. I turned to her, grabbing her arm gently, and pulled her under Richard with us.

"No, we are nice. Join us!" She looked up, embarrassed.

Her name was Willow, and we let her pick our collective poison. Tequila. We did a tropical tequila shot made from pineapple-infused vodka, tequila, and pineapple juice. We put our glasses high in the air for visibility. Glasses up, we came down to tap the bar for good luck and good folks before bringing them to our lips. I slammed my lemonade with the others, swallowing it in one smooth gulp. I came up sputtering in surprise, looking up at the glass in my hand. It had the little telltale black marker dot on it to indicate mine. I looked at Jason.

"Whoops. I marked the wrong one. I am so sorry, Amy."

Amber looked over at him. "You are in so much trouble!"

"Umm," I managed. My throat burned. I felt funny like I did when I heard Matt's voice say my name.

"Here's some water," he handed me a glass. "Drink it. All of it."

I tried to give a reassuring smile. "It was a mistake. He won't be too mad at you or me. It will be okay." I felt a funny, fuzzy feeling in my stomach. The crowd was loud, and many people were dancing, drinks in the air, where they stood. Jason looked at me nervously.

"Go now and do your thing before it hits you." His eyes were evaluating me.

"Okay good idea. How long is that?"

"About five minutes."

"Oh. I will be long off the bar by then." Jason got behind

me, his hands on my waist, and I jumped in the air as he lifted.

I was up. Wanting this to be over before it started, I took a running step and turned into an aerial and slid down into a slow side split, as was Johnny's request. The crowd was screaming, loving it. I turned my hips, repositioning myself to the front, and gave high fives to the three closest people in front of me. Someone farther out in the crowd reached in to touch me on the shoulder, nearly knocking me off balance. A pretty blond girl jumped on the bar to join me, motioning for me to dance with her. I looked at Jason. He offered his hand as leverage from the inside of the bar. I turned back to a side split and popped up to my feet. I needed to keep moving. I did a back handspring, turned, and looked for my friend. Jenn was just now on the bar, near the lone dancer. She moved past her and did two front aerials, and was next to me in seconds. We linked arms, and I felt the drink hit me. The song had changed to Madonna's "Like a Virgin." Ewww. Not a great song to be dancing to on a bar if you are exceedingly shy. Everything was exactly wrong. My head felt fuzzy, and I wanted Matt.

I jumped over some hands reaching out to touch my legs and rub my orange Keds for luck. Superstitious football fans. A man near the front ran his hand up my skirt towards my thigh. I brushed him away and did a backflip. Landing, hands up, I nearly tripped over two girls reaching to high five me. People were misbehaving. I looked up for Jenn, worried about how she was handling this. Jason had helped her and the other girl off the bar top, and I was alone. I did two aerials and was away from the aggressive part of the middle. People still with drinks high in the air were screaming out their football fandom. I looked for Matt and spotted him making his way fast to where I had just landed. I moved away from the crowd of arms and hands.

He looked up, and I mouthed to him, "I want to go home."

He motioned for me to jump, blocking a person's drink with his hand. I jumped, and he caught me in his arms. He must have had the same feeling. My purple backpack was slung around his shoulder. "Let's go."

"Tonight has been awful. I need to go someplace with you." I paused confessing, "this is not what I want. What I thought it would be."

"I agree. And I am so sorry; you don't deserve this. I have been in several altercations tonight—two of them over you. Let's leave. Pancakes?" His voice was angry but not at me, which felt good.

"Yes, please."

"Do you want to walk?" I shook my head no against his broad shoulder like a sullen child. "Okay."

He moved us steadily through the crowd. Coming out on a quiet side street, Matt set me down and took my hand. His knuckles had dried blood and cuts.

"Matt."

"Grazed the wall, tell you later. I will live. So, it's only 1:15. So I was thinking we can eat, and I will take you back to the garage after for your car."

He smiled, and I realized I had never seen his car before. Looking along the parking off Brazos Street, it was not hard to imagine which one was his. There were two silver four-door Hondas, an enormous black Ford double cab F150 pickup, a red minivan with Ohio plates, and a pink Cadillac with custom rims. As we walked, he fumbled with his keys in his pocket, stopping in front of the pink Cadillac. No way. I stopped short, my eyes wide. This pink car explained so much about his perpetual grumpy mood. He was talking about the evening, changes that he would make, impudently; he lifted his keys to unlock the pink door.

"Just kidding." He smiled and, turning, walked to the truck. I laughed into my hands.

"What? Matt, I was just feeling so bad for you."

"Aww, well, it's actually a great car, the color is not great, but it—" he stopped short. I was sitting on the curb, now stabilized from my unbalanced attempt to walk on my own.

"Hey," he rushed to my side. "Are you okay?"

"No, no. I am. But listen, we need to talk about something before I get in the truck with you. Ummm." I put my hands on my stomach, letting my face fall to my knees, despite the funny feeling originating in my head.

"Are you hurt? Show me." The humor drained from his face.

"No." I felt a familiar instability in the pit of my stomach, maybe from the alcohol, and definitely from talking with him about something he would feel the need to be confrontational about. "Matt, I know tonight has been hard for you. For me too. And I do not want any discord between you and the staff. And especially between us. I do not want any untruths between us. Anything separating us." He nodded.

"You have no idea how hard. We can talk at the restaurant." He paused. "No untruths. Good. I want that too. Tell me what's wrong with you." He looked worried and moved my hand away from my stomach, looking down and seeing nothing.

"You will be mad."

He smiled. "Maybe. But you can tell me anything. I only want to help you." I nodded.

"I accidentally took a shot at the bar. James made the shots, including the one intended for me but was distracted by my new friend, Willow. So he shot mine, and I shot his." He looked irritated but was maintaining an even composure.

"What was it?"

"A mixed shot, high alcohol content, the tropical tequila pineapple shot. It was an accident. Please don't be mad at him. I drank from the marked cup. I didn't do this on purpose." He smiled.

"I believe you. You don't need to say more. I've made a few of those; it's all alcohol. What did you eat earlier before coming into work?"

"Chicken breast and a sweet potato."

"Okay. Pancakes are the answer to everything that ails us tonight. I am bound and—" he blocked my ears temporarily, "....ing determined to have a proper date with you despite your crazy schedule and mine. Come on." He linked my arm in his, walking around to the passenger's side to open the door. The cab was high. He lifted me on the seat then, hopped up, reached around and buckled my seatbelt for me, and closed the door. He walked around, opening some sort of container in the back of the truck before stepping up into the driver's seat.

"Bubble water. Sip on this—little sips." He blotted his finger with a tissue from the center console. I looked up. "There is a little metal lip on my toolbox that I need to fix. Snagged my finger. I'm okay. First real drink, huh? Are you going to be okay?"

"Yes. It's manageable. Not like the...the bad night. This is a tenth of that, if that much."

"Okay. Good. Speaking of that night, I talked to the police earlier today and I have updates we can talk about later. Not tonight. I will roll down the windows a crack. That helps."

"Thank you."

"Hold my hand please, I want to touch you." He pulled away from the curb, and I squealed at the sound of his engine.

"Your truck is roaring! Like angry man music. Like three motorcycles." I was laughing, and he smiled in response to my excitement. This truck was honestly so much fun to ride in. Way more exhilarating than how it appeared on the outside. "It's like the music you listen to." He looked over and smiled.

"Like this?" He pushed play on the CD already in his sound system. I cringed, bracing myself for boy-speak and yelling.

"Garth Brooks? Really?"

"I'm from the hill country, Amy. I listen to a wide variety of music. My workout music is not your thing. It's okay. It won't come between us." I smiled. I was enjoying my buzzy tummy and working hard to make my behaviors look normal. I looked down. Seeing my backpack on the floorboard, I fumbled for it and reached in.

"Speaking of workouts. I have wanted to give you something. For a few weeks now, actually." I set a small booklet wrapped with a blue velvet ribbon on his center console. He released my hand momentarily to run his thumb over the corner of the colorful pages, never taking his eyes off the road. It sounded like someone shuffling cards. He picked up my hand, kissing the back of it.

"Thank you," he said, without knowing what it was.

"It's coupons for massages, near the stadium. It's color-coded. Some are for pre-workout, post, sports massage, and aqua therapy. It may help your attitude in gym environments." He chuckled, remembering a few of our encounters.

"How did you get these? I have trouble scheduling things."

"The university. And these are gifts from Stephanie's parents. From my parents too sometimes. More than I can use." He paused our conversation to parallel park on Kerbey Lane and turned off the ignition.

"Amy, have you ever heard of Kobi steak?"

"No. Is it good?"

"Yes. But my point is, it is very tender because it is well taken care of. The farmers in Japan regulate the diet and massage the animal before...well...slaughtering it. It is a piece of meat, what you do, how people objectify you. Did I watch a forty-year-old woman and her husband rub your leg for good luck tonight?" Eww. He saw that. Hopefully, he didn't see the other guy.

"I understand what you mean."

"Don't move." He walked around the side of the truck and helped me out of the cab.

"Because I'm little in comparison to the lift on this truck, or the shot, or because you are old-fashioned?" He looked me in the eyes as he grabbed my hand.

"All of it." The electric feeling of touching his palm was like closing a circuit for me. Only when we touched did I feel normal. "Feeling better?" Hmm...

"Yes. I still feel weird but not sick or bad or something. I feel kind of silly."

"Silly?" He smiled. "I guess that's as good a word as any to describe it." We walked into the cafe to find it nearly empty. Most people were either at the bars and had eaten before or would come in later. "Perfect." He smiled down at me. The ambient sounds of diners murmured conversations, and the sound of coffee pouring was relaxing me already. Matt gently pulled my hand as we walked across the old creaking floorboards and climbed into a vintage booth in the back. I liked this table immediately. The low lighting and the soft candle flickering were setting the perfect tone. We were going to make a memory here tonight—a first date memory. He glanced at the chalkboard, squinting to read the cursive handwriting.

"Well, that settles it then; I don't need this." He leaned the menu against the side of the wall. I looked over. "Gingerbread pancakes and coffee." I smiled warmly at him.

"Yes, please."

"You too?" I nodded.

The waiter came over, and as Matt ordered, I got up and mouthed "restroom" to him. The waiter somehow heard me and mentioned that the inside one was broken. He went on to say that they had a porta potty outside in the backyard. Matt stood, grabbing his hat and keys.

"Put our order in. I will drive her somewhere, and we will be back in ten."

"No, no..." the waiter gleamed. "This is Austin, Texas. Home of the brave, the weird, the smart, the creative, the drunk. This bathroom is bright orange with broad white stripes. It has a deck, ingenious mobile plumbing, and a chandelier. Fresh roses in the ladies'. And it's immaculate. It is mobile, attached to a trailer, and can be moved."

"Awesome. Thank you. I will be right back." Matt remained standing.

"I will walk you outside. There might be low lighting on the steps, bugs, or deranged Longhorn fans." He was only half-serious, I could tell. It didn't matter.

"Listen, this will not work for me. You being this way."

"Life is this way. You have an odd way of always getting into trouble." The waiter slunk away to the kitchen.

"Matt, I will use the restroom, wash my hands, and mentally compare the roses here to the most beautiful ones on earth, encased in my dorm room. It will be two minutes. If I take too long, you can send a brigade, but I will hurry. Please be good." I got on my tiptoes to kiss his cheek. "Please."

He responded by stooping down so I could reach him, then he nodded slightly and sat down. I sprinted down the steps of a multi-tiered deck towards a garden strung with colorful lights in the trees. No bugs. Why did he say that? Now I was looking for them. A few diners were chatting by candlelight at some tables to my right. There was an empty stage to my left and a small tiki bar with some men leaning against it, talking loudly. I bolted to the bathroom, wondering if it was even possible for a woman to enter and exit a bathroom in two minutes. At the sink, I washed my hands and rinsed my legs with warm soapy water. Matt, having noticed the couple, had made me feel the instant need for a shower. I checked my watch. I was on minute two. I bolted up the steps, and, breathless, reappeared at our table.

Matt pretended to check his watch and winked at me. I gave him a big hug, kissed him on the cheek, and plopped onto the bench in front of him, my ponytail swishing back and forth like a happy puppy tail. At this exact juncture, the waiter appeared with our coffee. Date moment number one had arrived: how he drinks his coffee. I was giddy with anticipation. The waiter set the coffee in front of Matt while he unloaded the creamer and sugar bowl on my side to sort and allocate.

"And for your sister." He handed me a small plate of pecan biscotti. "Go Horns."

I grinned up at him. "Thanks."

"She's not my sister." Matt's eyes locked on mine. His intense gaze was burning holes in me. "Thank Christ for that," he almost whispered.

The waiter lingered awkwardly. "Oh well, you guys are just sweet...and you are kind of protective." He nodded at Matthew. "So, I figured you were brother and sister."

"Nope. Not my sister." He studied me. "No. This is something else. This is the future love of my life," he continued. What was happening? "I've never been more sure of something. I've never felt this way about anyone." He looked at his watch. "We are seven minutes into our first date, and I want to define this. What this is. I want it to have a name. And I want to make it work. What do you want, Amy? Do you want to be my girlfriend?"

I studied him, my eyes moving over him quickly, trying to memorize this moment. I wanted to replay it all night on my pillow.

"Yes. I do want you...to be my boyfriend." His words immobilized me. I felt frozen, unable to speak or move. He smiled at me, broad and happy, eyes twinkling. Suddenly able to move and overcome my shyness, I bolted from my seat and ran around the table to jump in his arms.

"Aww. Honey." I smiled, laying my head on his chest.

"I like this. I want this. What is happening between us."

"Me too, babe." We kissed on the lips sweetly at first, and then like we had under the bank building. Matt stood and moved my coffee over to our side. Across the hall, I could hear the waiter talking excitedly to the waitstaff at the drink station.

"Oh, my goodness, you guys. This couple just fell in love!"

Murmured, hushed voices echoed from the hall.

"What? When?"

"Right now. Right in front of me. In my section."

"Awwwww." The cooing sounds like ten girls seeing kittens filled the kitchen.

"Umm." I smiled at Matt brightly.

"You are magic." He whispered into my hair and then took a slow sip of his coffee.

"Out beyond ideas of wrongdoing and rightdoing
there is a field. I'll meet you there." —*Rumi*

"Amy, stay here, Honey. Someone will come and
get you." —*Charlie*

CHAPTER FOUR

"Prepossessing"

It was my third night working at Azure, and I had gleaned so much about the bar in just a few short days: Namely, my boss Matthew absolutely hated me. I walked into the cool refuge from the heat that evening, bound and determined not to let his disdain of my general state of being have any effect on my spirit. Oddly enough, he wasn't at the door checking IDs. A possible good omen for how the evening might proceed, I surmised. As I passed through the crowds of merrymakers, making my way slowly towards the back hallway to check in with JR in the basement, I was suddenly aware of his voice ahead of me.

Oh, he was on shift then. That was okay. I was going to make this positive. I was going to make it all work. Eventually, he was going to like me. Or not. And I would be okay with it either way. I mentally composed my short cordial greetings in my head as I prepared to pass him. I would say, "Good evening," and nod my head politely. That would be all that would be needed. Keep it positive. Keep it short. As I made my way through the thickening crowd, I could see several patrons, drinks in hand, blocking my entry to the back hall. Matt's voice was undeviating and angry; I paused just beyond the crowd, listening.

"Walk. Now. You need to leave."

He held a large patron by the shirt collar, forcefully guiding his steps towards the alley. The man was in this thirties and heavyset with black hair and matching eyes. He seemed to have trouble keeping his balance. Or maybe the puppeteer behind him was causing this imbalance; it was hard to tell from my vantage.

His buddy suddenly emerged from the crowd trying to free his friend, and by doing so, pushed a man in the front. Yelling and cursing ensued as a drink spilled to the floor, glass breaking in a thousand directions.

"You too. Let's go. You need to keep your fucking hands off my staff. You're too drunk to be in here."

"At least I got a shot in, Kevin." The burly man from the crowd was talking to his friend, staggering in the hall.

"A cheap shot." Matt spit on the floor.

"You bleeding? Good for you, fucker." The patron named Kevin glared at Matt. "You was raised in a barn or what? Spittin' inside like that," he continued.

Matthew laughed, then grimaced, looking down and shaking his head. "You don't get to lecture me on being uncouth, asshole." He was still shaking his head, finding something about the situation risibly compelling. Laughing again, he looked up. "A matter of fact, I was. Spent a lot of time in my family's barn. Reborn and raised in there. A worn leather boxing bag hanging from the eaves. Teenage brothers and I beating the shit out of that thing for hours. Muay Thai lessons 'til we was cut and bleeding. Let's go outside, and I'll show you what I learned being raised in a fucking barn."

"Fuck you, man. We are leaving fast enough, ain't we?"

"No, you ain't. Move!" His voice thundered. They were facing the far wall, backs turned to the wide corridor, locked in bravado conversation.

I looked at my watch: 10:08. I didn't want JR to think I was late. I waited a few more seconds in indecision. Then as their backs were turned, everyone distracted, I snuck through the crowd, hugging the far side of the wall and dashing towards the basement, when I felt a hand grab my wrist and wrench me backward. I screamed.

The aggressive hand spun me around and then pulled me off the floor momentarily by my waist. I looked over at the unknown man, the one who was not Kevin, as he pulled me close to him, whispering something completely indiscernible in my ear. I screamed again, and not knowing what to, I managed to squirm away from him and sat down on the floor, my hands over my ears as yelling erupted like thunder booming, seemingly from all around me. Still sitting on the ground, I tried to move but felt confined by something. I fell back slightly as the man's hand, still on my backpack, was suddenly pushed back forcefully along with the rest of his body. The man spun around, and then there was a horrible smacking sound, like a heavy book being thrown forcefully onto an empty museum floor, as Matt's fist made contact with his face. The crowd oohed and aahed like they were driving by Christmas lights, cocoas in hand, merry and excited. He flew backward towards me, where I scrambled, trying to get to my feet, cutting my finger on the glass as I clambered, desperately trying to stand. Charlie appeared out of the back alley.

"Fucking get her out of here." Kevin was back now and getting thrown repeatedly into the wall. He groaned as a fist hit his kidney. Matt turned towards Charlie. "Take her to the basement and grab the zip ties for these clowns. Meet me in the alley."

I felt a hand on my shirt, and then I was lifted to my feet as Charlie and I flew down the staircase. In a state of shock, I sat on the couch, my backpack still on, and listened to Charlie cursing under his breath as he rummaged for the zip ties among other boxes scattered on top of the enormous safe.

"Amy, stay here, honey. Someone will come and get you,"

he locked the door fast and was gone.

Johnny was not here, and finding myself alone and locked in, I wasn't sure what to do. I looked at my finger. A piece of glass was painfully wedged in the pinkie of my right hand. I tried to get it out, but I couldn't get a good grip. I glanced again at my hands. They glittered faintly with a scintillating dust of fine glass. Walking pitifully to the sink, I washed my hands carefully, rinsing them in the cool jet of the spray before using liquid soap. I wrapped the glass close to my finger in a paper towel and looked for a medical kit.

This office was inexplicably both half messy and neat. It was odd. Certain legal documents and liquor inventories were posted neatly by date on a corkboard, and the office desk itself was a complete mess. I scanned the shelves and boxes for a little red or white box. Nothing. I didn't see a medical kit, so I looked around and spying a broom, careful to keep my finger tucked, did some light sweeping. Inquisitively searching around and finding folded cleaning cloths, I damped it in the sink by the wall and proceeded to clean the dust off the desk, chairs, shelves, and couch.

Something like fifteen minutes went by. I looked around and assessed that there honestly wasn't any other cleaning that I could do besides collapsing liquor boxes near the recycling. After completing this, I opened my backpack, pulled out my biology book, and re-read chapter fourteen, focusing on the highlights from earlier in the week. Another fifteen minutes passed. Charlie and Matt finally came down the basement stairs talking and laughing over each other.

"I just can't help it when someone says, 'Was you raised in a barn?' I mean, I am not much of a talker. I am more of a doer. But those exact words, man, I can't help but say something." Loud laughing.

Charlie's voice talked over Matt's. "You were on it tonight, Haymaker. Battle-tested again this evening, we was. We was." He laughed, slapping Matt's shoulder affectionately. "Listen, not that I feel sorry for them." He paused, laughing loudly. "Oh man, I like how that one guy, he kept swinging at us like three feet back. I mean, if you have no experience fighting, it makes sense. But we have thrown Kevin and that other guy out before. I still don't know his name. He knows how to fight, or I thought so. He was so far back, and I was laughing so hard I almost stepped face forward into his fist."

I closed my book and sat up.

"Oh no, honey, you were stuck down here." Charlie smiled. "I forgot to come get you, but it's okay. You cleaned down here, too, I can tell. We just wrapped up."

Matt shook his head. "You are such a problem." He made a face, glaring at me. "You have such bad fucking timing."

"What was wrong with those guys?" I tried diverting attention off of myself.

"Lots of things," Matt said. "Too drunk for one. Very touchy with Ashley downstairs. She was really upset."

He opened a water bottle and drank it all, tossing the empty in a box by the wall. Grabbing another, he uncapped it and walked over to a shelf. He opened a box of aspirin and, taking two, popped them in his mouth. Swallowing them fast and motioning for me to follow him, he informed me, "JR is off tonight. Just me. I gave Ashley the night off, so you and I are bartending upstairs together."

"You and me?" I moved my finger out of his view. He noticed, looking up at me.

"What's behind your back?"

"Nothing. Just a paper towel."

"Why?" He was not amused.

"I wanted to ask you if you have a medical kit down here." I spoke so softly, I was sure he hadn't heard me. He made a face from where he sat on the desk and got up, walking towards me. I walked backward, "It's okay."

"Let me see."

"I want to do it myself."

He looked down at me, seizing me by the wrist and holding my palm to the light. "Charlie, can you get the medical kit, please?"

Charlie reached on top of the safe for a red box that I could never have seen from my height. Matt's eyes were intensely focused on mine, and I looked away. Charlie opened it and handed me the tweezers. "Wash them. It's deep." Matt turned back to me, one hand on mine the other guided me backwards by the shoulders to better lighting. He walked me backwards a few steps, like we were dancing, and stopped.

Charlie handed me the clean tweezers wrapped in a paper towel. I tried to grip it, but it was at an awkward angle. I flipped my wrist to get a better view, but it was too hard to manage, left-handed. Matt looked at his watch. I tried again, but it hurt, and ultimately it slipped off. Matt kicked JR's chair into the center of the room and nodded at Charlie.

I looked up, alarmed at the sound. "It will probably be alright with a Band-Aid until I get home. I mean, then I will get it out." Matt shook his head. I nodded. He walked closer to me.

He shook his head again, "Amy, it's just a little piece of glass." He nodded at Charlie, who grabbed me from behind in a bear hug and sat in the chair. He pulled my hand out towards Matt.

"Please don't. Let me try again." I squirmed and closed my eyes.

"Oh man, that is a little bitty finger." Charles smiled.

"It's a big piece of glass, though. We need to get this out. Hold still." I made a slight whimpering noise. Matt froze. His intense eyes were lasers as he looked me over. Then he turned and walked back to the desk and opened the top drawer. Rummaging through it, he pulled out a watermelon lollipop and walked towards Charlie and me in the chair, unwrapping it. "No sad little sounds." He popped it in my mouth. "Finger." I couldn't sacrifice it to him. Charlie lifted my hand with his still holding me tightly. I felt betrayed by his hug. I closed one eye as Matt suppressed a smile, his eyes on me.

Was he enjoying this? Because that would be terrible if he were, this hurt. "One, two, it's out." I squealed, the lollipop muffling its full effect. I slowly blinked, evaluating his next move as he looked in the kit. He sprayed antibacterial spray, then dabbing the blood with a clean paper towel, put a bandage on it. "You can only put a bandage on something if you have removed the foreign object and cleaned it. Not before." I looked at him sternly, still stuck in a bear hug, a small white stick in my mouth. "Utterly ridiculous." He seemed amused by something as he turned away from me fast, hiding what almost seemed like a genuine smile. Was he mad, and this was sarcasm, or was he finding something endearing and funny? It seemed unlikely from what I knew of him so far.

"Let go of me!" I turned my wrath on my new enemy, still holding me from behind. "You betrayed me. Don't ask me for vanilla diet cokes for a while. A good long while."

"Don't be mad," Charlie laughed. "You can't live with glass in your finger, cutie." I ignored this, enjoying the first candy I had tasted in months before biting it impatiently and dropping the remainder in the trash can.

"So, Matt, I'm not that fast to manage half the bar with you. I'm so new. I'm sorry, I am just not that good yet. And you. Do you even know what to do?"

"What do you mean? I do everything as needed. Face bashing, liquor orders, taxes, finance, and budgeting, bartending, barbacking. All of it. Even fixed the banister twice."

"I'm sorry. I didn't mean that. I was really just referring to my inadequacies at this point in my training. I didn't know."

"Then don't say what you don't mean or don't know." I nodded solemnly. He shot me a look and pointed to the staircase. We walked in silence. Working with Matt all night together; this was my worst-case scenario for the evening.

When we reached the top, I tried to make it right. "I didn't mean to get in the way earlier, and I want tonight to be good; I'm sorry. I'm not very fast yet, but I will do my best."

"You were completely in the way. You are lucky you didn't get hurt." I lifted my pinkie in response. "Really hurt, kiddo. Stepped on, stomped on, ribs broken. Some people that come in here are dangerous. Mean. Looking for trouble of almost any kind. Some people won't be easy on you or stop a fight if you are in the way, even if you are just a little girl." I nodded, taking heed, slightly insulted by his description of me.

"Let's get to work, Matt. But first—" I went to the salt cellar and scooped a large spoonful in a shot glass, and topped it with warm water and a squeeze of lemon. I mixed it quickly and handed it to him. "Swish your mouth with this."

"Good idea," he nodded, emptying it in his mouth and walking to the restroom to spit in the sink. A moment later, he had returned, putting the glass in the sink for Henry.

"Hurts?"

"Naw." He flashed a smile, finishing his second water, and we both got behind the bar and began making drinks for waiting patrons.

An hour later, we were slammed with customers, impatient fingers in the air vying for our attention. Matt was surprisingly fast behind the bar, double-tapping my leg as he moved nimbly behind me, a silent indication not to step back. We danced around like that for an hour, like basketball players covering each other; we moved, grabbing and replacing bottles at lightning speed. His fingers hit the buttons on the computer like a blur of movement. This was harder for me, not having the computer memorized to find the domestic versus imports, top shelf, and craft liquors. But I was learning. I could tell I was faster tonight. Matt probably wouldn't notice, he was double my pace, and it was apparent to anyone. Eventually, the customers began to fall back, satiated by our hard work. "You need to work on your speed." He looked over at me, breathing heavily. "But your form is good. You weren't in my way at all, either. You're careful, and your drinks are correctly made. So, you will build it." I nodded, happy he wasn't entirely disappointed.

A couple of younger guys came up to the bar and, looking around, requested flaming Dr. Peppers. "I don't…I'm not…"

"I've got it. How many, man?"

"Ten."

"Okay, bring them to the bar." He turned to me, "Amy, pour ten beers halfway full. Guinness. Go slow with the beer. No head," he reminded, ringing up the tab. He filled shot glasses with amaretto and splashed 151 on top using a spoon to keep the separation. I watched as he arranged the drinks like a pyramid, beer on the bottom, liquor balancing on top of the glasses. I had never seen this. The patrons had gathered their assemblage and were leaning up against the bar. "Y'all scoot way back." He looked up, making a hand motion. "Farther." Matt grabbed the 151 and took a long sip, careful not to touch the pour spout. He lit a match, pausing to put his hand back towards my general direction, then he brought the flame to his lips, blowing 151 through it, creating a monstrous dragon flame that instantly lit the shot glasses as he turned his head down the length of the bar. "Little," he grabbed me quickly by the hand, "tap the shot glass on the left towards the center." I balked. "Do it now." I complied, and like dominos, the shot glasses fell into the beer extinguishing their flames in the plunge. The feral pack waiting a good five feet from the bar now screamed and rushed the countertop, angling for their prize.

Matt ran the credit card and looked over at Charlie, who had just arrived, apparently finished with restocking beer downstairs.

"Done downstairs. You need me up here?"

"Yeah, Man. Great. Glad you came up. I need to handle something at the door. The brunette at the end is drinking on the comp tab."

"For how long?" Charlie asked.

Matt's voice was low. "All night. Any night. All the weird shit she let me do. She earned it."

"When?" Charlie smirked.

"Last summer," Matt smiled and turned to walk down the stairs. Boys. Gross. He looked over his shoulder. "Amy, you don't suck at this, kiddo." It wasn't a compliment I could exactly thank him for, so I just smiled slightly and began wiping down bottles.

Charlie looked at me, opening his strong tattooed arms for a hug. "Forgive me for doing what was best for your pinkie?" I tossed some ice at him as he sang me silly compliments; then, considering his words, fell into his chest for a brief but forgiving hug. He was usually a bouncer but could bartend well, and to my surprise, he was slower at the computer than me. I was glad to help him with what I had figured out so far. We were having fun together; he was polite and playful. During downtime, he practiced basketball practice by throwing limes in my tank while I wiped down glasses. I shook my shirt, and two fell out.

"Stop." I finally laughed at him, ruffling his dark blond hair. "Enough. You will never get a basket."

"Um. I got two. That's why they are in your shirt, silly."

"Oh, right. Haha!" I guess this basic game had rules that were so obvious that he had clearly scored twice.

A man came to the bar and ordered nine beers. I put them on a round serving tray and picked them up slowly, checking for balance. Heavy, but I could manage. I followed him to a table and, to my surprise, successfully set them down without knocking anything over. "Amy!" I looked over to see my English lit TA select a Spanish beer, Estrella Damm, from the tray. "You work here? That's so cool; I mean, I love this bar."

"Thanks, Tim. It's a great job so far, and I'm hoping to find a balance with work and school. Of course, it's never easy."

"You have really strong arms." He looked at his friend.

"What's wrong with you man, you didn't help her carry that thing?"

"No, it's no problem." I blushed. Of all the things I had done today, working with Matt, biology class, not getting trampled by inebriated giants, this was literally the most comfortable thing. "No, no," I assured him. "My job, not his. Well, good night, you guys enjoy."

"Bye, Amy." I smiled slightly in response.

Upon returning, I found Charlie had gone, and Matt was repositioned behind the bar watching me walk through the crowd. I disappeared behind a large crowd as I made my way towards him and when I looked up, he had moved so he could see me. I sighed. Make it work, I said to myself as I stepped on the mat behind the bar. I smiled at him. He was unresponsive. I made a few drinks, but it was slower now, and I started loading glasses in a carrier for Henry, so when he came back up, it would be ready. Matt watched me.

"What?" I turned to him, suddenly irritated that happy, friendly Charlie was gone and replaced by someone who, for reasons unknown to me, disliked me immensely.

"You always find interesting side work to do."

"Well," I turned to him, "I wiped down bottles, I folded napkins, cut limes, there isn't much—" I was interrupted by voices behind me and the feeling of someone putting something in my back pocket, settling the note in with a little spank. I spun around.

"Hey, it's good to see you out of school. I thought maybe we could try that again sometime. Dinner or something. My phone number." My TA was standing in front of me, his group waiting offset from the bar.

"Thank you." I leaned in to speak discreetly, "I am so overwhelmed by work, school, and sports right now. To be honest, I think it would be unfair to meet someone at this time. So I am not looking for that." I smiled. "Please understand, and thank you."

He grinned, "I had to try. See you in class, Amy."

Smiling shyly, I started mixing shots for a beautiful brunette in a short silver dress. I watched Tim walk away, feeling badly he had asked.

I served her, ringing her up, and turned to Matt, who had his hands folded over his chest. He didn't say anything; he just shook his head. I picked up a lime wedge and flung it at him as he turned, pelting him in the back.

"Oh, yeah?" He turned to me, suddenly armed with a shot glass full of wedges himself. "Try to dodge me." I jumped out of the way squealing with laugher, missing two of his over-exaggerated assaults. He smiled broadly. "You're good. You have brothers." I shook my head no.

"Like ten cousins. All boys. Two of the older ones just enlisted."

He threw another one, and I jumped up in an air split, just missing it. "You are so good at this," he teased. "You could do this professionally."

I smiled then dodged him, as he tossed another. "Stop!"

"Never." He smiled as I jumped my hand over my face to suppress my loud squeals. "I'm goin' to get ya!" I dodged him again and he groaned as the lime hit the wall behind me, missing me by a foot.

A customer approached the bar, sadly cutting our game short. I made three martinis for her, and when I looked back, he was gone, replaced by Charlie. I was happy to see him, of course, but I felt like I had made tiny gains with Matt tonight. It was almost like he had been glad to be near me for a few minutes. Perhaps it was better he had left early before that changed. The end of the night went fast. We got slammed again twice, and closing out so many credit cards quickly could be daunting, but we managed.

Finally, the theme song for *The Love Boat* began playing, signaling last call and closing. Lights came on as customers were ushered to the street, and Henry locked the doors. After everything was clean and stocked, Jennifer and Charlie took the tall metal tip jars from along the bar and poured their contents on the table. The smell of this much cash in piles was like an old library book from the New York Public Library that had been exposed extensively to water damage. It smelled.

Despite this, it had to be the most pleasant and social time of the night. The bar was finally clean, restocked, and locked to the public. The girls put on their flip-flops, and sitting together, in lively conversation, began making stacks of hundreds. The boys finished the trash and re-stocking and eventually began joining us. Piles on piles of ones got counted, banded, and tossed in a box for Matt to allocate. Frank Sinatra was always playing after hours. Frank's voice was mesmerizing tonight, mixed with my exhaustion. When we were almost finished with the giant mountain of money, Matt came up from downstairs where he had been doing inventory. He began counting and stacking money next to James. Finally, we were done with the stacks and stacks of hundreds as it approached 3:30.

Matt looked around at everyone, remembering schedules and doing the math in his head, and began apportioning.

"It is what it is, ladies and gentlemen." He handed a sizeable banded stack to Charlie and James and went on down the table.

"This works for me," James said, fingering the band.

"Little Bitty, you don't do a timecard, so you get five percent more from the safe." He passed me a second rubber band of money. I nodded. "So, who's playing Pepita?" He asked, tossing the box on the floor and sitting down.

"Pumpkin seeds?" I whispered to Charlie. He nodded. "Just a dumb little game we made up," he said, putting sticky notes and pens on the table.

I looked at Amber for guidance.

"Everyone adds twenty bucks to a pile. We write four words or less describing all the people here, and they have to guess who said what about them. The winner gets all." I made a face. "Try it," she teased.

We tossed our money in a pile. Five of us were in. We quickly grabbed pens and wrote out the words, putting them face down in front of the person. I tried to be creative, but being new, it was hard not to be obvious as to what I might say about everyone. We allocated our piles, and Jenn read Charlie's first:

"Brawny Not Brainy," "Easy to Please," "Daft Dim Wit," "My Hunky Hero," "Always Happy." Charlie guessed incorrectly that Matt had called him a hero.

Everyone laughed, "I thought it was an obvious diversion." He chuckled, throwing the crumpled paper at Matt.

"Read mine." Matt passed me the papers.

"Big..." I paused looking up, embarrassed. "I can't read this." I could feel my face burning.

"Come on," Henry urged, taking a slow drag from his cigarette.

I moved to the next one, "I can't read this one literally because of the handwriting." I smiled shyly.

"It's okay," Charlie smiled, patting me on the knee.

Amber snatched them from me, petting my head like a puppy and flipping her strawberry-blond hair over her shoulder. "Big Dick Energy," "Callous Patronizing Fucker," "Probably a Good Guy," "A Fucking Asshole," "Worst Boss on Earth."

My eyes shot to Matt. He looked at me with eyes that twinkled in the low lighting. A smile crept slowly on the corners of his mouth. I noticed and smiled, immediately looking down. It was obvious I had said the only reasonably nice comment. And even that was tentative. When I looked up he mouthed, "definitely," to me, and I dropped my eyes again. He picked Jennifer incorrectly, forfeiting the obvious.

Amber went next and chose correctly that Jennifer had called her a "Category One Bitch."

"Amy and Henry still have a chance," Amber reminded.

Henry lit a cigarette, shaking out the match and blowing smoke over his shoulder.

I went next, and Charlie read them: "Innocent and Kind," "Looks Like Barbie," "Pretty N Sweet," "Unequivocally Prepossessing," "Pet of the Bar." Charlie laughed loudly. "Maybe you haven't worked here as long as Matt. But even if you have, I'm guessing nobody is ever going to say something mean about you." He grinned at me. "You are such a sweetheart." I smiled, glad I was making unlikely friends, then instantly, my smile faded.

I looked over at Matt, who was looking at me with a curious look on his face, the large table between us. I sat stunned. He had actually written something nice about me. I was dreading this silly game since its inception, waiting to hear his words: "Brain Not Developed" or "Don't Talk to Strangers." Something jeering. Something mean. What had he actually said? My eyes instinctively dropped to the pile of pale yellow squares by Charlie, and pressing evenly through the folded paper in perfect all caps was the word, "PREPOSSESS-ING." It was upside down, but I could still see it clearly through the fold. I recognized his distinctive handwriting from the office inventory forms. My eyes darted down; I hadn't meant to cheat. Wow, his handwriting was impeccable, and he pressed way too hard on the paper if I had seen it inverted through the backside like that. I looked up with confessing eyes, and his intense gaze held mine as he smiled earnestly at my knowing. I looked down at the table and took a sip of my water, asking Jenn if she had called me a Barbie.

Amber raised her hand guiltily. "You look like the one I used to have in my grandmother's basement. She was pretty, but she only had one leg." I blushed.

In the end, Henry won, which everyone was happy about, and we walked out into the night arm in arm, Jenn's arm linked in mine, Amber on the far side, as we turned out of the alley.

"Amy," Charlie was suddenly hanging over my left shoulder. "Come get breakfast with us this morning."

"I can't. Thank you. I have early classes." I smiled.

He kept his voice low, "Come on, Amy."

"I'm just tired."

Matt had finished locking the bar and had jogged up to us as we moved from the sidewalk and reached the street. "So, breakfast, who's in? I could eat a horse." Matt grabbed Charlie by the shoulders, shaking him.

Charlie spoke for the group, "Me, Jenn, and Amber."

"I have a kid." Henry sighed, resigning.

Matt looked at me. "Come with us."

"I'm tired." I smiled back.

"I will walk you then, come on. Past your bedtime, Little." His jeer finally came.

"Close your eyes, fall in love, stay there." —*Rumi*

"I am jealous of the strangest things. The water in your shower. Your coffee cup touching your lips." —*Matt*

CHAPTER FIVE

"Last Petal Pulled: He Loves Me"

He drinks his coffee black. And he drives an enormous loud black pickup truck. And when he is rude, he is actually worried. It's funny watching him pass over my cup and saucer; I realized that I already knew so many things about him. He seemed so mysterious, and there was so much I didn't know yet. Things I couldn't possibly know, but I knew them. If I paid close attention, most of the things I knew, like his great capacity to love, I had known them instantly the first moment we had met.

"Don't put that stuff in your coffee." He nodded at the artificial sweetener in my hand. "It's not good for you, and good coffee like this is like meat or anything else where you just want it unadulterated so you can taste its purity."

"Is this why you want to be my boyfriend? So, you can control each and every aspect of my life?"

He looked over, assessing me, and I smiled to show that I was being playful. He started to talk and then paused. "Amy, how do you feel around me?"

"Irritated." He rolled his eyes, so I went on. "Also, I feel adored. Protected. Amused." I paused, re-evaluating the question. "Happy. Hopeful. Safe. Cherished."

"Good. I feel those things and more about you. I think we can do this. We are going to go slow. Painfully,"—he almost winced as he said the word— "painfully slow."

Our pancakes were coming out of the kitchen. "Oh wow. Amy, don't look."

He covered my eyes. I could hear the sound of the ceramic plate being set on the table, first the left side, then the right, as it settled itself on the table with a familiar ringing diner sound. I felt the steam on my face. The heat. The cinnamon-warmth of the gingerbread.

"It smells like Christmas." Matt was pulling my hair away from my face. He dropped his hands from my eyes. Sparklers! The kitchen staff had come out, in recognition of us. They clapped as we smiled and waved from our seats. One girl blew kisses in our direction, and playfully bowing, they retreated to the kitchen. I looked at him.

"I am as surprised as you."

"This is so amazing! I can't believe they did that. How pretty they are." I picked up my sparkler at its base from the pale brown stack. Matt mimicked me, not inherently knowing what to do with it. I touched mine to his.

"To you, Matthew: may you always be happy and healthy as you are now. Locked forever in vitality and righteous well-being." I looked away from the sparkler, making eye contact with him. And now I couldn't look away from this man. I was locked in his gaze full of loving approbation and longing.

"To you, Amy: may you be blessed all of your days to remain just as kind and sweet and beautiful as you are now." Our sparklers blackened and died as our lips touched. I felt him take mine from my hand and slowly set it on a plate. "You. Amaze. Me." He paused, almost breathless after every word. I handed him his cutlery.

"You. Are. Hungry," I also emphasized each word, mocking him jocosely.

He smiled, winking at me, and started to cut his pancakes.

So completely unequivocally type A, even while eating. There was a procedure for butter. For how one should dip the syrup. For what to do with the side of nutmeg whipped cream, which apparently is to push it aside with a knife and not to eat it. He watched as I recklessly poured maple syrup in slow, deliberate spirals.

"No, don't! It will get mushy and too saturated."

"Opposites. This will emphatically work." I laughed adoringly.

He smiled, defeated. The gingerbread pancakes fed my soul as we talked, getting to know each other for practically the first time.

"Favorite color?" I took a small bite turning to him.

"Hunter green."

"Oh, love it too. Mine is a soft yellow." He pointed his fork toward the yellow floral curtains by the front window. "Yes, like a muted yellow."

"Butter yellow?"

"Yes, but like fourteen percent brighter than butter."

"I love how specific that is." He chuckled. I had never seen him so happy or relaxed. "Favorite dessert—go."

"Bananas foster."

"Oh, yum. With vanilla bean ice cream?" I grinned. "Very good. I would go with buttermilk cream pie."

"That's unexpected. I've never heard of it."

"My mother makes the best version, Amy. It tastes like the south and like happiness." I smiled at his endearing words.

"What book is on your nightstand right now?" His eyes lit up at this question like I had reminded him about a childhood treasure he had long forgotten about. "What's that look for?"

"Well, I like your question. So, when I brought you the flowers, I was laying them on your bed, and as I turned to leave, I noticed you have a book beside your bed. It's a collection of Rumi quotes. A very good book and in fact, it is the *exact* book that is on my nightstand at the moment." I blinked at him a moment and then rolled my eyes, grabbing my paper napkin, and speedily tossed the ball at him. He smiled, catching it, and then reaching for my hand, eyes locked on mine, he put the balled paper carefully in my palm. "It's not a line. We are reading the same book, sweetheart."

My hand wrapped slowly around my napkin. I suddenly felt the odd need to thank him for the tender way in which he had returned my assaulting trash. "Thank you."

"You're welcome."

"May I ask you something?"

"Yes. Please do. This is what this is about." He made a circular motion over his plate with his fork and knife.

"I like how you talk with your hands. I notice it more when there is something in your hands, like now, and you can't stop doing it." He smiled at my observation.

"I suppose you are right. What else have you noticed? What did you want to ask?"

"Matt, I've had nicknames all my life, but why do you call me Little? I am over five foot two and that is a reasonably sized person."

"Well, I started out calling you Little to remind the staff. Charlie and Kevin mostly. Just subtly, constantly letting them know that you are under eighteen and that I don't care what the law says." He paused smiling up at me, reaching for my hand. "But then later, I kept calling you Little to remind *myself.*" I smiled. His fingers ran over my wrist. "You also have little nailbeds and earlobes. And your voice is very soft when you are scared. All little things." His smiling eyes danced in the low lighting.

"Why do they call you, The Haymaker?"

"I think you have me confused with someone else."

"No. I'm certain of it. Almost all the staff calls you that. That and..." I smiled. I couldn't say the word.

"Maybe because I grew up in a rural area. Around hay."

I shook my head and he grinned. He simply wasn't going

to answer my question. "Matt, you are so happy in this diner. Next time we come here, I want this same table and to bring a tent and put it there, and we can stay all night talking." I pointed to an open space on the old wooden floor.

"What are you saying?"

"I like how you are right now. I feel like this is the only place I have seen you so relaxed. I want to always be here. You are so nice. You are less...dominant." I was not sure which word I was looking for to describe this, but thankfully he smiled.

"Watch me dominate this bacon." The waiter appeared with a side order of bacon apportioned for four people. "Thank you."

"You two enjoy. I am just here if you need something else." Matt acknowledged him with a polite nod.

"I feel like you are so unhappy everywhere, work, the gym. I saw you once jogging on campus. You looked unhappy then too. And there was a sunset and great happy weather."

"That's because I saw you jogging. Alone at dusk through west campus. And I was thinking to myself: I wonder how she gets by in the world. I hate that she is loose in society." He paused, dunking a slice of bacon in the maple syrup. "I was really thinking that."

"Oh. No doubt." I grinned. "Well, you could have said hi to me."

"I could have. I didn't, though."

"You didn't like me yet." I said it like a statement too sad to ask.

"It's not that. I didn't see you for what you are yet, but it was more about wanting to be appropriate." I searched his eyes, bringing my coffee to my lips. "Amy, you are very young compared to me. We have just over ten years difference between us. It won't be as noticeable when we are on the back porch having coffee thirty years from now. Gray hair, my arm around your shoulder. But here in this cafe with you, there is a pronounced difference." Wow. This first date was intense, just like our kiss, like everything about him. "And there is a law here in Texas, saying that you are of consenting age to be in a relationship with me but somehow you are still a child. You can't drink, smoke, vote, or go to war, but you are allowed to be with me. It's a dumb law and I think it's wrong." He rolled his eyes and took a sip of his coffee. "Thank God it exists in our case. I never really thought about it before, but I understand, in knowing you, the inherent intent behind some of these consent laws. Never applied to me before, so I didn't think much about it. My worry is that you will not be ready for a relationship six months from now after you are eighteen. Or even after another year and you are nineteen. That you need more time to mature."

"Are you breaking up with me?" I smiled, hoping this relationship could survive more than an hour and six minutes.

"No." He was distracted by his own thoughts. "No, of course not. We have so much to do together. There is so much I want to say to you, places I want to take you, to share with you." He paused. "Do to you." He smiled.

"Oh, great." I didn't catch his meaning, and he noticed.

"Amy." He paused and began again. "Amber mentioned you had a boyfriend in high school. Didn't last long...less than a year. How does that work exactly? How did he not kiss you and, uh..." He stopped. "...for a year? And how could you be with such a crazy, vacuous man for so long?"

"He wasn't all grown up like you. We were both fourteen, and it was more of a sweet friendship. Our parents were good friends from church. We took science together at our co-op. Homeschooled, remember? We would walk around the neighborhood together. Go to parks, feed the birds."

"Did you ever kiss on the cheek even, or—"

"Never. Never held hands, didn't hug, never kissed." He had a moderately concerned look on his face.

"And you called him your boyfriend?"

"I did. Before you, it seemed a lot more like a reasonable thing to say. We liked each other, and we talked a lot. He ironically goes to one of our rival schools, Oklahoma State."

"Probably a good idea for that guy. Oklahoma and that guy should get along just fine. Boring Oklahoma," he mumbled into his coffee. Then he looked up and smiled. I grinned back at him.

"Don't be jealous."

"I am jealous of the strangest things. The water in your shower. Your coffee cup touching your lips." He put his fingertip to my bottom lip a moment, "I feel like I am losing my mind sometimes." He smiled and quickly stole a kiss on my cheek. "However you want to define this relationship is okay with me. I can sit on my hands. I can be very patient. I want this to be right for you."

"Matt, I want this to be real for both of us. Not just for me. As it goes naturally is the course we should take—that's what we should do. I will need your help, I think, to tell me what that is and how things go. I like being with you." I paused, empowered by my own words. "I like you, and I am ready for a real relationship with a grown, handsome, and irritating man. I don't know many things about dating, but I am honest, affectionate, and I want to learn. You have to help me. Much of this so far, at least for me, has been ineffable, meaning incapable of being described in words. I think we should continue in that vein."

He smiled broadly. "Okay."

Good. He was happy to hear this, I could tell. I poured more coffee for him and then took a sip of mine. He nodded at his cup, then frowned, remembering something. He hung his head, running his hands through his hair momentarily, and looked up at me.

"I have to ask you a question. It's such a stupid question. But I have to ask now that it's on my mind. And I don't want you to be mad about it. I am not judging you. I just have this preemptive question before my other more prominent one." He was nervous, and I could tell because he was speaking carefully. I watched him curiously as he fought himself, choosing words and saying them slowly.

"Just ask, silly." I softly touched the tip of his nose, in a similar way as he had done the night before.

"Well, Amber told me a story you shared with her about two weeks ago, something pertaining to Christmas. Family traditions and stuff, she didn't go over the whole conversation. And the way you had phrased it, it was unclear, apparently to her about your *beliefs*." He paused at that last word.

"Matt, out with it."

"Do you know about Santa Claus and the Easter Bunny? You do, right?"

I paused, stunned, not knowing what to say. I had encouraged him to ask me anything, and now that he had asked, he had hurt my feelings. Shocked, I finally spoke. "Of course, I do! You think I am naïve, or twelve!"

"No!" His voice boomed. "No..." he was quieter now. "I think you are innocent, is the word. And not twelve, more like seven, sweetheart. And if you didn't answer this question appropriately, there is no way I could ask you the other one." He smiled broadly, taking a sip of coffee.

"Okay." I sighed. "I know that Santa and the Easter Bunny are magic. Magic methods of teaching young children to believe in the things that they cannot see, preemptively composing the concepts needed for faith in God. If we can believe in the magic of Santa, we can inherently open our hearts to believe in the magic of love and creativity that God has put before us. And in the spirit of fun and magic, I honestly cannot wait to creep downstairs on a cold night and fill stockings and set up pretty little things under the tree."

"You make that sound nice."

"It will be." I smiled. "What did you want to ask me?"

"Another time. I'm trying to go slow. It's hard for me. It's a marathon for the rest of my life. I don't want to burn you out on our first date."

"This date. Oh, my goodness, Matt, this date with you has been so wonderful. Thank you. You are so nice tonight. So relaxed and playful. Let's always be this way." I yawned and laid my head on his chest. He gently put his hand to my face, protectively pressing me to him. I listened to the loud drum of his heartbeat through his sweatshirt. It seemed louder than it should be.

"You know, Amy. We have not had a reasonable or normal environment to start a relationship in. I may be quite..." He paused, letting me define the word for him.

"Regnant, predominant, imposing, prepotent, preponderant..." He put his finger on my lips to stop my verbal assault.

"Okay, I am these words. I am a lot of other words too."

I moved his finger. "Charming, captivating, handsome, brave."

He smiled, eyes twinkling. "Our environment at work is unfair to you and me. We have to be smarter than our circumstances if we want to survive."

Remembering work, I gasped. "So did we quit tonight?"

"No. No...sort of but no. An ultimatum needed to be generated and discussed. So, my uncle and I had words. Boy words. Lots of them. He is only thirty-three, hard to tell with the significant premature hair loss, a late surprise for my grandparents at the time. We butt heads on things, but it will be alright. I broke the big mirror in the basement. He needs to apologize to you. You do not need to get on the bar top again unless you choose to."

"I will never choose that."

"I know. And he needs to re-write the upcoming August schedule, so our workdays match up. He put you on like six nights without me. I have exams too. Sometimes I need a break. After the June incident, I told him I want to be on schedule with you every night. He needs to listen to me. We usually make it all work. The bar is actually half mine."

"Oh, wow. I didn't know that, Matt."

"My dad gave him half the start-up capital and decided to gift me his share when it was paid back and after I started working."

"When was that?"

"When I was twenty, I started working at the bar. I'm a hard worker and do more than my share, so every so often, I guess I can afford to throw a tantrum and break a mirror. I bought it, anyway; I guess I can break it as well."

"I don't like it when you are stressed out or angry. I want to know this side of you." I touched his chest lightly with my finger. His hand slipped around my shoulder in response.

"I want you to know a calm, reasonable, loving man as well. And like I say, it is our work environment that is our biggest challenge. Guys just constantly approaching you every five minutes."

"Matt, I'm certainly not the only girl downtown that is in this situation. It's every one of us really. Just the environment as you have said."

"Well, you are the only girl I'm watching, and I don't like it." He winked at me. "And it's this." He touched the hem of my uniform top. "Under normal conditions, I am a relaxed, normally behaved guy. Nothing has been easy. It's been one thing after another since we met." He looked tired.

"What can I do to make it better?"

"I have thought about that. And if I am honest, and if I realize it's unfair to ask you to shave your hair, give up your scholarship, and quit going out in public, then nothing. You are perfect. You don't play games; you don't do anything provocative, that you can help anyway. You are kind and polite to patrons. No. We just need Johnny's compliance with my requests and some good luck."

I reached into my bag, "I was going to give you this tonight, but now I don't think you will want it. My mom is not feeling well, and I had gotten family tickets." I set four premier end zone football tickets on the table.

"The scrimmage. Right. They are opening the practice up to fans before the season kicks off. Two Texas teams. Quite a few universities are doing it this year. I was going to go with some friends. Tailgating, not this fancy. I will think about it. Is she okay? Tell me about your parents. There is so much we still need to talk about. So much I want to know about you."

"Yes. Chronic symptoms that we can control with meds. She has Parkinson's. She has, unfortunately, had health issues for years but is thankfully doing well considering. It was initially cancer, but a weakened immune system has led to many other health problems. The new meds she is on now are a real blessing."

"Good. I mean to say, I'm glad it can be managed, and I'm sorry to hear about it. I didn't know. Tell me more about your parents." I poured a second cup of coffee. He watched me forgoing the sweetener, giving black a try, and smiled. "It takes a while to readjust, but I think you will be better off," he said, nodding to the coffee. "Just do what you want, though."

I nodded. "So, my parents are good people. My dad is a lawyer with a high tolerance for hot sauce."

"That last part. I have been described similarly."

"You can handle the Texas heat?"

"Maybe your dad and I can get to know each other over a jar of salsa that no one else can handle." It was hard not to imagine them sitting across the table from each other silent and sweating, trying hard not to be the first to reach for the water.

"Maybe." I smiled fondly and continued, "and my mom is so kind and thoughtful but has had ongoing health issues that are debilitating. My sister is my best friend; she is three years my junior and wants to have a career in the medical field. We grew up in a very religious environment."

"So they can't come. That's a shame. I imagine you as a

child running around with long tapered hair and a homemade dress. I envision you picking flowers in a field and repeatedly praying in prayer groups. Was it like that?"

"Yes."

"This explains a lot to me, actually. And you are okay? Your childhood was good?"

"Yes. It was. Always had a kid on my hip. I could cook fried chicken and manage three kiddos before I could read. So it was like that." I paused, "I have a simplistic worldview on happiness. It's something that must be created with the heart and mind working together in the service of others. It's who I am, and to a considerable extent, how I was raised. Yours? I want to hear about your family."

"My dad is a state trooper." Things were becoming crystal clear for both of us. I smiled. I could have almost guessed this. "My mother is a homemaker. She is wonderful, and we are very close." I found this surprising and incredible to hear.

"Go on, please," I encouraged.

"My family bought a farm when I was five. My mom had inherited a large sum of money from a distant relative, unbeknownst to them at the time, and she was the only heir. They wanted to invest in land. Property. A hard asset. I have three brothers, all my size. I guess they thought raising Simmental and Belgian Blues—these are cows—would reduce the grocery bill as well. If you hit boys' growth spurts with copious amounts of protein—"

"You get a Matt," I smiled. So he wasn't created in a lab but rather a farm.

"Well..." He paused, thumbing the tickets. "Amy, I don't know if my heart can handle 100,000 eyes on you at once. What we go through at the bar is enough."

"Well..." I said, mimicking his propensity to put a slow "well" in front of things he found he needed a second to think through first. He smiled, noticing I had picked up on his slightest of his idiosyncrasies. "Well..." I began again. "If the

Darrell K. Royal Stadium is packed to capacity, that would be 200,000 eyes, wouldn't it, noting slight discrepancies for the injured. It won't be for a scrimmage, by the way. And this is about football, not girls. Which one of us is in finance again?"

He smiled and then, without warning, attacked my knee cap. I shrieked and realized the environment we were still in; then, covering my mouth with my hands, I threw back my head laughing. He readjusted his grip on my knee and attacked again. I jerked my other knee upwards, hitting the table and disrupting the cutlery and coffee.

"Oh, no, sweetheart. I am so sorry." He reached over, rubbing my injured knee. "Should we get ice to go?" He signaled the waiter that he wanted to pay out. "I want to find some derelict stone building and kiss you up against it." I smiled, remembering our kiss last night. "Then, I want to drop you off at your car and let you get sleep for the game."

"Will you come? Kickoff is at two." He fished a large wad of cash out of his pocket and paid the bill.

"Thank you." The waiter seemed pleased with his tip.

"No man, thank you. Y'all were great. We appreciate it." Matt leaned over to ask him a question.

"The yellow ones, of course, you can. There are too many as it is," the waiter responded ebulliently.

"Let's go, sweetheart." He pulled me to my feet. Some eyes at the tables near us shot to my uniform and stayed there, watching us move across the floor. "Yes, I will go, babe. Thank you for the tickets. Can I bring a few of the guys from work?"

"Of course. I gave you four, and they seat by the person, not by muscle mass," I teased. "Is four enough?" He grinned, looking down at me as we walked arm in arm.

"Yes, four is good. I was thinking Richard, James, and Amber are big fans." He nodded. "We will tailgate first, drink some beer, do the BBQ thing, then we will come up to the fancy area." He looked down at me for my thoughts.

"Okay. Hey Matt, if you feel overwhelmed, stop looking at

the boys and start looking for the families, the older alumni, the babies in orange onesies. I do that too sometimes. It's not always about what you think it is. Bevo is our mascot. But essentially, so are we. Think about it more in terms of animation. Like the Minnie Mouse or Cinderella characters at Disneyland. It's athletic and entertaining."

"Thanks, babe, that's good advice. Come on."

Under the broad porch canopy on the patio, Matt pulled out a pocketknife and cut a yellow rose from the trellis under the window. He held it up under the low porch lighting turning it over in his hands a moment. "Don't worry; the waiter said it was okay. This looks like..." He trimmed off the thorns skillfully. "The exact right shade of yellow." He handed me my prize.

I smiled brightly. "Oh, thank you, darling."

He wrapped an arm around me as we stepped out into the heat of the southern night under a thousand pinpricked stars.

"Start a huge, foolish project, like Noah...It makes absolutely no difference what people think of you."
—*Rumi*

"Let's go, Matt. This girl is kind of weird. Now we know." —*Jason*

CHAPTER SIX

"Rewinding Time: He Loves Me Not"

It was Saturday, and tonight would be my fourth night at Azure. I was relieved at the simplicity my weekend schedule afforded me: working out and going to work. No classes today suited me just fine. Having just completed two hours' worth of practice and drills, I had just parked my car on San Jacinto when I saw my newest dear friend hopping off a city bus, papers skittering in the wind.

"Amy, help!" she called as a paper went flying past me.

I ran after it, snatching it mid-air at the corner of a wall and concrete barricade. After reorganizing Stephanie's physics papers, we rushed into the building, talking excitedly as we entered the gym's sports medicine and strength training area, located on the lower level of the north end zone.

It was just after two in the afternoon, the first week of June, and everything in my life, and hers, was escalating exponentially. The workouts, the meets, pressure to keep our scholarships associated with them, combined with the condensed summer course load, was overwhelming. The goal was to burn five hundred calories in an hour and a half. This was not the university program but our own ambition driving us. In the newly renovated locker room, she prattled on about her roommate Jasmine as she helped me zip up my neoprene sauna vest. I slipped my loose tank over it, and we went out to the floor. Today was leg day: squats, lunges, quad extensions, calf raises, sumo squats, wall sits, and leg press.

Stephanie was the nicest girl on the team, in my opinion. Her ebony skin and toned muscular form made her exceedingly beautiful, a natural-born athlete amongst the elites. Everyone had been down-to-earth and kind so far, but there was something exceptional about her. She specialized in stunting and jumps. Her pikes and front hurdlers were always sharp and smooth. That was the thing. She was good at everything but remained humble and kind, always looking for a way to compliment someone else on their form, their jumps, and their style. I was drawn to her right away. And she was an absolute powerhouse in the gym.

"You ready?" She held the bar out to me. I nodded. We put the thirty-pound bar on our backs and began the slow production of squats.

"Your form is perfect," I gushed at her.

"Straighten your back. Here." She balanced herself while touching my lower sacral vertebrae.

"Got it. Thanks. Steph."

"Twenty-two, twenty-three, twenty-four, twenty-five. Hold. Low pulses."

"Um." I bit my lip; I was burning. If she was, she didn't show it at all. I held on for the duration of the count.

"And stop." I leaned the bar against the wall and wiped the beads of sweat from my forehead.

"I need water."

"After the next set." She grabbed her bar. I grabbed mine and resumed position. My traps were on fire as well. "You've got this, Amy. You can do this, girl."

"Okay." I shook my head, slowly pushing past the burn. I could imagine my muscle fibers on fire and being ripped apart so that they could be rebuilt stronger.

"Come on, Amy. You're a flyer, girl. You gotta be light as a feather. So back stiff as a board. Let's go." Funny, Steph. In cheer, there were three prominent roles: the flyers like myself, spotters, and bases. Steph was particularly strong and tall, so she was usually a base girl. We finished the set and put down the bar to start quad extensions. "One more of these sets left," she said encouragingly.

"I'm so glad you're driving today, Steph."

"Just keep an eye on that form. Amy, get some water. I've got my bottle here. When you go down, can you get us a couple of ten-pound dumbbells for calf raises?"

"Of course. I will be right back."

I grabbed a letter from my bag, hoping Maria was there. Selecting a folded white towel from the basket by the mirrors, I toweled off my temples first, then my aching shoulders.

I dreaded going downstairs. Even though this was one of the finest workout facilities on campus, on any campus for that matter, it was big, and the equipment was spread over so many levels and rooms. As I walked by the hallway to the staircase, I stopped by the sanitation cart and dropped an envelope containing a gift card to a store called Baby Boom Ba on the pile of clean towels. I smiled as I passed a heavily pregnant Maria mopping the landing of the stairs.

"Watch out, Amy, it's wet." She pointed.

"Thank you, friend. How are you feeling today? Did the crib setup over the weekend turn out? You look radiant."

"Yes. Took us nearly two hours, though. Like putting a tent up in the dark. The directions were so complicated, but it finally just came together beautifully."

"Bless you, guys." She smiled warmly.

"Bless you too, mija." I grinned at the sweet term of endearment and headed down the stairs.

It was a large space. I walked on, past the hydrotherapy room and sports massage rooms to the weight room. Inside there were rows of Maximus, Vibrogym, and other high-quality workout machines littering the floor. And everywhere, only boys. A couple of them looked up as I entered, keeping their eyes on me as I searched for the free weights—likely curious as to what I possibly needed down here. Most of them were jocks on scholarships, managing tight schedules and heavy weight, too consumed with their sets to notice a girl. Notebooks and huge gallon jugs of water littered the windowsills and tables near machines. These were the serious guys. Suddenly feeling serious myself, I made no eye contact, rushing to find what I needed and go. Dashing to the water fridge, I selected a cold mineral water. I drank half of it, my eyes on the wall. Remembering where the free weight wall setup should be, I turned and saw Matt over by the dead lift weights.

He had just dropped colorful weights, the literal size of my roommate, on the rubber flooring, and resumed fighting with his arm wraps when he looked up. Only having just recognized him, I immediately diverted my eyes, hoping he hadn't seen me. I turned to the far wall, finished my water, and threw my bottle in the blue can. Hastily I located the free weights opposite Matt and quickly grabbed them and bolted for the stairs, never looking up.

Upstairs, Steph and I completed our final sets in the remaining half hour. As I wiped off the weighted bars and replaced them, I was suddenly filled with dread at returning the free weights.

"Hey, Steph, would you mind returning the weights?"

"You got 'em out." She shot me a stern look, then smiled. "What's wrong with you? Did one of those muscle heads say something? If they did, just ignore them."

"No. It is a little intimidating in there, but no one was rude in any way whatsoever...everyone was fine. Nothing like that. There is this guy—"

"Ignore him. Some people in Texas don't know no better. And you know that, Amy. You, of all people, know that by now.

It is just—"

"I promise you no one was rude." I cut her off, as she was so off base to my meaning. "There is this guy who doesn't like me from work."

"From the bar? Why?"

"I don't know why. He is maybe just a grumpy person. Anyways he's in there, and I don't want to see him twice in one day. He scares me. Not really." I thought about it. "No. He does." I was making some progress, though. I thought of our silliness at the end of the night, throwing limes at each other. "Prepossessing," I whispered to myself, just now remembering this new development.

"Let's go together. It will be okay. Come on." We descended the stairs to the weight bar section, an air of girl power to our stride. To my horror, Matt had moved to the free weights and was lying on a bench directly in our path.

"It's okay," Steph patted my shoulder. "Beautiful chest presses," she said. "He's got perfect form."

The weights suddenly dropped to the floor as I passed by his head. Startled, I continued to walk past him when he stood up, blocking me. He pulled the earbuds out of his ears; a muted death metal raged as he repositioned them around his neck.

"What's this? Are you wearing a weighted vest?" His huge hand felt under my tank top to my sauna vest. Weights in both hands, unable to block him, I tried to step back. Eyes locked on mine, his thumb grazed my abs lightly as goosebumps instantly appeared on my arms. He pulled his hand away. I could feel the sweat running down my core. "Don't do that. It's dangerous. You are just dehydrating yourself for no reason." His tone was terse and authoritative.

"I'm okay. But what about you? Why are you listening to that angry music?"

"I'm angry." He replaced one of his earbuds. "It's not always a good place to be in here." He pointed to his head and replaced the second earbud. He lay back down on the bench and resumed his set without another word to me.

I returned the weights, not looking in his direction again, and grabbed Stephanie's hand as we ran to the sanctuary of the girls' locker room. After our showers, we drank mineral water and sat in the steam room.

"I am so glad this is not co-ed. Can you believe that guy?" She was at least on the same page with me.

"And you didn't help me. Steph, you didn't say anything," I said, suddenly accusingly.

She smiled. "He's a total jerk for sure. I just couldn't stop staring at those arms long enough to say anything, though." She laughed, shaking her head. "Next time, I will."

I smiled doubtfully. Matt had a way of silencing even the bravest of people. Apparently, Steph included.

"How tall is he?"

"I'm not sure, actually, but I know it's over six foot two—my guess is closer to six foot three or four, maybe. He is a big intimidating person. That's my best guess, only in comparison to Charlie, a friend and co-worker who is six foot one, and Matt is taller than him."

"Well, sorry, you have to see him tonight too." I looked at my watch. It was approaching five p.m. in the ATX.

"Yep. I have five hours of happiness left," I mused. Steph and I hugged goodbye and headed in opposite directions across campus.

After eating Thai in the dorm cafeteria with Kate and reading several chapters of biology, I went upstairs exhausted. I showered quickly and took a lengthy nap, waking up just in time to spend twenty minutes getting ready.

Driving downtown looking for parking and passing endless groups of students and flashes of bar lights and restaurants, I began to feel discouraged. Where to park? Turning left on Guadalupe, I found a little side street off Twelfth Street behind a gas station and a liquor store. Not perfect but, looking at my watch, I decided to settle for a brisk walk.

Cutting through a side alley and walking at a spritely pace, I became aware of a homeless man shuffling along behind me. He was talking to himself, and although not wearing utter rags, it was apparent enough that he was experiencing cognitive problems to some degree. I walked faster, turning out of the dark alley and onto the well-lit pavement on Colorado Street, my backpack repeatedly bumping me as I hurried. I stopped here under a restaurant sign and waited for him to emerge. He came out of the alley, and passing me, looked up at the buzzing neon sign and stopped.

"Spare some change?" He didn't look up at me; his dusty blond hair was lightly tossed front and backward in the evening breeze.

"Do you like tacos?" I nodded to the sign to my left.

"Sure. Sure, I do. Who wouldn't?" His eyes fixed on the pavement.

"Right? Who are these people? I love them too. What's your favorite?"

"You pick, lady."

"Okay." I ordered six beef supremes to go and handed him the bag. "Enjoy your night." He looked me in the eyes now.

"Hey, thanks." He followed me from Colorado to Trinity and across the main strip. He hadn't eaten anything from the bag yet but seemed to enjoy the clement chatter. "Where are you going, lady?" he asked me as we approached Azure.

"Work, friend. Enjoy your night."

"Okay, bye, lady."

"Bye!" I arrived at the door as he turned to leave.

"Bye," he called out again.

Matt was on the far side of the door checking IDs. He looked up. Richard gave me a hug, lifting me off my toes briefly.

"Good to see you, Amy. Come in." He looked at the blond-haired man standing under the streetlight, waving at me, a bag in his hand. "Is your friend joining you?"

"No," I answered, and entered the bar.

I greeted the downstairs staff and went to the basement to check in with Johnny and place my backpack on the peg near the desk. "Have a good night, Amy. I want you with Amber tonight. Okay?"

"Okay. Upstairs or—"

"Downstairs. It will be crowded tonight."

"Okay."

"You can do it. Stay close to Amber at the far end. Richard will be on your right after a while. He's at the door until Charlie comes in." I nodded.

A half hour into my shift, Matt approached me and motioned for me to lean in across the bar so he could speak.

"Amy, there is a vagrant outside who wanted to thank you for buying him dinner. If you want to do that on your own, do so. But don't feed strays and bring them here."

Strays. I sighed. "He was near the alley where I parked and followed me. I didn't bring him here in any purposeful way. I'm sorry." His eyes narrowed.

"It's okay. He has some sort of mental problem, and I have had to ask him to leave several times now. Some of these people are nice and need assistance, and most of them are not and do not. I think you should let authorities and social services deal with things like this. My opinion."

"Sorry, Matt." I resumed mixing lemon drops—shaker of ice, vanilla-infused vodka, lemon juice, simple syrup. Line the shot glasses with lemon juice, rim them with sugar, add a lemon wedge on the side. Shake. I looked up. Matt was still standing there watching me work. He frowned. I smiled brightly at him, and he turned, started to leave, but turned back on his heel.

"Are the little plates of kitty food in the alley you too?" I served the drinks and began folding napkins—side work.

"Yes," I didn't look up at him. He was frowning. I didn't

need to see it; I could feel it.

"No. Don't fucking feed anything close to the bar," I winced at his verbiage. "Things that eat tend to defecate. I don't want eating, defecating things, or people in the alley."

I blinked rapidly, wincing again at his words. He noticed the excessive blinking, and staring at me, started to speak, but stopped. As he studied me, he slowed his gum-chewing considerably so that it looked like there was a foreign object in his mouth that he must chew slowly, carefully, as to understand what it was, lest he break a tooth. I looked up, smiling. He stared blankly at me. I stuck out my tongue at him and resumed my work. When I looked up again, he had gone. Good. I felt my heartbeat quicken associated with the pride of defending myself.

I resumed my work, finding my pace and my stride.

"Behind," I tapped Ashley's leg as I rushed past her for the Jameson. Hearing myself, I smiled. I even sounded like I was starting to belong here. And the money was so good, several hundred dollars a night even on slower ones. If all else failed with my scholarship, I could continue to pay rent and tuition.

A while later the bar began to thin out. I climbed a stool and began replacing glasses on the shelf in front of the huge mirror. I turned around, scanning the bar top, and noticed Matt looking at me from where he stood leaning on the second-floor balcony. "Don't fall." I read his lips across the expanse between us. I diverted my eyes and made an old-fashioned for a customer. The crowds were coming back now, and I made several drinks and began wiping the large bar top when I felt him again. I looked up, my eyes meeting his across the sea of people. This time, I didn't look away. The heat of his gaze was somehow making my face flush from across the room. He winked at me and turned back into the crowd. Were we playing chicken just now? And had I won? Boys were weird. I smiled to myself, plugging limes in the beers and passing them over the bar top.

Half an hour later, we were low on Hendricks. Gin and tonics were popular tonight and call orders for Hendricks had made Ashley and I run through two bottles in under an hour. Tipped off to his location by Henry and horrified that I was actually seeking out my insolent boss, I reluctantly made my way to the basement.

It was nearing eleven o'clock, and Matt was opening mail in the basement when Jason walked in just ahead of me, the last staff tonight on a staggered shift. He was hanging up his hat and black backpack, talking incessantly about football, when he noticed a purple bag at the end of the pegs. He stepped back. It was a soft lavender bag with the words "buy local" and a pale yellow butterfly embroidered neatly on it.

"New girl's?" he asked, laughing. Matt looked up, scanned the pegs filled with black Jansports, and smiling indubitably, nodded. "So, how is she doing?" I had just been about to walk in, when curious as to Matt's answer, I hung back, lingering in the hallway.

"It's only been four days. She hasn't burned down the bar. But I'm not sure she knows how to use a lighter anyways." He tossed some junk mail in the trash.

"Is she working tomorrow?"

"Yes."

"Next week?"

"Starting Thursday. Why?"

"Well, she is hot, that's all." Matt looked up, studying him. "She has great legs, man. Really perky titties. I wonder if she—" I cringed, turning to leave, when a loud noise made me freeze in place.

Matt had silenced him by throwing an empty cardboard box across the room towards the recycling. It hit another box containing a few bar T-shirts, knocking it off a shelf with a pronounced boom.

"I want to know what is in this pretty purple bag." To my horror, he grabbed it off the peg and flung the zipper open.

"Don't be dumb, Man. Put it back," Matt said dryly. He didn't look up from the mail but added, "What do you plan on finding out from a girl's makeup bag and tampons anyways?" Jason shrugged.

"I bet she has porn. Maybe there is a laptop with pictures of her and her friends. Even better." What was a porn? I hoped I didn't have one in there and they were about to locate it and laugh. There was definitely a Koosh Ball somewhere. Maybe he wouldn't find it. I wanted to go but now I felt immobilized that they were talking about me and I didn't want to be seen trying to leave. "Laptop might be back here." Jason reached in the back of my bag looking for it.

"Don't." Matt was stern. He could always find a red line. Jason's hand felt the back pocket, and touching something that felt like confetti, he looked in.

"What in the hell?"

"Stop, dude," Matt didn't look up from the envelope. He seemed bored as he opened another letter.

"Seriously, what the hell?" Jason reached in and pulled out dozens of small folded strips of paper. "No laptop, but there are all these little fortune cookie papers. They're all crinkled up. There must be hundreds of them in there. Dude, she has like five hundred fortune cookie papers in here!" I sighed, in my hiding place behind the door, covering my eyes with my hands.

Matt looked at him and beguilingly walked over. He took the bag, set it on the desk under the light, reached in, and pulled out a crumpled paper.

"Pray Michelle can afford highlights," he read, "She wants them so badly." Matt and Jason exchanged looks. "These are all handwritten," he said, pulling out another one. "Pray for the squirrel that was hit on Salado Street. I hope it was instant. Pray the driver cared." He reached in for another. "Pray that Mrs. Fitzgerald in Hyde Park sees a brown-crested flycatcher. This would make her so incredibly happy."

"Let's go, Matt. This girl is kind of weird. Now we know."

"Shut up," Matt said flatly. He pulled out another one.

Jason smirked and headed upstairs as I hid.

"Pray that Mr. Ford at Bank of America can meet a friend. Maybe he could join an elderly club or a poetry group. He is very lonely. I hope the new friends he makes like to talk about trains as much as he does." Staring past the paper at the brick wall behind it, he slowly folded it back up and replaced it. Still staring at the wall, as if in a trance, he reached in the bag, compelled to pull out another one. "Pray for Matt. God, please make his head a happy place to be." There was a picture of Superman wearing headphones. Emanating like sun rays from the headphones were the words "ROAR, ROAR, ROAR," written in angry black lettering.

He folded this up, hovering his hand over the backpack to drop it in, but to my surprise, changed his mind last minute, pocketing the paper. He sucked in his breath but did not exhale, replaced the bag on the peg, and walked out the door.

"There is a candle in your heart, ready to be kindled. There is a void in your soul, ready to be filled. You feel it, don't you?" —*Rumi*

"Is this about the boy?" —*Kate*

CHAPTER SEVEN

"Paper Ball Falling"

I woke up happy and refreshed around 11:30 in the morning, sunshine flitting through the plantation blinds. In the living room, Kate drank coffee and watched *Nash Bridges*, her Spanish book open and highlighters unused in her hand.

"Good morning, Kate!" I gushed. My dreamless instant sleep last night made me feel like I had just stepped off the cafe porch, arm and arm, with my crush. I looked over at the vase containing the yellow rose and smiled. Our amorous conversation and the words we exchanged reverberated around in my head, making me feel immensely happy and free. I opened my arms, stretching wide, and spun circles around the room in the general direction of the coffee pot.

Kate watched, a sweet and almost mirthful look on her face. "What are you doing?"

I smiled a good morning at her. "I just want you to know how kind and accommodating you are. Honestly, you are so sweet. My schedule for sleep and study is so crazy, and you never complain, my friend. Please turn up *Nash*. You can barely hear."

She smiled as I handed her the remote. "My aunt, in La Grange, got your thank you email about the French press and was inspired to send us Texas pecan roast and honey buns from a delivery service here in Austin. They came in around 9:00. Here, try this."

"What! How nice of her. It smells amazing." The rich coffee color and the nutty aroma were enough for me to tell it was going to be delectable, and I might be able to forgo my morning crutch. Kate passed the pink packet of sweetener over and handed me a spoon.

"I am going to try it solo."

"What? You always use this stuff."

"I know." I looked at my cup. "Trying new things."

"Is this about the boy?"

"Kate..."

"He is sort of controlling, isn't he? My advice—drink coffee the way you want."

No. Don't, Kate. I wanted to gush to her about all the beautiful things from last night. My head was spinning with all the words he spoke, my heart brimming to the point of spilling over. I looked at my watch and set the alarm to relax for twelve minutes.

"Well, he's not wrong. They are chemicals, and I needed someone to remind me about that." I peered over my coffee cup.

"I don't know about all that. I know you've always had your coffee that way." She shot me a look.

"He is opinionated, not controlling. So far, I agree with his opinions." I felt my strength coming back with my fifth sip. I wanted to defend him against the world that only saw him how I used to see him. "But I appreciate you looking out for me. I do," I said warmly.

She smiled, and we settled in on the couch, legs curled in, hot mugs in hands.

An hour later, I was showered, dressed, and bicycling towards the Darrell K. Royal stadium. I saw Stephanie stepping out of the sauna in the locker rooms, wrapped in a burnt orange towel, her tight black braids sparkling like glitter from the moisture. "Good morning, beautiful." She reached out to give me a friendly side hug.

"Afternoon actually, love. I have so much to tell you." We looked at our watches simultaneously. Roll call stretches, coach prep and talk, sets formed, final checks...soon enough, it would be game time. Above us, the roar of fans already clattering to their seats for pre-game drinking and fandom was only a faint vibration. Though informal and playful as it was intended, our first run at this was causing my head to race. I wondered if Matt was in the parking lot with his friends, starting the grill, having actual fun. To think he could relax in multiple places and not just our little cafe seemed incredibly errant for me. I was hopeful and full of heart.

We dressed quickly and rushed to meet our group in a room dedicated to stretching, just off the main gym. Orange and white groups assembled, ready and listening. One of the assistant coaches came in and divided us into smaller groups. Some were divided to prep rally for the tailgaters in the parking lot. Their goal was to encourage fans to get involved in the game, take pictures with fans and promote the agenda: a Longhorn win. I closed my eyes momentarily in a brief prayer. I could see Matt so much sooner this way. She addressed the orange group first.

"Anthony, Emerson, Sampson, Jennings, Riley, Matherson, Bailey, and Thompson, y'all are going out the tunnel just before the football players. You need to incite the crowd to their arrival. Go high V approach; back tucks at positions, toe touches are sharp. Hurdlers left, and right pike is a full extension, so sharp moves. Pop it back fast." She demonstrated the move in slow motion. "Kaplin, (Stephanie) Shroder, Langford, Dawnson are on tailgate joining the orange." I made a sad face to Stephanie that we would soon be separated.

"Tell me if you see him," I whispered to her.

The coach continued, "You will be in front of the band marching the parking lot. The giant five-hundred-pound orange and white drum, Big Bertha, will be directly behind you. Keep form. Smile. Focus on the crowd. Get them involved. Y'all got this. Our first taste of the fall. Proud of you all!" Soft talking amongst the groups. "Everyone else is going to follow the football team out of the tunnel. Handsprings. flips. Tight moves and eyes on the crowd. People! Focus on your stunts looking spot on and sharp. It's back handspring, round-off, then handstands...walk out on your hands about ten feet towards your first stunt set on the end zone." Heads nodded.

"I miss him. Say hi for me if you see him. I wonder what he's doing now."

"Hell ya. I'll be your spy."

"No, you don't actually need to—"

There was more from the head coach. "Look sharp. Remember to keep your motions tight and snap them into place. Keep your claps on the beat and in front of your nose. Ashley. It's right here." She called a freshman out, showing her the specific motion.

We stretched in our small factions, ate a small snack and hydrated in a room littered with tables that was dedicated to the band, cheerleaders, and pep squad groups, and did a final check.

"Who are we going at today anyway?" I asked Jenn as we walked towards the tunnel.

"Texas Tech. The Red Raiders...they are pretty good. Not a lot to do up in the panhandle. Except eat steak, drink beer, and play football."

"Oh no," I groaned.

"Yep. They are enormous. And they love being the best in Texas if they can, so they fight us extra hard apparently."

"Geez."

The whole city morphed into an utterly despondent, depressed mass when we lost a football game. Even a scrimmage, open to the public like this, would not be great if we lost. It was too official to be unofficial. If we lost in the fall, there would be a depressive vibe in the air that would spread from the scoreboard to the bars, through the banter between couples, to erupt into fights, and would eventually end as a calamity finale of excessive drinking and various forms of debauchery. This was not the best situation for the city, and it was not the best situation for going into work tonight.

I hadn't thought of work. Were we even going in tonight? I hadn't talked to Matt. He was probably still sleeping when I had gotten to the stadium. He was here by now, though. Probably on his second beer, turning something on the grill. Knowing we were in the same vicinity, even a place as big as the stadium, made me feel euphoric and excitedly blissful.

We were in the tunnel now, a clear view of the bright sunshine hitting the grass and illuminating the endless bleachers and fans. It looked full on our side from the visibility we had—a sea of orange with an occasional oddball dot in black or red. Apparently, not everyone got the figurative memo to wear white if you didn't have orange.

The band had started. From above, we could hear the trumpets and drums inciting the crowd. "And out of the engine came the flame with a name. It burned up my mind; it made me insane." Behind us, like bulls at a rodeo, the football players were packing in, succeeding us. The stomping overhead of thousands and thousands of boots created the intonation for the lyrics being broadcast. "The Eyes of Texas are upon you...all the livelong day..." The loudspeaker blared, creating a soft murmur heard in the living rooms and back porches of homes in a radius miles thick. "Get me a bottle." The crowd cheered wildly. Many of them had one in hand and could relate. "Get me a bottle, get me a smoke. I gotta kickback. Gotta let it all go." I looked over at Jenn, who had put her hand on my shoulder, stabilizing herself in a stretch. I nodded to the football players whooping behind us, jogging in place.

"Close your eyes for a second." We closed our eyes. "Do you feel like we are in Barcelona?"

She popped her eyes open, staring at me. Matt would have known my meaning instantly. "What do you mean?" She shouted out over the music.

"Running with the bulls. You feel it, right?" I made a subtle nod at the giants behind us. We laughed hysterically.

"I smell it. They smell like animals." She wrinkled her nose.

"That's the new rubber." I pointed down at the flooring.

"Almost go time."

I felt the nerves start to shudder through my body. It felt like being excited, but with a palpable anticipation of something unpleasant mixed with a certain edge like too much coffee. "Give 'em hell. Give 'em hell. Make 'em eat shit..." The crowd was roaring, overstimulated, already tipsy, and waiting. The announcer broke through the song that was silenced instantly: "Please welcome the University of Texas at Austin cheerleaders." We ran out, popping the movements in big, exaggerated moves, making the most of ourselves for the cameras and the crowds in the nosebleeds. Matt had heard this. Even if he were outside a three-mile radius struggling with parking, he would have heard the muffled words, even if they were indiscernible. I wondered if he was thinking of me.

I ran past the cameraman, and he focused on me as I made an exaggerated Longhorn symbol with my fingers. Our mascot sign language understood by all was reflected in his lens. Instantly my face popped up thirty meters into the sky on the projectors behind either side of the goal lines. I slowed and smiled brightly into the camera, then jogged to my position near the twenty-yard line.

When we were safely in position, the sports broadcasters introduced the football players. They broke through a swath of orange paper that now covered the tunnel to charge the field and take battle positions. Texas Tech arrived to a soft, and then roaring, onslaught of boos mixed with sporadic applause from the crowd. They were a great team too; this would be a fair fight. Everyone hushed for kickoff. Just off the grass on the turf, I made a sweeping glance for Matt in the stands.

Not seeing him relaxed me, and I began my routine with Jenn, Lindsay, and Ashely. For the first stunt, Jenn and I were up, the two flyers on the top of two bases. We reached for each other, eyes not leaving the crowd, holding hands. Our free arm stretched out, one-legged like flamingos, on the count, and in unison, we jumped up and then were caught by the girls at our base. Spotters on either side stood by, ready.

The broadcaster's booming voice was excitedly calling out the plays for anyone's eyes off the field.

"And Triggs delivers a strike in the first down of the leading receiver..." Cheers from the orange; silence from the red. The voice boomed on, "...confident throw from KeShawn Smith as he brings another first down inside the fifteen." I smiled at the crowd, joining my group with a highly choreographed pom-pom routine. Moving together as one unit, the crowd in front of us was flashing cameras and calling out to us.

"Go, Texas. Love y'all," a woman's voice called out in our direction.

On a verbal cue from the head coach, I ran with Lindsay to a box just off the turf. Grabbing two Texas T-shirts rolled tightly and wrapped in thick rubber bands, I looked up into the bleachers. The fans near us stood instantly, vying for our attention.

Arms were waving. "Up here. Babe, up here. Right here, sweetheart." Lindsay and I held hands and, holding up a shirt in each hand, spun around facing the crowd. Then, smiling, we diverged. I went right, and she went left. I tossed a shirt up in the stands towards a group of excited students. They all lunged for it, contending aggressively to be the winner. A student in a white hat held up the shirt, giving it to the girl next to him.

"Thank you, darlin'. Love you!" I waved at the group, grabbed another shirt, and tossed it higher into the stands. Hands reached out, and the victor raised it over his head. I recognized him instantly.

James had caught it. Recognizing his face made my heart beat faster. My eyes flashed to either side of James, and I found him. Eyes locked on me. He smiled. He seemed like he was handling the crowd well. Great. He was wearing sky blue, naturally going against the hackneyed color choices of thousands and thousands of Longhorn devotees. Same sweet Matt from last night looked down at me and winked. He was trying.

"So proud of you," I mouthed up to him.

He put his hands up in a gesture of ambiguity. It was too many words to mouth to someone at two hundred feet of separation.

I responded by moving closer on the track, forming my hands into a heart shape. "You," I silently mouthed.

"You," he responded, handing James his beer and emulating my heart. I turned back to Jenn.

"What the actual fuck?" She nearly yelled in my ear over the speakers.

"Be nice." I tried not to cringe at my friend.

"That guy? He is so mean to you, Amy. I won't be your friend if you date that guy."

"It turns out he is nice. We will talk later." We were positioning ourselves for stunting.

"I have met him, remember? On two occasions, I go out. I've been to y'alls bar. He is not nice, actually. He is hot. Hot as fuck," she continued her sailor speak. "But, no, babe. He is not nice."

We rose into the air together, grabbing hands for balance. On count, we caught our heels, extending our legs in front of us, our gleaming white sneakers as close in proximity to our ears as possible. Hold. Smile. The count was in my head. Back straight. Drop foot, jump up to a toe touch, and then basket toss, down to our base girls, catching us on the ground, still trying to finish our conversation.

"I like him," I looked up, breathing hard and wondering what he thought of my stunt. He smiled, his eyes never finding their way to the field.

"No, Amy. Just no." Jenn patted my shoulder.

Despite my friend's warnings still in my ear, I smiled up at him and pointed to the fifty-yard line. His eyes met mine, and he smiled, laughing, and shook his head. Uninterested in the game. Me too. Maybe he was starting to see how hard this was. This wasn't just weigh-ins and outfits he disapproved of. This was hard on an athletic level and seeing this was good for him.

I smiled and rushed, obscured from view, to the awning for a water break, for a mental break from his intense gaze. I thought of work. I came back out, hydrated, with a few seconds to talk.

"Matt, do we go to Azure tonight?" I mouthed silently to him. He paused, then, in understanding, shook his head no.

"Not yet. Negotiating the situation still." He smiled broadly. "Your friend Stephanie found me."

"What?" I couldn't understand him. He put up a finger to signal he needed a moment.

At this exact moment, the Longhorns scored their sixth touchdown against Texas Tech.

"Emerson, Pattison, go now, six. You're awesome," my coach called out to us. I looked up at Matt, and he smiled, waving at me as I took off towards the goalposts. Six back handsprings were representing the six point gain, in unison with Kelsi Pattison. I looked at her, and we took a running start and ran, ready to turn into the back handspring.

"One." The entire stadium, minus any Tech fans, counted along. "Two. Three." I focused on my form. Nothing else right now, even him, could distract me from my current focus. Everything needed to be sharp. Kelsi and I made our bodies move together. I knew her pace and cadence. "Four, five, six!" The fans cheered wildly. Our smiling faces and accompanying high five were suddenly broadcasted on the enormous teleprompter. We stopped short, popping up in the air as we finished, raising hands in accentuated hand waves. Catching our breaths, and holding hands raised to the sky, we strolled back to the base camp near the twenty-yard line.

I took a sip of water from the hydration station, and coming back into view, looked up, searching for Matt. I found him, arms around Jason and Amber, singing the fight song. Wow. He was having fun. I was so stunned and happy about this that I turned back to my team, intent on my gaze not changing anything for him.

"Two and a half. Amy, Jenn, Tisha, go." The assistant coach beckoned me towards the thirty-yard line. We had fifteen girls now, divided into lift, spot, and catch groups for the pyramid. Up. I held my body tight as I felt a lift towards the second tier. Hold. I looked over and saw Stephanie.

"Did he tell you yet?" She was gleaming. I knew who she was referring to but not anything he might have said.

"No."

I was up to third-tier with Jenn and me alone on the top. Flyers. We mounted into position, and arms raised, held. The count was loud in my head. One. Two. Three. Four. Five. The sequence was descending. This was a fast-paced move full of tricky transitions, release moves, and dismounts. I was down on the ground before I could count to three. We dissipated to the appropriate groups, ready for the end game show.

I looked up at Matt. He signaled to me that he had something in his hand. I smiled and ran directly beneath him. From the sky, a balled-up piece of white paper fell to the field. I caught it and running to my group, tossed it by my bag. Lottie, the assistant coach, patiently went through the end game layout. Water break. I ran to my bag and, breathing hard, unrolled the paper. "Beautiful, beautiful girl. Proud of you this afternoon. JR and I have not made right. We don't go in. Steph invited us to a frat party, a 'bubble party' on west campus. Apparently, you have been invited to many things like this but have never gone because of your work schedule—poor girl. Let's go tonight. I have tickets for the three of us—ten p.m. I will pick you up. Matt." I crumbled the paper, threw it in my bag, and ran out from under the awning. I smiled up at him and made an "okay" sign with my hand and then a heart. He winked at me and turned to leave.

The game was nearly over, and they wanted to beat the existing crowd, no doubt. I looked up and waved at James and Amber. They turned, waving sweetly at me. I tossed a shirt up to Amber last minute, she caught it, blew me a kiss, and they were gone.

I went on to finish with three more stunts, mostly basket tosses with the male cheerleaders and then a group cheer as we exited, jogging back through the tunnel. I linked arms with Stephanie.

"We did it! The fall is going to be awesome," she said.

Her arm was around my shoulder now. "You dear, dear friend. You invited him to a party, and he said YES! What have you done?" I hugged my arm around her neck. "I cannot believe this is happening. Tell me everything," I squealed with unknown delight.

Stephanie detailed the party situation in the dressing room as soon as we were out of the showers. "Who is hosting this, Stephanie?"

"A frat near my house. I forget which one. Delta or Kappa or something." She smiled. "It's a bubble party. You need to be there at ten with Matt. I will be outside exactly at ten but can wait around a bit for y'all to arrive; I live two blocks away, you know. Actually, why don't you guys come over first? She scribbled her address on my hand in ballpoint pen. We can have a drink and then walk over."

"I'm not sure if I will, but he might. I am super grateful. I haven't seen your place."

"Amy, I am so happy to party with you and Big Guy. He's actually nice. He recognized me from the gym as your friend and waved. Then, he ran over from the BBQ and fed me a bite of steak as we passed. We talked for a short bit." Haha. I was laughing, astonished at this image of him doing something so endearing.

"Awesome. I love that he can be sweet and normal."

Now she was laughing, "I think you're right; he's maybe not so scary. I mean, from how I have seen him behave today, he's like any guy."

"Right? I mean, he will never just be any guy for me." I was immediately loathing her word choices. "But I understand what you're saying, and I am encouraged."

This was so out of character. Or was it just that I was getting to know Matt for the first time? I hugged Stephanie again out of gratitude and ran towards the side garage where I had parked my bicycle.

"I once had a thousand desires. But in my one desire to know you all else melted away." —*Rumi*

"I heard you say you trust Matt. That's good. He will look after you, and you can let go, relax for once." —*Stephanie*

CHAPTER EIGHT

"Bubble Party"

Riding my ten-speed speedily through campus, my mind jumped from new memory to new memory. I felt like I had lived a lifetime's worth of happiness and adventure in half a week. My head was spinning. I parked my bike outside my building and entered the dorm room in a state of utter exhaustion and triumph. It had never occurred to me that Matt might enjoy the game and glean a sense of discernment for my sport's actual athleticism. It was nearly seven.

Inside our cozy dorm room, Kate had ordered us Indian food and was re-heating a plate.

"Oh, wow. This smells so yummy." She watched me put a twenty dollar bill under a magnet on the fridge. "Thank you for ordering and picking up coffee beans." She smiled.

"It's delicious. It may look like baby food, but it's spicy well-rounded flavors. Here." She had made my plate. "How was the second scrimmage, and why is your hair wet?"

"It was fun. I think the nerves will be gone for the fall season. I showered at the stadium." We talked about her classes and her crochet projects. She was making seat covers for the breakfast chairs. Always on a craft project, she had completed three out of four, and they were a perfect fit of soft purple loops. "This was just what I needed. You?" She nodded.

"I love this new place. Let's order again next week."

"Yep." I washed my plate, brushed my teeth, and collapsed on my bed for a two-hour nap. I woke up at nine and joined Kate for a coffee.

"Amy, your friend Stephanie called; there is a color code for the party tonight." She looked at a scrap of paper by the phone. "You need to wear—"

"Orange," I smiled. I had been in Austin only a couple of months but understood there is always a burnt orange dress code. "Got it."

"No! No, actually...it says white only or no entry."

"Unexpected after a big win like today." I changed into a pair of white jeans and a white T-shirt. I blow-dried my hair, and after brushing my teeth and doing my makeup, I sat on the couch with Kate.

"Are you sure you don't want to join us?"

"No, I am pretty tired from running around doing errands on the drag and doing lunch with friends."

"Are you sure?" I smiled.

"Of course. I am just impressed you are going to a party and with him. You have known each other for months but only in the last forty-eight hours have you started doing anything that could possibly resemble normal dating." I smiled at her insight.

"You are right. And there is a marked difference between us. He is so different now. So nice and charming. I see him trying."

"He has fallen in love. You have tamed a wild beast."

I didn't say anything, choosing to pull a cuticle instead, thinking it over. It seemed too early for that, but I felt like she was right as well. At least on some level.

"And what about you. Do you feel that way?"

"I don't know." I needed to be honest. "I think I do. I admire him. I feel so happy around him. I have never felt this way about another person."

"But..." She sensed my hesitation.

"So, the thing is, he has only recently become a nice man in my presence. I know that man is who he is. A small part of me is still scared of him. Intimidated. Like only four percent, but I cannot call it love until he makes that go away completely for me."

She looked up from her purple yarn, concerned. "Well, I think you are smart to be mindful, to go slow."

"Yes. That's the plan." It seemed impossible. Even during the chaos of the game, the way we had both connected was intense energy. This was going to be the most challenging part of our relationship—going slow.

"Well, I'm so happy that you are my dearest oldest friend, and honestly, I am just so happy to see that you are happy, Amy."

"Oh, thanks for being excited with me," I smiled kindly at her. "You and I have known each other since we were eight. Hard to imagine we are here in college together. And with all this work and studying happening, it is a super rare treat going out on a Saturday night like this. I don't know when or if it will happen again. I'm always working. And I enjoy work, but this is something so different. I am honestly stunned. Stephanie invited him, and then, even more, astounding, he said yes."

I looked at my watch and dabbed some perfume on my wrists. Stepping out to the balcony, I looked outside, expecting to hear the roar of a giant pickup truck. Instead, I saw him stepping silently out of a taxi and walk towards the lobby.

I kissed Kate on the cheek. "Bye, honey."

"Enjoy your bubble party, whatever that is."

"Not sure either but thank you. Just a cute name, I think. Oddly, I could be back much sooner than normal, but I will be a mouse. 'Night."

The elevator doors opened, and I stepped out to see him

waiting for the elevator.

"Amy!" He was instantly in front of me, lifting me in a giant hug. He smelled like he had just gotten out of the shower, the faint smell of soap still clung to his hair. He had a single red rose in his hand.

"Matt, what did you do? Thank you." I was noticing a theme with him. "Have you given me a flower every day since we kissed under the bank building?" He smiled. "Is this something you do? Like with past girlfriends?" My tone was kind and nonthreatening. We hadn't talked about this before, and suddenly I felt as if I had asked a crazy paramount question, not the little question I had initially intended.

"Amy, I have been with many girls."

"Mmm." My heart sank. I knew I was not his first girlfriend, but it was still painful to hear.

"I have pursued girls for a long, long time now. Like any man, I guess. No more or less, really. And though I have dated and had a few healthy, lasting relationships, it hasn't been many. And no to what you are thinking."

I smiled, "and what is that?"

"Have I ever felt this way about someone else? Am I just doing the same monotonous routines?"

"I didn't ask this. I asked, essentially, are you always this thoughtful?"

"No." He smiled. "I am not. I am always honest and respectful, though, when I am with someone. But you are very, very different. And the path we are on is a new one for me too. I want to enjoy things with you and through your eyes. Your pleasure. Your happiness is what I want to pursue." I reached for his hand, silently letting him know I was okay with what he was saying. That I wasn't jealous, and I was grateful for his honesty.

"I think I understand. And I appreciate your honesty."

He went on, "And to fully answer your question, I want to say that I plan on giving you a flower every waking day for the rest of my life. And when I give it to you, I am saying silently in my head, every single time, saying to myself…" he smiled, "Be worthy." I smiled slowly. "Be worthy," he repeated softly. "I said it last night on the porch by the yellow roses. I was so tired I almost said it out loud." He smiled brightly. "Come on." He linked my arm in his, and we went to the waiting cab.

I gave the driver Stephanie's address and settled into the back seat holding his hand. "Where is your truck?" I asked as the driver sped away from the curb towards Guadalupe. He smiled, holding my hand.

"I drank beer earlier at the football game, and James's place is near you. We ate dinner and had more beer. I feel fine, but I would never do anything that would endanger you."

No. Mr. Safety would not make bad choices like this. "You handle beer well. I couldn't tell. I think I saw a Shiner Bock in your hand at the game, but your behavior was normal." After working at Azure for just over two months, I felt like I was an expert at distinguishing drunken behaviors. I could spot them way easier now than in May.

"I have been doing a lot of things, obscure to you, for many years now. I am a good drinker. I'm responsible, I know what I like, I keep hydrated, and I seldom overdo it. It's all so much to figure out when you're new to essentially everything." He laughed.

"Are you laughing at me?"

"Yes."

"Why?"

"Honestly, you are so cute, Amy. And also, I just remembered something about last night. I am so sorry about the Santa question! I am honestly so relieved, I knew it wasn't true, but she had me so worried. You knowing the truth about Santa is a starting place we can build a foundational relationship on."

We both laughed, playfully pushing each other, as the taxi zoomed through a yellow light. The soft glow of businesses and homes created streams of light, like shooting stars, whooshing on either side of us.

"Matt, I want to tell you something." He leaned down so I could whisper in his ear. "Thank you for my flower. Thank you for what you said about its meaning. I liked it enough when it was just a flower. Now I want to save it forever. Maybe." I was suddenly feeling shy.

"Maybe?" He whispered as he turned to me, grabbing my chin and lifting it so I could face him. He leaned down, his seatbelt extending out as far as it could go until it locked, and kissed me—long, slow, passionate kisses. I felt a soft trembling all over my body. It started in my stomach and moved outwards like a ripple in a stream rushing headlong to my extremities, where it stayed, leaving my fingertips feeling vulnerable.

We were interrupted by our cab stopping in front of a cobalt blue duplex with a large concrete front porch filled with red geraniums. Matt paid the driver, and we got out. Stephanie must have heard the cab door shut because she opened her door as we approached the steps. Soft ambient lights like flickering candles flooded our eyes from behind her. There was the earthy smell of bergamot incense burning in the hallway as we entered.

"Come in here, Amy." She excitedly gave me a big hug as we came to the living room.

"I am so happy to see you," I smiled warmly. "I love this place!"

She turned and gave Matt a welcoming hug as well. After a quick tour of her small apartment, we settled in on the soft gray couch, fanned by two blue lounge chairs and lots of tables with potted succulents and cactus. I smiled, looking at the vast array of colors and textures.

"It's the only thing I can keep alive, with this crazy schedule. Let's have a quick drink before heading over.

"Yes, please." Matt walked to the kitchen to help her carry

a sizeable, prepared tray into the living room. I looked around at the mint-colored walls and orange-trimmed room full of happy, bright things and family pictures. This room was a felicitous place to be. I smiled, feeling glad for my friend. She walked in behind Matt, who was carrying a large acrylic tray, which he set on the coffee table in front of us. On it, she had bowls of mixed nuts, a glass of salami sticks that shot out in all directions bending over the glass, and the makings for martinis.

"Martinis or beer?"

"I will go with two beers, thank you, Stephanie." He pulled an opener out of his pocket.

"Amy, would you make me a martini?"

"Of course, love. How do you like it?"

She turned on the radio to Jane Siberry and K.D. Lang's "Calling All Angels," which filled the living room. "Vodka and wet."

"Okay, honey."

Most people ordered dry with olive juice. I turned, trying to remember what the wet connotation referred to in this drink. Vermouth. Right. I proceeded to her bar tray and shook ice, a local vodka called Tinos, and a drizzle of vermouth. One more drizzle. I opened the shaker steadily and let the icy liquid spill out slowly into a glass. Little ice shards, making tinkling sounds like jingle bells, made them look up. As I handed her the glass, I realized that they had been discussing something very particular while I was preoccupied.

"What?" I smiled. I wondered if he doubted my adroitness at this classic. "Matt, I make good martinis. I learned from Johnny Ray during my first week. Steph, tell him."

She took a sip. "Yes, it's perfect. I make these all the time. I know what I like, and this is better than mine." I grinned.

"I will just ask her then." Steph was talking to him now.

Matt nodded to Stephanie, who opened a jar on the coffee table tray. It was a small white jar with a star on the lid. She passed it to Matt. He opened, looked in, and closing it, held it in his hands.

"What is this?" I asked, suddenly feeling uneasy. "You guys look so serious. I thought you only could care for succulents? Stephanie, are we burying your late hamster tonight before the party? I will speak a few words if needed." Matt threw back his head and laughed loudly.

"You are so funny! Everything you say."

I smiled. "Okay, not really. But what's going on?" My eyes shot from Stephanie's deep brown eyes to Matt's. No one said anything, so I stood.

"Steph, I am going to go to the restroom before we head out. Whatever scary thing is in that jar better be gone when I get back, Matthew." I shot him an attempt at a dirty look, but it came out as a smile anyways.

He laughed and nodded. When I got back, it was clear they had finished discussing whatever it was that needed more saying.

Matt looked up as I entered the room. "You are so beautiful."

"She is, isn't she?" My friend was coming out to bat for me. "Can I just tell you, Amy has her own fan base. Some people show up time after time to practice, just to try and speak with her. The scrimmage before last was closed, but there were some friends and family that came. And this guy dropped roses with her name on the tags down onto the field during practice."

Matt smiled. "Oh, I believe it."

"My rose, oh no! It's in the cab. I had wanted to dry it and keep it forever. Shoot."

Matt shifted slightly in his seat to reveal it beside him. "Come sit with me in this huge love seat; there is room."

I stood and paused at the coffee table to refill Stephanie's martini on my way to him. I stood listening as he spoke, still wary of the jar.

"Amy, where I envision us years from now when school is over for you, is far, far away from all this. I have experienced a lot of parties and different things," he paused, "that you do at parties during my high school and undergrad years." He was purposefully vague. "And I don't want you to miss any of the fun, more prudent aspects of this time in your life. Especially when I am with you to help you. Sweetheart, you can say no, but I think you should try some different things during your college years, within reason."

I smiled. "Okay, but I have no idea what you guys are talking about."

"To be clear, there are plenty of negative things to experience if you are unsafe, but Stephanie and I talked at the pregame, and we thought you should try one of these." He opened the jar from the coffee table.

I timidly reached in and pulled out a tiny brownie. "Okay," I said flatly. They were staring at me. "I am happy you made these, Steph." I brought it to my lips quickly, hoping they would stop staring once I took a bite.

"No!" "Stop!" They both cried out.

"Aaaah," I screamed and dropped it on the floor, standing up fast, a chair between us. "What is wrong with you?" Matt was roaring with laughter. I had never heard him laugh so hard.

"Amy, these are pot brownies. I didn't mean to scare you. But you need to decide. We were thinking, it's a safe environment for you to try one, with us."

"Drugs?" I was confused. "Matt, I thought you never took drugs or condoned anything like this. You have always said as much."

"Well, pot is marijuana. It is legal for medicinal purposes. It is a drug, that's true. But it comes from a plant and, when used in reason, can be fun."

"No." I shook my head. "No, I can't do this." I imagined myself sitting alone in a desolate alleyway, drug paraphernalia scattered by my bare feet.

"Amy, this is a very expensive, very pure hybrid. It has a name, Purple Kush, and gives a very relaxing, blissful sort of high. I bought this from James this afternoon, and Steph made brownies with it for you."

"You tried this today? This afternoon?" I couldn't believe what I was hearing. I never thought about doing drugs before. Drugs with names. And yet, I was considering it now.

"Yes, honey, we smoked at the game. While tailgating. I wanted to make sure it was perfect if you wanted to try it tonight."

"Will you have some too? Again?"

"No, sweetheart. No, I want to be able to handle myself. Keep track of you. A football game is fun for something like this but not a frat party with you two. Frat boys are unskilled, but they'll come at you by the hundreds, like ninjas, if you step on their ant pile." He smiled at his own inane analogy. "I don't expect that, but I have to anticipate trouble to some degree. I will keep my head and stick with beer. Stephanie?"

"Matt, thank you, I am in." She reached in the jar, took a two-inch by two-inch brown square, and set it on a plate. "Amy, I am going to eat one, maybe two, but we thought you might like to try half."

"I'm...I...I'm not sure." I had tears in my eyes. I didn't know how to respond. I smiled at them anyways; I knew their intent was kind. These were my people.

I stood up, taking my rose to the kitchen along with some dirty dishes, and began setting them in her sink. I put the rose in water. I hadn't expected this, and though I knew in my heart I would likely live through this night no matter what I chose, I felt overwhelmed. Pulling my hair into a ponytail, I added a drop of golden liquid soap to a sponge near the sink. I turned on the warm water, thinking. He came up behind me and, leaning down, kissed my neck. He didn't speak, but it was clear enough that he was waiting on me.

"I don't want to embarrass you, but I am trying not to cry."

"Oh no. Come here." I turned to him, wet hands trying not to touch his shirt as we hugged. "Why would you cry?" He smiled sweetly. "And that wouldn't embarrass me."

"I always thought people who do drugs are bad people. And I don't want to be...like that in any way...to be bad. I want a purposeful, happy life and I am feeling overwhelmed." I had to be honest, even if it felt shamefully nerdy. He kissed the top of my head.

"Your childhood. I understand. Listen, it's not that simple. Not all drugs are equal. And irresponsibly, like driving and using or excessive use, is not okay. People who hurt people using the lens of addiction as an excuse. People who are using serious narcotics which are dangerous. That's different. Amy, soon enough, you are going to be married," he paused, running his hand over my shoulder, "Happily married, living happily ever after, in a place far from here. You are going to have babies and little kids running around pitter pattering barefoot on the floorboards. I don't want to be the guy that put you in a tower, even though I really wanted to." He grinned at me.

I could see what he was trying to say to me, what he was trying to give. He continued, "And I think it would be okay to try this. Plant-based, natural. Not too much. Within the safely net of being with me. If you don't want to, that is fine, of course. It's okay. Whatever you want is fine. I personally do not believe what we are talking about for you tonight is a sin."

"Umm." I nodded into his chest as we hugged. I still hadn't decided as we turned and walked back into the living room.

"Are you good, girl?" Stephanie had changed into her white shirt and was drinking a second martini.

I smiled shyly. I hadn't meant to be dramatic; I was just so wholly taken aback suddenly by a situation I never thought I would be in at any point in my life. Matt opened another Lone Star beer and looked at his watch. 10:30. I squeezed his hand,

and he looked over at me. "I trust you."

He smiled. I opened my mouth and popped in a quarter of the brownie. I am not sure what I thought it would taste like, but it was seemingly just like any other confection of its kind that I had ever had. Wait, no. Maybe there was an aftertaste of some sort, like hay or grass from a newly mowed lawn.

Steph smiled at me, "You are not going to go to hell over this." I smiled; tears came anyway. I worked hard, so they didn't fall. I didn't trust words, so I nodded. "Your other quarter." She handed me another tiny square. "This will be fun. It will be okay."

"I don't want to feel scared or out of control."

"Amy, come here," Matt gently pulled me onto his lap, whispering in my ear. "You're thinking about June. I won't let anything bad happen to you. It won't feel anything like that, and you won't feel overwhelmed with this much. It's okay." I nodded; he had answered the question I hadn't wanted to ask.

"Okay, Matt." He stood up and brought his bottles to the recycling.

"I heard you say to Matt, that you trust him. That's good. He will look out for you, and you can let go, relax for once. Everything will be fine. I'm meeting someone there, but I will help you if you need me."

I was suddenly aware of the music. Duran Duran's "Hungry Like the Wolf" was playing. Matt had just gone to the restroom and returned to find Stephanie attempting to teach me how to hold and strum her ukulele. I looked up at Matt. "I think my brownie was broken. I feel normal. But don't worry, I am still having fun."

He smiled at me, laughing as he put his hand on my shoulder. "Well, saying your food is broken, that verbiage, is the first hint it is working."

"Oh, no." Haha! He must be right.

"Should we go? If we hate it, we can just come back to my place. But first, Amy, I want you to try just a sip of my martini.

It's still cold."

"Good idea." Matt opened another beer.

"Just one or two sips, and you will be perfect. It's not too much tonight. Okay? You are okay." She seemed so confident.

I wondered how she had eaten an entire brownie and had three martinis with her tiny figure. I was feeling something. I looked at Matt, and he smiled brightly.

"Okay." I brought the thin glass to my lips and took a sip.

"A bigger sip," she urged. I took a bigger sip. It burned, and it was hard to swallow.

"Oh, my goodness, why would you like this?" I was coughing. "It tastes like seawater! Exactly like the ocean. Specifically, the Mediterranean, if I recalled a trip fondly three years ago."

"Haha," she laughed. "I made this one dirty, and you are right actually...sea water!" We both laughed.

"Steph, do you have a travel toothbrush I can borrow? It's so salty." Laughing, we disappeared in the bathroom, emerging a moment later minty and groomed.

Matt grinned at me. "Let's go."

We walked out onto the porch, and though it was a couple of blocks away, we could already hear the soft buzzing of party revelers talking and the faint drum of music. "How do you feel?" He was holding my hand as we traversed the side streets together. Stephanie was on my right, singing along to a song playing on repeat in her head.

"Good."

Suddenly, I was aware of how big his hand was.

"Matt, your hands are enormous." I released my grip on his hand to rub our palms together slowly. I looked down, stunned I had not noticed this before. Maybe I had actually, but tonight it was shocking visual information.

"They are in proportion to the rest of my body. I have big feet too." Stephanie reached around to pop him hard in the chest.

"Don't scare her." They both chuckled softly.

Instantaneously, I felt like I was a child, walking with my parents. And they were having an adult conversation directly in front of me. One I didn't understand, nor was I invited to participate in. I felt like they had given me a shiny red balloon, and I was watching as it floated away—farther and farther away. I looked up at the stars—a prayer for tonight, for my mixed emotions, and my sin. No stars welcomed the words I sent up from my thoughts.

Matt grabbed my hand as we stepped up the stairs of a giant grassy lawn. Beyond the landing, an enormous white house with oversized white marbled columns seemed to vibrate from the life within. The sprinklers were on, and at least four Slip N Slides were set up on a far side of a vast grassy expanse. Several young, intoxicated pledges were already hurdling themselves down the shiny lanes like bowling balls towards pins, rolling off the end, and tumbling into the grass in a fit of laughter.

"I am understanding the dress code. I figured as much. Men are such conniving assholes." He had lowered his voice and turned to talk to Stephanie. "Are you sure you are good?"

"Yes," she said. "I know what I'm doing, what I want. We've been talking for a while."

"Okay." He continued to lecture her but in a less chastening tone than he had ever used on me. I looked up at the giant white house. Greek letters for the frat in substantial black letters hung thirty feet above us. Matt handed the unfortunate pledge assigned to door duty the tickets.

"Shirt off, man. White only."

"Who wants to look at me?" Matt smiled. "Point him out; I want to be polite about my preferences." Not knowing how to respond, he parroted the only jargon he had been told.

"White only is our Greek party code tonight. You can lose the shirt, of course. Just go shirtless."

I turned away, not wanting Matt to see my face. I was

feeling the euphoric feeling from the brownie and the buzz of my salty sip. I couldn't trust my face not to reveal my elated anticipation and almost fear of seeing him shirtless.

As I turned from him and towards the door, I could see thick plastic sheeting beyond the partially opened entrance. I walked towards it, pushing it aside with my finger. Behind it, like a huge writhing mass, was something that looked like mounds and mounds of glittering snow.

"Oooh. Aaaaah." I took a step towards it and scooped some with my finger. "Bubbles. Heaps and heaps of them," I whispered to myself. I remembered the invitation and, suddenly excited, pushed the door open, and walked inside.

Instantly, I was swallowed up to my waist in a magical sparkling glittered froth. The music from the stereo on the wall was the only object in the room other than a disco light flashing color across the white sea foam. "I Want Candy," by Bow Wow Wow, was playing filling up the air space in the room that the bubbles had not yet occupied as they rose quietly from the floor to meet the music. On the left and the right of the grand room were hallways with more bubbles pouring out, flowing like ebbs in a river towards the elegant space.

I looked down at the illuminating bubbles that clung to my white jeans like a second layer of clothing. And suddenly feeling the effects of the evening, I jumped forward and did a front flip, the bubbles whipping up like soft cream from my feet and hair as I moved. Landing on my feet with a dull thud made me wonder what was under me. The high from my confection and the soft sparkling sensation was overwhelmingly interesting. I suddenly started parting the soapy foam, its strawberry smell more aromatic as I popped bubbles in my attempt to dig. Finally, several feet down, I could see the wooden floor for a moment before the enormous mass overcame the empty space and buried it completely. Of course, it was a floor. Why had I even checked? I smiled to myself.

Two boys wearing white shorts and no shirts passed me, heading towards the kitchen.

"Want something?"

Looking around at the other twenty people in the room and unsure who they were talking to, I didn't answer.

"Hey, babe," one of them came over, putting a glow stick necklace around my neck. "Can I get you a drink?"

"No. No, thank you." I wanted to play in the soap.

He smiled kindly and disappeared into the kitchen. Suddenly I heard my name being called from a booming voice outside. I spun around to see Matt and Stephanie entering the house abruptly. His face was panicked like he had lost a child at a fairground. Scanning the faces and moving through the soap quickly, his eyes locked on mine. I waved at him. "Matt, Steph...bubbles!"

He had his white undershirt on, his blue folded one was hanging from his pants. "Amy, I was so worried about you. You can't walk off." He put my hand to his chest to feel his rapidly beating heart. "Don't leave my sight for even one minute, okay?"

"Okay. I didn't mean to. I just saw some bubbles by the door, and I couldn't help but touch them. Look how sparkly they are. I didn't mean to leave."

"You need to stay close. All night, sweetheart." He smiled, forgiving me. He didn't want to lecture me; he wanted me to have fun. The scintillating bubbles had risen to my core.

"Matt, how did they make this bubble bath without the water? And is it all over the house?"

"It is all over the house. The pledges have to clean it in the morning. They have a bubble machine upstairs and one off to the kitchen, apparently."

I turned to my friend, "Wow. Stephanie. So amazing, right?"

She grabbed my hand to dance with me, her answer in her swaying hips. The song ended, and a DJ set up outside on the lawn announced that anyone wearing a glow stick needed to take off an article of clothing and toss it out the window. I spun around and noticed some pledges had opened the high windows.

Steph touched my necklace. "That's you."

"Where did you get that?" Matt sighed. "You were missing for literally two minutes or less." He took my necklace and tossed it across the room like a frisbee, where it sank slowly out of sight. "I need a beer. I am already stressed out. Do not let go of my hand. All night."

"Don't be stressed. Bubbles." I reminded him and scooped some up, blowing a kiss as they sprayed in all directions.

Grinning, he held me firmly by the hand, pulling me towards the kitchen, past the dancing masses. A foaming wake was rippling out from either side of him as we moved. In the kitchen, the bubbles were very high. We must be closer to one of the machines. He looked down at me, the glittering white up to my armpits. Not letting go of my hand, he made a swiping direction over where he guessed the countertops to be. Correctly finding them, he lifted me onto the counter.

"Don't move." He winked at me. "Now, to find the fridge." It was the only thing that was clearly marked in the kitchen. Transparent packing tape held thirty glow sticks on the perimeter of the entire fridge, a clear demarcation to find beer. I lifted my finger towards the unmistakable glow slowly as I lay down on the counter. The suds were one inch thick on the counter now and rising. I looked up at the ceiling, listening to the soft popping around me, my leg hanging over the edge of the counter, swinging back and forth kicking the suds.

"Well, well. Hello there." Five Greeks walked in from the great room into the kitchen. Somehow their seemingly friendly hello was wolf-speak for, "I think I see a drunk girl."

I picked up my hand and waved it, watching my fingers move like they were slowly playing an invisible piano. I waved again, this time at the ceiling, looking at my fingers, fascinated by their movements.

Matt rose suddenly from in front of the fridge. "Beer?" He asked cheerfully to the approaching mob.

"Sure. Thanks, man." He tossed some cans over and walked to me as they exited out the back.

He set his Tecate down behind my shoulder and began unearthing my core and shoulders from the glimmering white that was attempting to overtake me. I wiggled around laughing as he leaned into me, speaking in my ear over the music.

"You look so good lying on this soapy table." His hand was softly brushing over the bubbles on my skin. "All my life, I have never seen a more desirable, beautiful girl."

He leaned into the cabinetry to kiss me. I made "mmm" sounds softly and touched the soap on the smooth, cool marble with my fingers. I looked up and smiled. He met my smile, and taking a bit of soap, touched my nose with it playfully.

"Haha!" I didn't attempt to remove it. Instead, I sat up as it slid off and moved to my knees, so I was above him on the countertop. "It's my turn to say, 'don't move' to you."

"Oh, really." He turned, facing me. "Well...I better not move then."

"No, you'd better not." I scooped some gleaming meringue and dolloped some on his head, making a little hat. "Don't move," I bossed him a second time.

"Yes, ma'am." He closed one eye as suds ran down his temple. I noticed in time and stopped it with my hand, protecting his eyes. I added more peaks to the first scoop and heard Stephanie's voice.

"There you are. What are y'all doing?" She smirked.

"Playing," Matt answered for us, remaining perfectly still. I added more foam, and it ran off the back of his head almost immediately.

"Y'all are so cute."

"You still good out there?" Matt called to her, still not

turning his head.

"Yes. Thanks. He's here now, came late, but it is going well. Very happy." I looked up from my work and smiled. "Amy, I will tell you later." I grinned back at her. She grabbed two beers and blew me a kiss, retreating to the front room.

"All finished." I sat down and wrapped my legs around his waist, kissing him.

"I want to move now."

"Okay." He turned his head, angling for a better kiss as the suds ran off him.

"Lay back. I love the height of this countertop."

We kissed sweetly, slowly, the passion building in both of us. His fingers intertwined with mine up against the smooth tile were pinning me in place. I squeezed his hand, and he kissed me deeper in response. Somehow the act of kissing while lying down had deepened the effect he had on my body. Tingles as small and numerous as the popping bubbles around us filled me. I wondered if he felt the same way. Every so often, he needed to unearth me from the shimmering milky waves. They were rising very high now. The vast whiteness all around us was somehow creating tunnel vision for us both. There was only him and only me. No one else existed; only distant laughing and muted screams suggested otherwise.

Suddenly the sprinklers came on above us; I screamed, sitting up quickly and looking to the ceiling and laughing with surprise, my hands held up trying to catch the droplets through open fingers. The water flooding down on the kitchen eradicated millions of tiny bubbles, popping them instantly on contact with the cold water. The foam sank three feet, and then immediately, the water stopped—bubble control. I was giggling incessantly from the shock and sheer exhilaration of it all.

"Now I won't lose you. Good." Matt reached over and replaced his forgotten beer with a cold one from the fridge. He took several sips. "Do you need something?"

"A water if they have something so boring." He smiled and passed me one.

He drank a water then more of his beer, and not knowing where to put the bottles, tossed them into a foamy mass at the side of the fridge. He walked a few feet over to me and stopped suddenly. He didn't move, frozen in the foam, his gaze moving from my body and back to meet my eyes. Some Greeks passed through the kitchen on their way upstairs; talking loudly, they grabbed drinks and fumbled up the glistening steps. He hadn't moved yet, brown eyes locked on mine, a serious look on his face. I laughed and threw some suds in his direction.

"Mother may I...yes, you can walk," I joked, wishing I could suddenly be in my twenties. My upper twenties. I should have said something else.

Eventually coming out of his trance, he treaded to me, putting his hands on my waist, his lips to mine. His kiss was full of affection and desirable wanting. Tempestuously he kissed my forehead and whispered in my ear through the music.

"Oh no. Really?" I looked down. My shirt had ultimately become see-through and his odd behavior was obvious to me now. A thin pink bra was now visible, and attempting to rise from the cotton fabric, excited by the sudden cold water shower they had just endured, were my nipples. "No, no, no, no." I reached to cover myself with my hands.

"This is the entire reason for this party. All the furniture they had to clear out and put in some storage unit. All the prep and cleaning. It's essentially about this." He nodded towards my chest. "You understand that, don't you? About this place. We are not in a nice place." I looked around at the sparkling magic around me. It felt like a winter wonderland. He could see it his way, but I would see it mine.

He slowly moved towards me and put his hand carefully on my collar bone. Letting his hand drop to my heart, he leaned into my ear to whisper. My heart was beating very fast now. He opened his hand carefully, avoiding my breasts, and leaned his forehead to mine. He was silent, but I noticed his lips moving. He was praying. This was the second great shock of the evening. We had not discussed his faith before, and I had wanted to ask him at the cafe about his religious views, the multiple fights he was in, his grazed knuckles, more about his family. Instead, we had just let ourselves enjoy the date and it had gone naturally in any direction it wanted. We had abandoned any verbal agenda, somehow brushing over all the things we were going to say, and instead went with our hearts. This was another moment like that. I put my hands over his and leaned into him, my face on his shoulder; he spoke above a whisper, now allowing me in his prayer and thoughts. When he finished, he embraced me tighter, and I tugged his arm softly; he leaned down so I could reach his ear better.

"You are so wonderful. The best boyfriend in the world. I want you to know." Sighing and then rising up on my toes again to reach him, I said, "I guess I couldn't have known it could be like this. I'm so happy."

He kissed my forehead and leaned down to look at his watch. It was just past 11:30. "Maybe I'm not the best boyfriend, Little. What do you think Kate would think if I dropped you off like this?"

"Oh no! I hadn't thought of that." I grinned. "It's such a silly fun night. I can't wait to tell her about it, but this mess...we can't even get in a taxi like this. It's so rude." He smiled at me, uncovering my waist from suds again as I sat on the counter.

"Sweetheart, I brought another brownie in a baggie in my pocket. Do you want half again? Or a quarter? After a while, I can take you to the hotel we passed in the taxi, three blocks over. We can get a room and shower. You can go first and then me. And we can go to bed. To sleep, I mean to say. I promise you I will be a gentleman. You can trust me. Only kissing as we have been. Is that okay with you? I hadn't planned that we would be this messy."

I nodded, so he pulled out his phone and made a phone call. He looked at his watch. "Perfect. Room twenty-three, by the main office; great. Last name is Abernathy. First name, Matthew. Cash. Good. Thank you too, goodnight."

"Matt, I have been well-behaved, and we are hiding in the kitchen having fun. People have been nice."

"Correction. No one is nice here. I scare people away from you. Go on."

"Maybe we should split the brownie. I think we can handle it together. Something to laugh about sometime on the front porch in thirty years."

His eyes shot to mine, and he smiled. "Okay, sweetheart, but I want to leave in about an hour. Is that okay? This party is only going in one direction after a while, and I don't want you to see that."

"Yes, that is perfect. Fine." We opened the sweet morsel, and popped it into our mouths. Holding hands, we glided to the fridge and downed some mineral waters. "It's so stiff; look at this." I set my empty water bottle on the foam where it stayed without sinking.

"It's light, but it's the weight displacement that is causing—"

"Matt," Stephanie came running into the kitchen breathless. "Are you guys okay?"

"Yes. Are you? Why are you running?" She was pulling a giant man with cornrow braids behind her.

"Yes! Just excited. I wanted you both to meet Trevor. Trevor, this is my bestie, Amy, and her boyfriend, Matt." These words, these titles so newly associated with us, were wonderful to hear.

"Her boyfriend," I repeated in my head, but it came out a whisper on my lips. I felt him squeeze my hand lightly, indicating he liked it too.

"Trevor is a fullback and majoring in computer science."

He waved at us and put his hand in Stephanie's back jean pocket. He seemed nice.

"Matt, do you still have my candy?"

"Yes." He pulled out a second double-wrapped baggie with two brownies in it.

"Thank you." She gave us hugs.

"I love you, Steph." She smiled as I leaned on Matt for stability, and additionally trying to block my shirt from view.

"You had more!"

"Little bit." I made an inch with my fingers, blushing that she could tell this information so easily.

Matt's voice startled me. "Trevor, glad to meet you. We are going to be leaving soon. So you are good? With her getting home?"

He nodded and made an okay sign with his foamy fingers. They hugged us again and disappeared down the hall, where a dining room might have been under normal circumstances. As the door opened, the pulsating bodies of the dancers sloshed more foam through the door.

"Matt, I have to pee."

"Okay. Come on." He pulled me up to the banister of the stairs helping my free hand find it. "You feel okay, Amy?"

"Yes, I think I am just now feeling it again. Maybe."

He smiled, "I am so glad you are having fun. Don't let go of my hand."

I looked up the stairs. Foam, the size of a refrigerator, was oozing down the staircase. Alarmed at its size and descent on us, I screamed. Matt looked up. "Pretty bubbles, remember. Be brave. Walk through it with me." He gave my hand little pulses, reminding me we were connected.

Somehow easily coming out the other side of the giant glimmering cloud, we found a long corridor. Several glowsticks arranged to form a "B" were taped to one of the doors. He knocked on the door loudly, waiting a few seconds, then opened it. The foam was in here as well but less than any other room. Mostly suds that had fallen off of people's bodies. Matt moved to the shower and pulled back the curtain. A condom wrapper was floating on the foam; he closed the curtain and shut the door behind him, speaking through it.

"Okay, go ahead; I am right outside the door."

"'Kay. I'll be really quick."

I peed and, finding the toilet paper swollen and soaked, decided to sadly go without. What would be the point? Everything was wet. I dressed again, looking in the mirror at my matching bra and panties glowing like a sunset under my soaked clothes. Geez. College memories, I said to myself, excited I was making some. I rinsed my hands. Ironically, there was no soap. I reached down for some suds, a goofy smile on my face. I opened the door, and Matt walked in. I tried to move past him to exit.

"My turn. And I'm sorry, you have to stay here."

"What? Why? No!" I protested.

"You can turn around. You cannot go out in the hall."

I complied, my face blushing, listening to the sound of him unzipping his pants and the sound of the fluid hitting the toilet. There were so many new experiences this night. Even this was something so intimate and so strange. A boy peeing. I stayed as far as possible from him, facing the door, frozen in place even as he rinsed his hands.

"Funny, there's no soap, right?" I asked and he laughed.

"Come on." We walked to one of the upstairs rooms. Matt opened the door a crack, looking in a moment and then closed it quickly. "Nope." He smiled. He took some mints out of a metallic tin in his pocket.

"You have so much stuff in there."

He laughed. "Want some?"

"Yes, please."

The foam was exceedingly high as we walked down the hall towards the other end of the house. A crowd passed us in the hallway. Matt pulled me behind him. Too late. Eyes on my ghost of a shirt followed us into the next room.

This was another large room with no doors and three entry points. The music was coming from a speaker near us as we entered. The bubbles were very high here. The second bubble machine had to be close. There were just a few people here. I spun around in circles, face up to the chandelier's soft light, hands outstretched, the high hitting me hard again.

Matt stood, leaning by the adjacent wall, a contented look on his face as I spun circles, round and round. The soft crushing of the suds mixed with the sound of my laughter. I felt someone approaching me from the far wall. Matt whistled where he stood and shook his head no. The lone dancer, whoever they were, retreated slowly into the white oblivion. He watched me a few minutes then walked over, the foam rising swiftly now.

"May I have this dance?" I extended a sparkling hand, deformed of shape. He blew on it, revealing my skin, and then kissed it, pulling me to him. We shuffled and turned, swishing effortlessly through peaks like sparkling diamonds. He leaned down to kiss me. The lyrics to Roxy's "More Than This" urged him on. The rising suds were at my chin, and I had to let go of him to swat them back with my hands. He was a surprisingly good dancer, moving easily and confidently.

"Matt, the foam is too high." I had fought it, but it was winning.

"On my feet."

"What?"

"Put your feet on my feet." I smiled, finding them blindly.

We moved slowly in little movements just as we had, my head higher on his chest than normal. Slow, soft circles, our bodies close, my body aching to be closer. Our song finished. Roxy. I would need to remember this band. This song. This moment through the fog of my mind. I would need to remember. To write it down. The thin veil of soap covering his jeans. The way he let his eyes drop quickly to my chest for seemingly the first time, returning them to me with an endearing smile. His handsome smile and bright, intelligent eyes. I remembered what I had told my roommate earlier this evening, and the four percent vanished from my heart and mind.

"I will remember this song and this dance for the rest of my life."

"Me too." Our lips touched. "You really are drowning, aren't you, Little Bitty?"

"Yes!"

"Crawl up." He bent down, offering his thighs as stairs to his body.

We moved to the wall, where he pinned me in kisses. We stayed this way, our bodies buzzing with longing, with the THC running through us like electricity, and the augmented trappings of a young, strong love. His hands ran down the sides of my shirt, sending an almost magnetic energy field from my nerve endings to my heart. The foam was rising so high that even Matt had to swat it away.

"Will we die here?"

"No. No, sweetheart." He grinned. "I am tired of fighting it, though. If we can't fight 'em we could join 'em. Close your eyes. We're going in."

"Okay. I'm scared."

"No, don't be. It's not as crowded here. We are up against the wall, and my body will be over yours if someone steps back."

I closed my eyes holding my breath as if we were plunging into a deep sparkling blue sea. He scooped me up, laying me gently on the wooden floor. He lay on top of me and fought the foam, momentarily creating a little cave, a small pocket of air. He pulled a water bottle out of his back pocket. "Keep your eyes closed." He supported my face at an angle, rinsing the foam from my face.

"Thank you." I opened my clean eyes to the foam cave, my

eyes adjusting to its soft light. "This stuff has surprisingly good structural abilities." I blushed. "Tonight has been so playful and fun, Matt. Thank you."

His hands held mine, our fingers entwined. Our lips locked as the opening we created by our sinking bodies closed above us, leaving us hidden in paradise.

"Amy." He was almost breathless. "Can I touch your tummy? I can see your abs lightly through your wet shirt. I promised you and myself actually that we would not advance our cause tonight. It's not okay with the brownie I gave you and with our plan to go slow. But I can feel your shirt being pulled up, and your wet clothes are revealing a little bit, and I am so curious. I'm dying to touch you."

My stomach. Really? Hum. "It feels like you are touching me all over as it is."

"How do you mean?"

"Those little tingles all over my body that happen when we kiss. You may touch. Promise not to tickle my ribs though, please," I said, remembering his expertise at this.

He smiled, and never letting go of my right hand, our fingers interlocked, he moved lower down my body. I felt his fingertips brush my skin to lift my thin wet shirt and gently pull it high on my chest. I could feel the bottom of my pink bra exposed to the cool air. His hand disappeared to fight the white cloud, creating another temporary air pocket for both of us. Then I felt the warmth of him come back to me, softly resting his hand on my tummy. I heard him make a sound, like a giant sighing, exhausted and overcome. His fingertips were barely touching my skin, tracing the faint long lines of my hard work. He opened his hand fully, allowing his palm to cover most of my core with its warmth. He kissed me gently here and on my hips, and then after quite some time spent blissfully in this way, I felt him re-covering my shirt as he rose on his elbow to meet my face.

"You are so beautiful." He sighed. "If we brought in halter

tops as a concept to Azure, we could all retire in six months."

I wasn't sure what to say, so I remained silent.

"Amy, can I ask you a very personal question?"

"No." I took a sip of water that he handed me.

"Please."

"No."

He leaned into my ear to kiss it. "Please."

I felt his tongue push into my ear like he was kissing my mouth. I squealed loudly, writhing around on the floor, while his free hand fought to keep me in one place. I bumped my hand on the wall.

"Ouch." He rubbed it gently, not leaving my ear alone. "Fine." He smiled and fought us another air pocket.

"So, do you get your period?"

"What? Eww. Gross Matt, you're not allowed to ask that. And wait...you think I haven't had my period, and I believe in Santa. Get away from me." He laughed.

"No, no, you misunderstand me."

Too late. I had sloshed foam on him and fled. My memory of feeling like a child while in the company of my best friend and boyfriend was still a fresh wound in my mind. I visualized the balloon floating upwards. This was too much, and I was gone. I just needed a moment to think. "Amy!" Matt's voice boomed to the left of me. He had gone in the other direction. My eyes were closed, and I was sitting cross-legged in the white nothingness fifteen feet away. He called my name again. "Amy, stand up! You are going to get stepped on."

I didn't care. I needed to think. Why would he even like me if he thought these things? I heard him whistle loudly and by the sound, he was farther away. Good. Go. I tried to be mindful, but my thoughts felt muddled. It was hard to think properly. I opened my eyes after a few minutes, and suddenly he was there. His boot anyways. I tapped on it with my fingers, finally ready to talk. Finally mature enough to be mad and be able to articulate something about it. The drugs were having their way with my ability to form coherent thoughts and complete sentences. Suddenly, I felt a hand reaching down, and finding my arm, lifted me up. I shook the foam off my hair and face, though it clung to my clothes.

"I'm sorry." I started first. "I want to be on your level. I don't want you to treat me like a child. I'm not sure what your meaning was earlier, but you're right, it's true that some seventeen-year-olds haven't had their periods yet. Probably rare. If you must know, I am one of them. I mean to say, I got mine last year, but it was just that one time. My friend says it's not a real period because it lasted one day. Not sure. Not that I needed to tell you that embarrassing detail about me. I think it's the drugs right now making me mad, or you are very rude. If I am honest, I can't tell. I just needed a minute to think. To think if I am angry or not."

I looked up at him, hoping I had made sense. A tall, brown-haired boy who was not Matt was staring back at me.

"Oh," I stammered. "Oh, I am so sorry."

He smiled. "No problem." His hand touched my forearm comfortingly. He felt cold and foreign. Rebarbative even.

"Sorry," I repeated, stammering, and ran across the room, trying to put as much foam between this stranger and myself as possible. I instinctively dashed off in the direction I had last heard his voice at the edge of the room. "Matt!" I called out loudly into the hallway. No answer. From behind me, I felt someone approaching me quickly. I turned as two strong arms wrapped around me fast and tight, pulling me back in the room and pinning me against the wall with an assertive touch.

"Amy." He was out of breath. "You cannot do that here. This is not a safe or reasonable place for you to get lost. I know you are not in your right state of mind right now and that I did that to you, so I cannot be mad at you, but dammit, I am!"

"I'm sorry you think these silly dumb little kid things about me, and you want to kiss me anyways! So explain yourself!" He could see my perspective and immediately went defensive.

"Listen, Amber and me. There is history. She and I were together for a bit early on, like six years ago. It didn't mean anything to me then, and she certainly doesn't now, to be clear. I do not like the kind of person she is: manipulative and bitchy. She knew that I was attracted to you earlier than anyone. She could tell somehow, and anyways, she almost had me convinced about that Santa Claus thing. Brought it up a lot. She can be convincing sometimes. I didn't naturally think that you thought that." I put my arm on his forearm, and we sank slowly in the foam, sitting down our backs against a wall. He made an air pocket, and then he continued. "The period thing. That was not her. And I was not trying to embarrass you or anything like that. It's just that you have a visible six-pack, you have very little body fat, and I was wondering if you even get your period because of your athleticism."

I sighed, "I'm sorry, I didn't mean to take offense, but earlier tonight, I felt like you and Steph were talking about adult things, and you just left me out of that."

"I remember. I picked up on that. Listen, I'm sorry, Amy. You are the youngest person I have dated and with the biggest age gap. And you are different in many ways. And I just want to be a good boyfriend. Not vulgar or too much for you. I didn't mean to make you feel that way. I was attempting to keep you out of that world as long as possible."

I turned to him. "Listen; I want an authentic relationship with you. A mental, spiritual bond between us. I feel that growing even now as we argue. And I feel like it is growing every minute we are together. But I feel like you stop that growth if you treat me differently because of my age."

"You are different and perfect. And part of this is a credit to your youth. But listen, I adore you. And I am so grateful to be with you. And I am unbelievably attracted to you. To your witty mind and your unbelievable body." His words worked on my stubborn heart.

"Forgive me." I squeezed his hand.

"I was never actually mad," he laughed. "Just worried when I lost you. Three minutes lost in here is like thirty minutes in the real world. On a bad side of town." I turned to him.

"Let's kiss and then leave."

Bubbles popped softly around us—millions of them like the crackling of a distant fire. We kissed our forgiveness, our amends, our apologies. And then we left through the main corridor and out into the main room.

"I'm embarrassed about my shirt," I admitted as we sloshed towards the exit.

"I lost my blue shirt about a half hour ago. We could have used that. Up." He bent down, and I climbed up into a bear hug. I could feel my breasts getting lightly crushed by his chest. He must have been aware of it, too, because he whispered in my ear, "You feel so good."

I lowered my head on his shoulder as we descended the stairs outside the front gate towards the hotel. "Can you still carry me this long?"

"Sure. I prefer holding you like this. Your cute see-through clothing would be pretty noteworthy outside the context of this party."

"Thanks, Matt," I laughed, a nervous tinge evident in my voice.

Entering the empty hotel grounds, he set me down, and we walked towards the office where he had instructions for late-night check-in. After getting the welcome letter and key, we walked to our room. Our room. How many firsts were we having tonight? And yet we were both actively digging in our heels at futile attempts to go slow. The room was surprisingly nice, with a sitting area, rainforest shower, and enormous king-sized bed.

"Amy, you can go first in the shower. Take your time. I am going to run to the late-night food place a couple of blocks away. I have a key; don't open the door to anyone."

"Okay. Which one?"

"There is a little Mexican restaurant that is still open. It is pretty good; I forget the name. What do you want?"

"Horchata, please, if they have it."

"They do... let's drink horchata in bed and click through late-night TV." I smiled at the idea of this comforting notion.

"Sounds really good."

"But first." He walked to the thermostat and lowered it way down to the lowest possible setting. He picked up a pamphlet by the fireplace and read it over, then lifted a small brown latch opening the flue on the fireplace and looked around for the wood. He built a little fire, the perfumed cedar crackling softly, as I disappeared into the sanctuary of a hot shower.

"Forget safety. Live where you fear to live." —*Rumi*

"Amy, trust me, please. You insult me. You are hurting my feelings." —*Matt*

CHAPTER NINE

"All Night Long"

The steamy shower was wonderful, almost instantly bringing me back to my cognitive self and awakening heightened senses. The events of the night had been fun, but I was ready for normalcy and to put our drugged-up memory in the past. I opened the complimentary toiletry bag and selected the citrus-infused shampoo and conditioner. It seemed strange to be adding more soap to my body, but Matt said he would be gone for almost half an hour, so I figured I had time for the works. I lathered my hair with the shampoo, envisioning the white soapy lather on my head and remembering our time spent together in the kitchen. I put my hand on the cool white tile, remembering the marble cabinetry and all the intimacy we had created between us in just one evening.

"I'm falling in love," I said to the smooth tile, water streaming steadily over it like a stone in a river. "It's actually happening to me." My voice cracked, and I hung my head as the tears fell, mixing along with the water that streamed down around me. This was unexpected. I hadn't been emotional a few minutes ago. Maybe the drugs were wearing off, or perhaps the grave seriousness of what I knew was the start of a long road with no exit in sight. A road that if there were an exit available to me, I would shun and even build blockades to prevent my trajectory change. The tears continued to fall. I rinsed the shampoo and added half the bottle of conditioner. I wasn't sure if men used this or not, but I didn't want to be greedy if they did. I lathered and shaved my legs. The toiletry kit had two toothbrushes and a sewing kit. I took a toothbrush, freeing it from the protective plastic sheeting, and brushed my teeth, taking the time to add everything else back to the kit and set it on the rim of the tub. Stepping out of the shower, I dried my hair and spun it up in a terry cloth twist on my head.

Wrapping a soft towel quickly around myself, I opened the door a crack, calling his name. No answer. I laid my shirt, jeans, undergarments near the crackling heat of the fireplace. The burning wood was creating a therapeutic scent, permeating the small room. What in the world would I wear to bed? What would he? This wasn't planned, and it was suddenly making me incredibly nervous, occupying every thought in my head. He promised to be a gentleman, and I believed his words. He might not have thought about it either. I retreated speedily behind the safety of the closed bathroom door. Locking it, I sat at the stool before the giant mirror, thinking, and began to blow dry my long tresses. This took some time, and thankfully the warm towel and heat from the fire had helped me through half the process. Almost finished.

Ten minutes later, through the loud whooshing of the blow dryer, I heard him knock on the bathroom door. My heart began beating fast.

"Matt, I don't have anything to wear." I unplugged and set away the drier.

"I brought you something. I have something for both of us. Unlock the door, and I will pass it to you."

"Okay." I slowly opened the door six inches, and he handed me a folded shirt and what looked like a kid toy in a round plastic ball. "Thank you, Matt."

"No problem." I closed the door and opened the folded

shirt. "Little Nina's Yummy Tortillas" was written under a giant cartoon cactus with flowers as hands. Size large. Okay. It was soft and clean. I gratefully put it on and was instantly swallowed by the soft cotton. I cracked the clear ball into halves on the sink counter. It popped open loudly to reveal thin white cotton panties that tied at the sides. Okay. Great. Weird. Where did he get these? I put them on, carefully tying the ends. I opened the door a crack.

"Babe. Come out. Eat with me. I didn't know what you wanted, so I ordered a variety of different stuff." I stuck my head out, unsure of how to proceed. "You're in a T-shirt, honey, and think of the underwear like bloomers. Not that I can see them in that big shirt. Not that I won't try."

I gave him a sideways grin. "Okay." He was right. I walked over on my toes and sat at the little table he had pulled by the fire. "It's so cold in here."

He smiled. "Well, it's cuddling weather."

"It's hot outside." I scolded.

"But in here, we need a fire and a place to cuddle to stay warm. I didn't know what you wanted. But I got salsa, chips, and fajitas. Oh, here's your horchata."

"Thank you, Matt. You are very thoughtful."

He winked at me, then focused on wrapping up another giant fajita. We ate slowly, talking and laughing easily about the events of our second date.

"Do you know how they make this?" He lifted his drink, the ice clinking together softly muted by the Styrofoam.

"Yes, actually. It's rice water with sugar, vanilla, and cinnamon. Is that right?"

"Yes."

"So weird how good it is."

"Well, it's carbs plus sugar." He winked at me again. "So, it is always going to be reasonably good. You only had part of one." He watched me stand and put the trash into a plastic bag.

"I'm perfect. Thanks."

"You are." He grinned at his own obvious line.

I ignored him, smiling to myself, and went into the bathroom to brush my teeth for a third time this evening and came out to find him gone. Not knowing what else to do or where to sit, I sat in a large love seat near the fire. The flames leapt high, making soft crackling sounds as the door opened and closed.

"Hi, where did you go?"

"I went to put the trash in the dumpster out back. It was delicious, but now I don't want to smell it or see it." I nodded. "I am going to take a shower now." He handed me the remote. "Find us something."

I smiled, and he was gone. I could hear the water turn on and tried not to feel timorous at the thought of him being naked in such proximity to me. A door between us. Would it always feel like this? I would die of a heart attack before I hit my thirties if I couldn't figure out how to manage it. I listened to my beating heart, remembered what I had told the cool white tile in the bathroom, and smiled.

Picking up the clicker, I began flipping through the channels. What in the world would a person like Matt watch on TV? Something scary. Something violent. Maybe something with a plot. Probably, something I would not like. Flipping through, I noted super weird shows were on at this time of the morning. I clicked from one unknown dated show to the next. *Mr. Ed*, I murmured to myself. It was just after two a.m. now—an early night for us. We could watch an entire movie and not fall asleep, if I could find something. He was right about what he said the first night we met. "'Welcome to the night. We don't sleep.'" I whispered it to myself as I heard him open the door.

"Amy, my boxers are dry, thick jeans, I'm guessing, but my shirt is was so soapy and I just now rinsed it. Can you bring me my shirt from the restaurant, or is it okay for me to be shirtless?" An arm reached out, handing me clothing. "Can you put this by the fire for me?"

"Of course." I couldn't decide. I wanted to see him, but I was so scared for some reason. I felt like his chest was a gateway drug to an unknown land. A foreign place that I knew nothing about and needed to read up on first for safer travel. I passed him the shirt from the restaurant and took his wet one. He came out moments later, and I laughed into my hands.

"The homemade tortillas were so good. I am not ashamed to wear this dumb shirt. The people working there were really nice too. I like that place." He grinned at me.

I realized I had never seen his legs before. They were tan and very muscular with angles and sharp cuts in his calves and thighs that would have inspired a DC cartoonist. Superman. He kissed the top of my head and walked around to the far side of the bed, pulling back the top comforter and revealing the soft white sheets. I stood frozen.

"Get in," he urged, arranging the pillows on his side. His side. My side. I couldn't move my legs. I tried, but they wouldn't do what I wanted. I felt a soft ringing in my ears. I blinked quickly, trying to urge some part of my body to do something. Something normal. I stood there broken, ashamed at my shyness.

"I see," he said gently, getting up and walking around the end of the bed towards me. He sat on the comforter, pulling me softly onto his lap, his voice in my ear. "I am not going to hurt you. I won't even tickle you, even if you beg me to. I only want to feed you and," he paused, looking at the television, "watch *In the Heat of the Night* with you." He smiled. "Interesting choice." My eyes were on the ground.

"I didn't. I wasn't finished looking through—"

"Amy, trust me, please. You insult me." He pulled some blond hair back from my face. "You are hurting my feelings." I nodded, still unmoving. "May I help you? I know it can sometimes be challenging to pull back the sheets of a bed set you have never seen and then climb up into it." I laughed weakly. "Don't be nervous around me. Look at my dumb shirt; look at yours. Remember our kisses in the bubbles." He entwined our fingers and kissed me.

It worked. I felt better. I smiled, releasing my tight grip on him, my fist full of twisted cloth at his shoulder. He lifted me up and placed me in the center of the bed, pausing to fluff and reposition my pillow. He pulled the covers up high over me, and winking, walked over to the coffee table and picked up the clicker. Thank goodness he was normal. Why couldn't I just behave like a normal reasonable human around him? He looked over at me as he adjusted the volume and put more cedar on the fire.

"Are you warm enough? It's freezing."

"It's so bad for the environment what we are doing. The fireplace and the air conditioning." He smiled.

"I know. And I feel moderately bad about that." He closed the metal mesh, fighting to keep the wood in place, and climbed into bed with me. He lifted his arm to the ceiling, silently inviting me to come closer. "Let's see what's going on here." Our eyes reflected the flashing pixels of the car chase on the television. "Bad guys, good guys." He made a right-left motion with his finger. "Oooh, eighties hair. Look at that awesome mullet and Members Only jacket." I laughed. He looked down at me and grinned. He wanted to say something, but he stopped himself and sighed. A boxy brown Honda Accord flipped up in the air and caught fire.

"Oh no." I giggled. The stunts were so bad.

"Let's see what happens." More police arrived at the scene. "Are you nervous?"

"No." I blinked.

"Well, the bad guys are doing well, and," he looked at his watch, "there are only seven minutes for the good guys to make it right." I smiled up at him.

"You make everything fun, Matt. I am having just as much

fun here watching this dumb show with you as I would if we were in Paris or London right now."

He laughed. "I haven't been to Europe yet, but I know what you mean. I was just thinking essentially the same thing. Have you been?"

"I have."

He softly brushed my eyebrow with his thumb. "Tell me about it. But first I have a question. Why are you so beautiful? Why?" He whispered. I rolled my eyes to the ceiling and smiled.

Rolling my eyes at him at triggered some sort of aggressive playful mode within him. He pulled me down onto the bed off my pillow, and we kissed—the act of kissing while lying down in bed was exhilarating. I felt myself shaking softly from the inside out. I felt like at the start of a football game when it was almost go time. That buildup of excitement mixed with performance pressure of some kind. It was new and fun and hard to describe.

"Can I say goodnight to your tummy? While you tell me about Europe."

"What. Why?"

"Well, it's fascinating to me, and it is my second favorite thing that I have seen so far, minus your beautiful brain, face, heart, etc., etc., etc."

What was his favorite thing? I couldn't think about it, for fear of turning colors. He disappeared farther down the bed.

"We landed in London earlier this summer. My best friend Kate and I."

I felt him pull my shirt pulled up and then carefully lift my hips, tucking the sheets in around my waist, tightly covering me. I could feel his breath on my abdomen and his lips softly kissing above my belly button.

"Matt, the good guys are winning." I felt him move to look at his watch.

"Such a shocker. Three minutes out." He smiled. "Go on;

you landed in London. Your family was with you as well?"

"No. My best friend Kate and I went alone."

"What?" He popped up from my middle, an irritated look on his face. "Go on."

"I had just gotten news I had been selected as alternate for cheer and was going to be given a scholarship. I was so excited, but it was irritating to go on this trip, this food and cultural tourism, knowing I wanted to lose weight. I set a goal for myself to lose fifteen pounds in Europe." He sighed.

"You're perfect. You would be better with more weight, actually. I am attracted to healthy, happy, confident women." This was a surprise. Maybe not, actually. He seemed to have a code of some sort, and when I knew more about him, I might be able to break all his secrets easily. "We need a conversation about that sometime. Not now." I smiled, thankful. "England," he prompted.

He was lying with his face resting softly on my stomach, his hands at my sides gently running his fingertips over my skin. I tried to keep my voice even as he touched me.

"Well, we went to stay in Titchfield, England, with a friend, Alex—Alexandra, a friend I met once when I was very young on a seaside vacation. Anyways, we stayed pen pals for years. Her family hosted us for two weeks, and then we went to Florence and Rome. A week in each Italian spot. Titchfield was magical; their home was beautiful, very rustic. Oh, Matt, you would have loved it. A quintessential English countryside estate an hour train ride from London!" The inflection in my voice was rising as I spoke. "It had seven bedrooms, all with fireplaces and beautiful old floorboards worn smooth by use. There were formal sitting rooms full of old photographs. I sat with Edna, her mother, and listened for hours over teatime to the shenanigans of the rascal aunts on her mother's side and the grandfather who lost a leg in the Second World War. The gardens were very formal, with low-lying boxwoods trimmed just so. The hedge helped to define the rose gardens and the informal vegetable garden. We took the train into the city twice a week. The stables, the gardens. I did a lot of pre-reading for my current English lit class in the grass of the rose garden." I sighed, remembering the crisp cool weather and the sun on my face. "We went horse riding in their village and we picked strawberries for English trifle, that's a sort of pudding served commonly at teatime. Oh, honey, we had a fancy English teatime service inside the old library in town. It was amazing, everything was just so, with fancy doilies underneath the tea cakes and little biscuits with clotted cream and berries. We were reading and trying different perfumed teas. I loved it! It was such an afternoon. Lightning outside, reading for hours as the rain poured down. Oh, I wish you had been there."

"Amy, I am so glad you have been to Europe and experienced these things. The inflection in your voice as you speak is so sweet. If I was with you in Titchfield, London, Florence, or Rome, what would we see together? One or two places in each."

"So, in the Titchfield area, we would ride horses towards an old pub called McDonald's. Ironically it's near a beautiful farm." He laughed. "We would tie them up out front near the antique fountain for watering animals. We would eat a traditional meal of bangers and mash, and depending on when we went," I paused, "we could have a beer on tap together and then ride home."

"Bangers and mash? That don't sound like food, honey. The British are weird."

I smiled, remembering fondly, "oh, they are! A super fun bunch of tarts and blokes." He smiled at my try at an accent. I hid my face momentarily in my hands, shaking off the embarrassment of my impression, and continued, finding my confidence again. "So bangers are a variety of sausages, usually local organic and yummy. And mash is mashed potatoes with peas and gravy to the side. After we ate, we could stop by the farm and see a few animals. Maybe watch the sun sink, reflecting in the lambs and sheep's soft fur. And the second thing we would do is rent bikes and go trail riding through the countryside. We could stop for lunch and then again a few miles later for a pint. We could go thirty-five to forty miles easy through the light and shadows of beautiful trails peppered with old homes and estates in view. What locals do when they can."

"When in Rome, right. Did you do this in March before we met?"

"Yes. I did. Kate is not much of a biker, so I got up early several mornings."

"Amy." He army crawled up to my face looking down over me. "You are implausibly beautiful. Especially when you are talking about something you are emphatically interested in, like travel, culture. I want you to know that I cannot wait to travel the world with you. I love how interested you are in life. You make me happy. Go on."

He disappeared back down to my stomach, where I heard him whisper, "I missed you," to my tummy. I shook my head at him and continued.

"So in London, I would take you on a tour of Windsor Castle. We would listen to the rich history from the tour guide, and we would leave two hours later through one of the formal gardens, feeling glad to be Americans and glad to be free with our rights written out by brave men declaring them a gift from God, not a king. I love that our constitution works around our rights from God, as not to limit them." He smiled broadly at me.

"You are patriotic?"

"I am. Very much."

"Me too. Very much. You like Locke? Hume?"

"I do. They inspired the founding fathers. Locke can be complicated. Well, they both can be. But for me, David Hume has more practical application in his philosophy and speaking.

I am a constitutional patriot."

He shook his head slowly. "Umm. So attractive. So then what would we do?" He was beside me now, cuddling me in his arms, my head on his chest.

"We would naturally be tired needing refreshment, so we would go to a fish and chips place. We would order fish and chips, and they would serve it wrapped in a cone of newspaper, and we would sit in the sun at Victoria Park. I would have brought a large cotton blanket in my backpack and maybe a bottle of Bordeaux. We would spend the afternoon sunning, eating Cadbury something or other. Probably chocolate Flake, and I would read you my favorite parts of Tolstoy's *Anna Karenina* while you laid your head in my lap. The shadows and sunlight dancing on your face. I would slip some cheap sunglasses on you and read. My hand on your heart."

"Amy, you're killing me. You have excellent taste. That book is like a thousand pages. I liked it too, actually. Russian royalty," he muttered, smiling at me a new look on his face, one that I had not seen before. I was exciting him. I was exciting him on an adventurous and cognitive level that he wasn't used to, or hadn't expected, and it warmed my heart and encouraged me.

"Okay. So next, we would take a short two-hour flight to Florence, Italy. Our first destination upon arrival would be the Santa Maria Novella. Here we would hold hands and kiss as we witness the frescos detailing the lives of Mary and St. John the Baptist. The majority of the art is from the Renaissance, so essentially a strong rebirth of art, literature, politics, and music. You can see the difference in the color usage, the light, the angle of the body, and the figures' posturing. A young Michelangelo would have likely worked on some of these. We would be witness to his strokes of genius. The light on the skin, the gesture of intimacy between the figures. The perfect proportions of the figure and the hues mixed to perfection in the frescos. The art would have an effect on us. It would creep up slowly; we wouldn't notice it right away. But after some time, we would be changed; bodies trembling, eyes moving over the art, in classical eye candy artistic adoration. We would order wine on the balcony café if you wanted it, and we would be introspective. Silent except for the sound of my heels on the stone floor. We would need to leave shortly, to exit the south side of the building towards a back alley, and we would need to kiss passionately behind a stone garden wall. Tears would well up in our eyes, at least mine; art does that for me. Our hearts would be filled with hope, inspiration, and passion, and we would take that out on each other." He sat up now, face severe but untelling. Eyes searching mine. I didn't care what he thought.

I continued, "We wouldn't care who saw us. We would only care about our kiss, the art, the pastel hue of the color in the fresco, the conviction the creators of this art had about God and beauty, and the taste of wine on our lips. Witnessing it would make us fall deeper into love. And far in the future, we would tell our children about some of it over dinner, one night, talking on about the art of this quaint venue one simple lovely day when we were young."

I paused; he didn't say anything. He was staring at me with a serious look on his face. "Don't. Don't stop talking, sweetheart." He managed a smile. I took hold of his giant wrist and turned it, looking at the watch.

"I will tell you our plans for Roma, and then we will snuggle closely. It is freezing in here." He smiled to know his plan was working. "So, in Rome, we will see the Colosseum. I know you know about this history, so I won't narrate further, other than to say we will take a walking tour of the underground chambers where the slaves and animals were kept. Much of it will be roped off, inaccessible to enter, but it will have a clear view. And as the tour continues towards the north side ruins, we will linger behind because we are spiritual creatures, you and me. Our hands touching lightly to the stone walls and each other, we will pray together for the poor, brave souls who waited here, listening to the roar of the Sunday crowd gathered to see their blood spilt for their entertainment. We will reaffirm a vow then and there never to be the kind of people who find pleasure in someone else's suffering. It is one thing to hear the facts about this time period or see statistics on war; it is something else to be spiritually present in these places. On this historical ground."

He nodded slightly. "Go on, honey. Please. Don't stop."

"Well." He smiled at my use of his favorite word. "Well, after the tour, and feeling very introspective, maybe implosive from the experience, we will go out into the night, hand in hand, seeking comfort in the form of comestible edible pleasures. We will go to a small intimate eatery, just off a side street, five hundred years old, this old stone building—this place. Ristorante La Luna Sotto il Sole Imperiali is the name of this restaurant. And we will sit on the same side of the table in order to be closer. We will both feel a little more vulnerable from our time spent inside the Colosseum, and from our prayer, and our walk, and our growing affections. And we will spend the next several hours eating and talking, laughing, your hand resting on my knee until it's all better."

He was smiling at me, love and respect in his burning gaze. "That word you used at the cafe. Our first date. Ineffable, no words. I feel that now. I have no words that would accurately describe how I am feeling towards you. Tonight is our second date, and I am trying hard to slow down, but my mind has me racing. We only have fifty to sixty-five years left together, at least in this lifetime, and that suddenly doesn't feel long enough." He smiled slightly. His nose was pink, and his eyes looked watery.

Was he going to cry? I couldn't look. I lay on his chest, giving him the privacy of a moment without my gaze. My head moved up and down softly with his breath. We lay in silence for some time.

"Matt," I whispered as l lay on him, my head on his chest, my limbs spilling off of him in a bear hug. "Are you okay?" Silence. Then finally, he spoke.

"Yes." He was quiet, a moment more. "I'm just thinking, sweetheart. Maybe we don't go slow. Maybe we go fast as hell and enjoy every minute of it. Every moment we get together."

He reached over and clicked off the muted television, creating instant darkness against the glow of the embers. I moved up to him, my body shifting, oversized cotton on cotton, my mouth finding his. His face was wet and salty. I kissed him passionately. He let me have "my turn, my turn, my turn," my body aching in the seconds I pulled my lips away from him and only finding blissful pleasure as we came back together to kiss; and suddenly, without a word, he flipped me over on my back in the darkness. Aaaaah—that oceanic cadence of our lips. "His turn, his turn, his turn" was pushing me into the soft mattress. His mouth telling mine solemn promises, forged that night, that he wanted to keep. Exhausted emotionally and physically, half an hour later, we fell asleep. Our bodies embraced in a burning caress of entwined feet and fingers partially covered by a tangled white blanket. Two hours later, in the chill of the early morning, I awoke to feel covers carefully wrapped around me. I turned over towards him and fell into a deep, sound sleep.

"Moonlight floods the whole sky from the horizon to horizon; how much it can fill your room depends on its windows." —*Rumi*

"I saw it all in your eyes last week, and the week before." —*Matt*

CHAPTER TEN

"Buttons"

A soft light was moving across the sheets, flashing a muted purple across the soft white cloth. It was like light on water as the wind blew pecan trees back and forth outside. I blinked my eyes open to find him gone. Smelling hot coffee, I turned over, tangled in the sheets. He was in the lounge chair behind me, reading a magazine and drinking from a steaming paper cup. "Good morning." He smiled at me, bringing me a cup from the coffee table. "Colombian roast. From down the street. This place manages to roast it without making it taste bitter and burnt. Apparently, that is a challenge, my experience at most coffee shops anyway." I took a sip. Yummy.

"Thank you so much. Matt, what time is it?"

"Noon. We got late checkout. Stay." He smiled.

I shook my head, "I need to study all day today and the day is half gone."

"Me too, to an extent." He looked at his watch, handing me a bag containing a bagel. I looked in. I hadn't had a bagel in years.

"Matt, dating you, I am going to fail out of school, lose my scholarship, and lose my job, my sobriety, maybe even my mind." I blinked up at him, smiling. "And for some unwonted reason, I don't care." He laughed, eyes twinkling.

"Umm. Good. Everything will work out, Amy. You don't need to worry about anything. Listen, do you remember our conversation last night?"

"Which one?" I laughed, thinking of the ample range between idiocy and intimacy throughout the evening.

"The part where we change course completely. The part where we don't go slow anymore or waste any time not embracing the way we want, kissing every moment, dancing, speaking over dinner. You have changed me. Fundamentally. And I need more. I want you to meet my parents."

"Oh." Oh wow. This was unexpected and wonderful, actually. I instantly blushed, feeling flattering adulation.

"Tonight at the ranch, we are doing Sunday dinner."

"Matt, I would love to, but really, I have to study." I shrugged, feeling defeated.

"I will drop you off now and pick you up at 5:00. You can sit in the middle seat so I can put my arm around you, and you can study on the road up." I smiled, calculating the time. Might work. I thought of my course load and mentally added an hour to the early morning on Monday.

"Okay!" I smiled, my heart beating faster. "I would love to meet your parents." I ran my fingers over his hair playfully as I went to the bathroom to change.

Ten minutes later, the taxi pulled up to my dorm, and I got out laughing loudly from our tickle session in the backseat.

"See you at five, Amy." And the taxi pulled away.

Back in the dorm, Kate listened to my account of the evening with a face vacillating between consternation and felicity. We made coffee, and I took my cup into the shower with me.

Five minutes later, I was in shorts and a T-shirt, hair dripping down my back, biology book open, highlighter in hand. The afternoon passed slowly, and I was making clear strides in science and math. The majority of the more challenging work complete, I went to the kitchen. I was suddenly trembling with hunger. Shoot, I had forgotten my bagel in the cab. I wouldn't have eaten that anyway. Slicing an apple carefully, I smeared almond butter on the slices and put them on two plates, handing one to Kate, as I entered the bedroom study nook.

"Thank you." She smiled. She twirled her short curly hair around her pencil as she worked.

"Hey Kate, I told him about England. All the fun we had. I'm so glad we went together when we did before everything got so busy and complicated."

She smiled back at me. "I still miss those elaborate enormous English breakfasts."

"Yes, I remember that too. Not that I was able to partake much on my trip."

"You pushed yourself so hard. I woke up a few times in the night, and you were working out on the balcony in Italy." I grinned. That was an excellent memory actually. I was all alone in Rome. The city was completely mine amongst the sparkling stars and streetlamps. The only one awake doing planks at four in the morning.

"Well, that was for you, Kate. I didn't want to take time away from our touring, so I worked out extra at night. He seemed to like England best from my descriptions. Oh, Matt would love the breakfasts there. Remember that one place on the corner, Tallsman's, that served it on that huge platter. Like a serving tray." I spread my hands out, reminding her.

"I mean, it's for one person but could clearly feed like six people." She smiled, suddenly hungry enough to nibble from her plate.

"He would absolutely love that." I smiled.

I looked at my watch and grabbed my English lit work and moved to my bed. My timer went off, and I got up, closing my book. I would finish this in the car, and I would bring *Romeo and Juliet* and the play's Cliff's Notes to read alongside it. I hadn't read it in high school yet, and there were several plays to choose from, and discussion groups had been set up in accordance. Feeling the precocious trappings of love, I had selected this classic, inspired by my own beating heart for the first time.

Packed with work for the trip, I raced to my closet in a sudden panic. I looked at my watch—half an hour.

"Kate!" I screamed, my eyes scanning my clothes. She rushed in, her earbuds on her neck.

"Are you okay?" She searched my face for the emergency. "Spider?" She whispered, looking around. I laughed loudly.

"No. No. Worse. I am meeting his parents, and I don't know what to wear. I am thinking conservative but cute. And suddenly, I don't know what that is."

"Oh, that's easy." She smiled, relieved it wasn't an insect, a rolled-up magazine dropping from her hand.

"Sorry. I need your help."

"What will you be doing there?"

"Having dinner, maybe looking at a cow. I don't know."

"Okay, I think you should go with this cotton dress." She reached for a forgotten garment in the back. "It's a perfect fit on you. Or jeans and this loose silk shirt."

"No, the dress. It's perfect."

I put it on quickly, letting Kate help me button in my haste. The fabric was worn-soft cotton with Navajo southwestern designs scattered on a background of soft sky blue.

"You and your sister took that handiworks class with Mrs. Henson, right?"

"Yes," I recalled my first sewing class fondly with our homeschool co-op. "This jersey cotton dress was one of many projects we completed with her. The lesson was buttons."

She smiled thoughtfully, "Well, clearly, you passed." She had started at the hem, and I had worked top-down; our nimble fingerers met at my waist.

I looked at my watch; dashing to the bathroom, I rubbed

some vanilla lotion over my shoulders and legs and grabbed my bag of work. "Bye, Kate."

She waved at me, her hand blocking the receiver on her phone. "Be good, have fun."

I opened the door to the hall, and he was just turning down the main entrance hall towards me. A massive bunch of daisies swung by his side as he walked. Upon seeing him, I dropped my bag and ran towards him.

"Sweetie. Jump!" He bent down, and I flew into his arms. "Aaaah, you smell so good, and your skin is so soft."

We kissed, and he set me down, handing me my thick spray of white petals. He gave them to me slowly. His lips were moving slightly, his eyes on mine, reminding me.

"Thank you, Matt. When I take these from you, I tell myself: 'And I will also be worthy. And I am so grateful for you.' These flowers are one of my favorite kinds." He smiled warmly, a beholden look on his face.

"You make everything good. Let's get your bag."

"Let me put these in water quickly. I don't want them to die in the truck."

"So many many flowers are decidedly going to die for you in this life. You have no idea. The floral death that awaits so many..." I looked back, and he winked at me.

"Well, these will live through the night," I opened the door and put them quickly in a vase in the kitchen. I waved to Kate, who was on the couch, the phone in the crook of her neck, speaking loudly and crocheting, and closed the door.

Stopping at a vending machine in the lobby I ran my finger down the buttons and selected A4. Moments later, a small clear ball dropped to the receptacle at the bottom.

"Earplugs," I looked up at Matt. "This is so rude for our third date." I wrinkled my nose. "But honestly, just on the way there. I need to read. This way, you can listen to the radio."

He nodded approvingly and reached his hand out for me. Approaching his truck in broad daylight only made it bigger and more exaggerated looking. He walked around to the side with me and helped me into it, handing up my bag.

"You know," he nodded to my earplugs as he sat down and pulled on his seatbelt, "that is how I got your underwear last night."

"Oh." I blushed. "Well, I was going to ask you about that."

"Seat belt, honey." He nodded at me. "There is this little dive bar across from the Tex-Mex place, and it sells different things in the vending machines in the bathrooms. I remembered that when I was trying to come up with something proactive for our unique situation. I went in the men's, but it was mostly..." He paused. "Well, they didn't have ladies' underwear."

"So, what did you do? I mean, you cannot possibly—" I paused my speaking to silently squeal at the roar of his ignition.

"Well...I went back out to the bartender and asked her if she would go into the women's and get them for me. She did, but I guess she was messing with me a bit. She was asking why yours were lost."

"Oh, my goodness, Matt!"

He grinned, pulling onto I-35 south, "well, I was honest, and I told her yours were wet, and you needed new ones."

"Oh." I sat frozen.

"Well, it's the truth. And as I said, she got them for me, as you know. And as I am leaving, she tells me to wait and come back to the bar. She makes us a Maker's Mark shot. So, we are holding up this shot of bourbon in the air, and she pauses to let me speak. And I said, 'To Amy and Amy's panties.' I lift it to my lips, and I hear her say, 'May they always be wet.' Well, we took our shot, and I tipped her and left. Austin, it's a weird place, ain't it?"

"Oh, dear." Recovering slowly from the heat that had flushed through me, I smiled and patted his leg lightly.

"You're so shy." He pulled my hair back slightly to see my

face.

I responded by putting in my earplugs and mouthing, "I can't. I can't hear you." He spoke louder, exaggerating his harassing words.

"You are all cute and pink." He laughed.

"What?" I made a gesture of confusion, embarrassed by his accurate observation.

"Fine, study then, brat. I did promise you."

Reluctantly and still giggling, I pulled out my English lit, piling binders on my lap. I reviewed my notes on the last two lectures, put them away, and pulled out Shakespeare. "What's in a name? That which we call a rose by any other name would smell as sweet." It was slow, tedious reading, but it was pretty, and it matched the scenery as we turned on to Ranch Road 12 heading north. His hand rested on my shoulder; the caliche gravel's sound under the tires and the sunshine all contributed significantly to the literature on my lap. The perfection of the words, speaking straight to my palpitating heart, had an effect I couldn't deny.

I cuddled into him at a red light as he read over my shoulder, "Did my heart love till now? Forswear it, sight! For I ne'er saw true beauty till this night." I smiled and popped out my earplugs, putting away my work for the evening.

"I'm finished, for now; I just went back to review and highlight. I want to see where you grew up."

"This is it." I looked out towards endless hayfields catching the golden sunlight on each stalk.

"Matt, it was nice reading in the truck with you. I don't think I was prepared to read Shakespeare while having the feelings I have for you. With the sunlight on my face through the window, it was a very beautiful thing."

He squeezed my hand. "Well, *Romeo and Juliet* is a clear classic, but far from my favorite. In my opinion, he's not worthy, and he falls in love so quickly that it's clearly only physical. He doesn't know her. He hasn't watched her from across the room. Night after night, a sea of space between them, and seen definitively how she is both kind and beautiful when no one notices the details of her in that vastness. The poetry in how she moves. He hasn't seen her push herself, work so hard she's sweating, right here down her temples," he touched me softly, "or to find her weary-tired in the early hours of the morning, where she might collapse right in front of him. Any moment he might need to reach out and catch her in his arms. He watches, and he waits. He hasn't seen her laugh at his jokes until she wipes the corner of her eyes and smiles up at him. Or seen her vulnerable in his arms. Barely conscious," he whispered. "He hasn't seen her at all. But I think I understand," he pulled over to let a Mustang pass and resumed driving.

"Um. So, Romeo is clearly not as romantic as some modern men." I cleared my throat slightly, my heartbeat quickening at his words. "And I do understand seeing it that way. And it can be cliched at first glance, but at second glance, if you were to describe wanton love and attraction, this might be it. It is a timeless desire, and for me, feeling like I understand what that is for the first time in my life, it is so special. That I'm not on the outside looking in anymore. And I am included. It is beautiful." I blinked a tear back.

"Oh, sweetheart, come here." I snuggled in, and his hand moved around my waist. "What is this thing you are wearing? It's so soft, and you look so beautiful. I didn't even tell you yet."

"You look nice too. You are more Clark Kent tonight." He looked down at his white dress shirt and jeans and grinned.

"I made this dress when I was fourteen. It was my fifth sewing project that I ever made. I would say maybe forty percent of my closet is handmade stuff." He was changing lanes now. "It used to be more, of course, but I mostly wear workout gear and athleisure wear."

The truck was pulling off into the grass into a meadow off the old farm-to-market road. "Stay." Stepping down, he grabbed something from the back of the double cab, went to the tailgate, and then to my side. "Here, slide down to me. It's muddy." His arms reached out to catch me, putting me gingerly in the back of the truck. "Okay, lay down."

"This is the most unorthodox date, Matthew. Honestly." I sighed, suppressing my giggling but complied anyway, adjusting the blanket and lying down. He joined me, leaning back on his elbow to face me.

"I just wanted to see this pretty dress you made. It's so sweet on you, and I just wanted to pull over and give it the attention it deserves." I smiled, shrugging off the compliment.

"It's not a big deal. My sister is way better than I am."

"Shhhhh. Close your eyes."

I closed them, suppressing the urge to peek. I felt him run his fingers from my forehead and slowly down the bridge of my nose to my lips, where he lingered, replacing his finger with his lips. Then lips on mine, his roving finger moved down my neck, past my collar bone, to my heart covered by my first button. Bump, bump, bump, bump. His fingers moved slowly over them. He left my lips to move down my dress over every cloth-covered button to the hem where he stopped. He touched it, momentarily flipping it over.

"This is very well done. Do you still sew?"

"Thanks, Matt," I turned out the hem on my right sleeve, confessing the unsteady stitches of a novice. "Sadly, my sewing machine is in its box in the closet where it hasn't been unpacked yet." I signed. "I miss it." He frowned, remembering something.

"You made this at fourteen, correct?" I nodded. "Well, two things are stressing me out right now."

"Oh no." I sat up. He gently pushed me back down with his kisses and his free hand, and we repositioned ourselves on our sides, propping up on our elbows.

"You still fit in a dress you made for yourself at fourteen. I have been watching you for a while, and to be honest, you worry me. The weigh-ins, the pressure you put on yourself. That don't feel right to me. And we have never talked about it before. And I am trying not to be controlling, but I feel the need to give you paternal advice: you are beautiful. But beauty is healthy, happy, engaged. That's what is attractive. To me, anyway. My last long-standing relationship, she was a size eight, ten maybe. She was pretty, and she was healthy. And last night, when I was stoking up the fire a bit, I moved your jeans and noticed they were a size two. That's really little. And I don't want to lecture you, but I want you to be healthy. To be okay." He smiled, reaching over and putting a hand momentarily on my chin.

"I agree with you. Every word. No comment." I smiled through my lashes.

"Another time then." He was serious. I nodded. I wasn't trying to avoid this conversation.

"I just. I just." How to make him understand? "What can I say. It's a scholarship, based on athleticism, some social pressures, maintaining grades, and is literally contingent on hard work every day, like the military in some slight regard, in terms of health and monitoring. They have weigh-ins too. And ninety percent of my weigh-ins are me solo, just working hard. The university has been great. Really supportive. I am getting the support I need, but I will tell you that sometimes it hurts. I hurt myself, push myself hard. Not because I am asked to but because of my position. I am a flyer. And regulating my weight, balance, and form is essential in this very specific position. It drives me to push myself."

"This pressure is not coming from the university? What is a flyer?"

"No, not at all. It comes from me; as I said, I push myself hard. It is more intense than high school athletics at any university level, but I feel supported and feel like I have the resources I need to be successful. The balance of school and time for sports is the hardest aspect. It's mostly measuring or weighing my food and counterbalancing calories and work-outs. I eat the same things all the time. Oh, a flyer is a girl who gets tossed in the air. The highest on the pyramid. My particular problem is I am too tall to be a flyer at almost five foot two. So I have to regulate myself. But you, Matt...you work hard too. You hurt for what you've earned to make gains. We are similar."

"It's different, actually. There is a practical application to what I do. It's useful, logical, and I eat so many calories, honestly like 4,500, sometimes 5,500 a day. Yes, there is some pain. Some teardown and rebuilding of the muscle fibers, but it's very different, in my opinion. I'm just worried about you."

"Well, don't be. I am trying hard to manage difficult things in my life. University is a lot for me. Maybe because I am a year younger than most freshmen. Or I am unprepared somehow. Also, I have always been athletic and little. But it's true, that this is hard on a new level, but it is not much stranger than how I have always lived." I smiled. "Thanks for the paternal notes, Matt. I can manage this. At least for now. It's getting harder with the classes ramping up."

"Aw. So that was the second thing that was bothering me. Well, you talk a lot about handiwork classes—sorry that word is new for me—and you talk about art and poetry classes you enjoyed. Did you take a lot of core math and science classes?"

I shook my head slightly, "No. I didn't show a great propensity towards science or especially math. We are opposites sometimes, Matt."

He smiled. "Sometimes we are. So, hey..." He paused so we were looking at each other. "That makes me really mad, actually, Amy. You are smart, honey, and you are a quick learner. You deserve every choice and chance that anyone should have. Honestly, that hits a stereotype nerve for me and pisses me off. I can help you. You got a high enough score on the SAT or ACT for the university application process?"

"ACT, I got a twenty-four."

"Okay, that's good, actually, so I can work with you, and we can rebuild some foundational basics."

I was so relieved in finally telling someone my struggles; I couldn't help feeling overcome. Someone who cared about me, instead of judging and shaming, wanted to help. Tears spilled from my eyes.

"Oh no." he kissed them away.

"I have to go over everything twice in math and science. I am constantly backtracking because, honestly, the foundation isn't there. I just went to public school in the afternoons to meet up for athletics, a dual enrollment for homeschoolers. I often wonder if I would be having an easier time if I had also taken core classes, too. I think I needed one more year." I was confessing my long-standing struggles now.

"Amy, listen to me. You are smart. You are beautiful. You weren't set up well for success, and this must be so much pressure and stress...and with the bar. I honestly don't know how you are doing it."

I nodded, untrusting of words.

"If we have kids, I want you to homeschool them; that's how smart," he paused, "how sapient you are."

I smiled at his word choice. "Matt, I took some great classes. I know lots of families who were very successful at homeschooling. And they are not experiencing the problems I am. Kate, for example, is doing well. I think my mom's illness and my inability to self-teach and self-assess math were the biggest factors." I smiled as a tear fell down the curve of my cheek, speeding up its descent.

"I understand. Listen, we will be one of the successful parental groups. The thing is, we will be fair. Girls need to be strong in math and science as well. And boys need to learn to sew patches on their own pants they tear up."

"You can?"

"I can. It's not pretty, but yes, I can."

I nodded vehemently, "I agree with everything you said

tonight. Thank you. I don't think anyone knows this about me. Not my coach or parents. Only you and God, no one else. That it is so hard, running bleachers in a weighted vest, before my workout starts, studying until three a.m. on nights I don't work. You saw it all in a dress." I winked at him, grateful he was my friend.

"I saw it all in your eyes last week and the week before." He paused, putting his fingertips over my heart. "I've been praying for you."

"I have been praying for you since we met!"

"I know! I mean to say, I can tell. Amy, I need you to trust me. To tell me when it is too much. I don't want to take anything away from you. But if or when it becomes unbearable or unsafe, trust me enough to tell me. I can make a lot of things different for you." He didn't elaborate, and I didn't ask. I didn't need to ask. I trusted him instead.

"Thank you. I promise." I wiped my eyes, feeling better than I had in weeks. "Your sweet parents...we are going to be late...Let's go to dinner."

"Set your life on fire. Seek those who fan your flames." —*Rumi*

"Gotta be passionate about what you like to do in your free time, Amy. I love to cook. But it takes time and burning things to a crisp sometime to get it right." —*Sheridan*

CHAPTER ELEVEN

"Finding Our Way Home"

Driving past miles and miles of wooden post and rail fencing, hands held on the seat, Waylon Jennings on the radio, we finally turned onto a long gravel road winding up a hill lined with live oaks. Pulling up to park in front of a large free-standing garage, we got out and walked through the soft light of the evening towards a large white house with a deep front porch overlooking a yard brimming with white magnolias and camellias. The air was so sweet as we ascended the steps; it was almost hard to breathe it in. Big wide floorboards creaked as we walked across the porch past a quintessential southern porch swing on the left and a sitting area anchored with a jute rug with benches to the right. We stopped at the door. He looked down and smiled thoughtfully at me before knocking and opening it. "Everything is fine." He winked at me, his handsome face quieting my sudden nerves.

"Hello, hello." He called out to the hallway, stomping his boots on the crimson mat outside. We were immediately greeted by two sizable dogs in a teal-painted hallway lined with antique copper hooks for hats and bags. Framed black and white pictures hung neatly above these.

A sign near the boot rack said, "Leave your holster at the

door and come on in y'all." To my surprise, there was a 45 sitting in a holster, complying solitary and inert, in a large rustic wooden bowl on the table. Even more shocking, I watched as Matt lifted his shirt and unstrapped a thick leather shoulder harness holding a gun tucked under his arm, and set it casually in the bowl next to the other one. "My older brother is here."

I thought it was just a kitschy sign, and here he was literally doing as it directed. I looked down at my sandals and smiled. Born and raised in Texas.

The two silvery Weimaraners that had met Matt initially now eagerly greeted me. A wet nose moved from my leg to my hand as I reached down to touch them. Twin tails were hitting against me in unison as I petted. Matt pointed to the one on the left, "Action," he said, "an excellent upland bird dog. And Bolt over here, he is a deer-loving dog. Absolutely obsessed with deer hunting. Bolt is very special; he has a conductivity trait for hunting."

"How do you mean?" People were walking down the hall, hands beckoning us kindly to join them in the kitchen.

"It means, in short, that he has good natural hunting skill sets. The way he follows us in operation and in what capacity. He has the cognizance to look for wounded game, for example, if that's what we are doing. He watches and learns. In other words, good intuition and smart."

"Fun to have in the country, I imagine."

"Absolutely. I love taking them with me in the fall. Bolt has his specialties, but Action can kick up a covey really well. He ain't useless. Come on, Bolt. Come on, Action." He patted his leg, inviting them to follow.

I put my bag on a peg in the hall and reached in pulling out a small bundle wrapped in red floral cloth and tied with ribbon. We walked into a large kitchen that was fragrant with roasted duck and some sort of wild game.

"Oh. Here they come, y'all. You must be Miss Amy." A

petite woman with shoulder-length curly brown hair, styled like the 1930s, walked over and gave me a warm hug. Matt must have gotten his height from Darwin and his father. She wore a simple long blue dress under a black cotton apron. Her smile was bright and warm, and I immediately liked her. "Hello, honey. I am Sheridan, Matt's mother." She evaluated me quickly with her eyes and reached out to put her hand on my arm. She smiled up at her son "Oh, I like her, Matt."

He hugged his mom in response. "Mom. It's good to see you. How have you been?"

"Good. Good."

I handed her the bundle, "I brought you some honey soap from this farm co-op near my dormitory. I hope you like it!"

She smelled it through the package. "It's huge! Must weigh a pound. Oh, I do like it; thank you so much, little darlin'." She set it on the table and warned her son, cutting ribs on an enormous butcher block, not to touch it.

"I'm almost finished with these, and my hands are so dirty, and I am going to come after your soap, Mom." She swatted him on the shoulder with her hand towel and moved it to a higher shelf near the pantry. "You better move it higher," he teased, and then turning to speak to me said, "Hi Amy, I'm Luke. It's really good to meet you."

I smiled and said hello, turning to wave to the three people sitting at a table peeling potatoes. "Amy," Matt was ushering me towards them, "this is Victoria, Luke's wife, and my other brothers John and Samuel."

"Hello, everyone. May I join you?"

"Yes, of course." Samuel stood up, moving his seat so I could pass by him to an empty one.

"She's got us peeling too many," Victoria leaned in.

They talked over each other in the sweet way that families do. I began peeling potatoes and getting to know Matt's family. They were wonderful, good-natured, and witty. I liked them immediately and soon felt at ease talking about the animals they had, and a litter of kittens born recently in the barn. They promised we could take a peek at them later.

Doing something with your hands while meeting new people makes conversations more comfortable and more natural, it seemed. I attacked the potato I held a little too aggressively, and a peel flipped off and alighted on Samuel's forehead. It was giant. He must have noticed it, but he talked on and on, seemingly unaware while Victoria and I laughed quietly until our sides hurt. Suddenly, without warning, he grabbed some from in front of him and lobbed them playfully at us. Peels flew like confetti all around us but somehow missed. We squealed with laughter. Potato peels can be fun like that sometimes. I turned my head and saw Matt wink at me as he stepped outside. Finishing the potatoes, John picked up the giant bowl of golden faceted tubers while I started wiping the spilt peelings into a pan with a cloth. Mrs. Abernathy began pouring a mixture of rosemary, melted butter, and garlic over them. I looked up from my filled pan.

"Sheridan, where would you like these?"

"Would you like to feed the chickens with me?"

"Yes!" I had to be careful with my excited tone. "Yes, thank you," I said, my voice more subdued.

She grabbed a coffee tin full of breadcrumbs, green bean tips, and carrot ends, and escorted me out the back door to an expansive deck. "It's just over here," she pointed.

Outside Matt and his father William were talking on the deck overlooking vast fields of golden and green.

"Amy, come meet my dad." I walked over, readjusting the large bowl of peelings to my hip so I could reach out and shake his hand.

"It's very good to meet you, sir. Thank you so much for having me." He was tall, and even with the distinct silver peppered in his hair, he looked like Matt. His full-faced beard was unable to hide his charming smile.

"Well. Well. I have heard some very flattering things about

you." He smiled. "You are such a pretty little thing. Excuse me." He turned to address his wife at the gate, raising his hand to his mouth. "Watch out for the rooster. Sheridan, watch out for that damn rooster."

"I'm on it, honey." She had a large wooden mixing spoon in her apron pocket. She pulled it out as we entered the gate. I stepped behind her. "I am going to put that cockerel in a pot one of these days. He takes his job too seriously." She pointed at him with a spoon. "We are here to feed you, birdbrain." "Honestly. He is young and so, therefore, a little stupid; he needs more time to figure it out. But I'm not going to give him much more time." She shooed him away as he pecked at her dress, pushing us back towards the fence.

The girls gathered around us as we scattered delectable bits around the yard.

"These are Ameraucana chickens, Amy. After we feed them, I will show you what makes them so special. These are just for the family and friends. This is my little project. You always got to find something fun for yourself. Have myself a nice little kitchen garden in the back with raised beds and all the stuff I like to cook with growing as well."

"Oh yes." I smiled at the sweet girl-to-girl advice she was giving to me, having just met.

Suddenly she shrieked, "He is going to tear my dress!" She picked up the spoon and hit the bowl with it loudly at the rooster, temporarily sending him across the grass. "Come on, let's go to their house."

I stopped short in surprise, looking up. "Sheridan, I am not sure what I was expecting, but this is simply the most beautiful chicken house I have ever seen."

She laughed warmly. "It is, isn't it? Clark Gable and Vivien Leigh would be jealous of it."

It was a white two-story classic with a porch up top and room enough to walk in. Gleaming white lime-washed walls didn't hide the craftsmanship of the woodwork. The front porch had a screen door as well as a chicken door.

"It's beautiful. A person could almost live in here." It was hard for me to get over my shock of its beauty and charm.

"So, I tell you what, my sons made this for me for my birthday about five years ago, and I absolutely love it."

"Unbelievable."

Inside we stepped over the soft hay as we approached the nesting boxes. Amazed that I didn't need to stoop inside, I looked to the far back wall to see a tiny ladder. Overhead, exposed beams stained dark were the only color contrast to the light bright interior washed in lime. I followed the little ladder with my eyes, watching as it led to more roasting boxes and an upstairs great room. From the ceiling upstairs hung a rope with a cabbage hanging from it.

"Amazing." She watched my gaze.

"Chickens have personalities like any animal. I adore these girls. When the kids aren't here, I come out and spend time with them. They are very playful. So, snack time is playtime." She nodded towards the cabbage.

"It's endearing."

"Amy, look at this." She opened the partial lid to a nesting box to reveal a wreath of hay. Inside the golden straw, lavender and white chamomile flowers mixed on the soft nest. In the center of the nest, tucked in amongst the flowers, was a sky blue egg.

"Oh, it's beautiful. It's blue! And you have added herbs. Did you do that to make it nicer for them or to keep away bugs?"

"Both reasons, actually. I like to do simple things with great attention to detail and enjoyment. It just makes it more fun for me."

"I understand. I like that very much. It feels God-inspired to put creativity and hard work into everything you do like that. I hope it is okay to say that."

She smiled, nodding, and handed me a galvanized pail from a hook on the wall. "William and I are Catholic. Most of the kids have followed us in this. Luke and Victoria. Matt has gone his own way. Here, honey." She pointed to a wooden box. "Open this one."

I wondered what she was referring to about Matt but was instantly distracted by the pastel pink egg. "Sheridan, I don't understand. Everything is so magical here. What is happening? They lay Easter eggs?" I laughed, not knowing how else to describe it.

"Yes! The informal name for this breed is Easter Eggers."

"Oh, my goodness. I am loving every second of being on your property! Thank you again." We opened box after box finding purples, blues, deep browns, soft burnt reds, and pinks.

"Let's go on inside, honey." She linked her arm to mine as we managed our full colorful pails.

I had meant every word I spoke to her. It was eminently clear that this farm had started a rural passion in me that would never leave. I was seeing the pastel hues in the eggs and the promise of kittens later and not the backbreaking work associated with this lifestyle. But like anything, once your passion has been sparked, the work that follows is often pleasure as well.

We were seated at the table now, discussing this very thing as platters of food were set upon a buffet. We bowed our heads in a prayer that Sheridan said briefly and organically. Her easy way of speaking was relatable, and it was clear she was someone seeking a lasting friendship with God. She followed the prayer with reciting excerpts from Corinthians 13.

"Ladies," Sheridan pointed at Victoria and me, "go on and get your plates, please. There will be nothing left when Luke or Matthew go through, and I want so badly for you to try the spareribs. Amy," she singled me out now, proud to show off the farm, "the ribs, the chicken, and the veggies are all from us. From the farm. And the duck, dove, rabbit, and deer are from a hunting trip awhile back and been in the deep freeze."

Everyone finally plated and reseated, we resumed a lively conversation that lasted over an hour. Matt was so charming and relaxed around his family. I looked up many times to find him laughing, eyes twinkling, his hand on my knee under the table. I loved seeing him this way. I will always remember you like this, I promised myself. Our first fight, our fifteenth, I will remind myself of this night, and it will prompt me towards compassion. I will forgive you if and when you deserve it, but this night will remind me to look for the good things, like your laughing eyes and your witty banter.

Matt, Luke, and William went back for seconds. While they were up, Sheridan asked me if I cook. This was more than a simple question. She loves him. It must be so hard to be a mother, I thought to myself. Even when they are adults, you worry and want the best.

"Yes, ma'am, I do, actually. I took classes growing up, and with my mother's illness, I found the time and need to do it. It was one of my chores, I guess, growing up. I would also say I have a lot to learn. Thai food, wild game, Indian food, coddled eggs. These are things I would like to know more about before I call myself proficient at anything. I have a lot to learn, and I am excited about that, because I like to cook."

"Wonderful. Gotta be passionate about what you like to do in your free time, Amy. I love to cook. It takes time and burning things to a crisp sometimes to get it right. I would love to cook with you sometime."

"Oh, I would like that too."

Matt was back from another round at the buffet and seated next to me. Eyeing my plate, he made a solemn expression and whispered in my ear.

"Eat that venison and ALL your tomato avocado salad, and you can have dessert."

"Matthew, no secrets at the table," his mom scolded.

"Okay, Mommy." He smiled warmly at her, a threatening hand on my kneecap.

"So, what was Matthew like as a child?" I almost wanted to cover my ears, afraid to know.

"Well…" I guess I knew where that came from. "Well, honey. He was similar to how he is now, actually. A very kind and affectionate child. He always picked me wildflowers when he was little." I smiled, imagining him. "Played with just a handful of toys. Serious sometimes. Most times, honestly, though, he laughed and played. Hardworking. Disciplined like he was in the military, not the third grade. Immaculately neat room. Never had to get on him about that. Honestly, he was my favorite child." Forks dropped to plates like bombs falling. "I'm teasing. I'm teasing! Seeing if anyone was listening." She laughed brightly. "No, I love all my children, of course. And they were all so sweet and cute. With Matthew, he was always barefoot running down that gravel road. Had to shake the rocks and snakes out of his pockets before letting him come in the house."

"Matt." I smiled warmly at him. He leaned over and kissed my forehead.

"Now, you know what to look for before you let me inside."

"Excuse me," Sheridan went to the hall returning with a large black and white frame. "Honey." She handed it to William to hold. It was a picture of a little boy in a cloth diaper. He was leaning against a tree and had turned around to look at the camera like someone had called his name.

"Oooh! Matt, you are so cute!"

She looked at the picture affectionately. "He was, wasn't he. Look at his little Indian markings under his eyes and his holster."

"I did your war makeup with Mom's lipstick." Luke was laughing. "I got in trouble over that, if I recall. Coco Chanel or something. You have a half Indian and half cowboy thing going on there," he laughed. "I hadn't noticed that before."

"I guess I couldn't decide who was the good guys and who was the bad guys. That's a tough one. Cowboys are awesome, but Indians...well, they can be pretty cool too." He chuckled. "That quintessential childhood impasse. I can't decide as an adult either."

A half hour later, we had cleared the plates for coffee and dessert. William handed me a plate.

"I'm too full. Thank you." I tried my best to be convincing.

"So actually, this one is buttermilk cream pie," William said.

I looked over at Matt, who was pouring more coffee. His favorite, and I had never had it. I hadn't even heard of it until a couple of nights ago.

"Amy, share it with me if you can't finish a whole slice." I nodded.

Taking a sweeping glance for his mother, I leaned in, whispering, "Matt, we have only been dating for three days. Three days. It feels like three years. Wonderful ones. We are going so fast, and we always have been."

Aspirating slightly on his coffee, he paused to turn his head from the table and cough repeatedly in his arm before coming back to me. "I can't stop it. I tried, and now I won't. Are you okay with everything? Is this still good?" He touched my hair and I kissed his cheek in response.

"Yes. I am so happy, honestly. Your parents are wonderful and I feel light years away from where we were a few weeks ago, with me doing cartwheels on the bar and you being angry."

"Oh, I know. The bar is not good for us, but we can make it work. Or not, sweetheart, I was thinking—"

William interrupted us, serving the dessert. First impression: it looked like an ugly cheesecake. But it smelled good, like vanilla and cream, and tasted even better, sort of like sweetened sour cream but with an eggnog aftertaste. I set my fork down and took a sip of coffee.

"You don't like it?" Matt whispered.

"No, I do, actually. It is very, very rich. Like edible eggnog, maybe. Very good. I am going to have to work so hard tomorrow."

Matt looked at me flatly. No smile or even anger was present on his face. I realized at this moment: many times, when he had done this before, and I had evaluated him only as being angry, he was just being solemn. Thinking. He broke his gaze to drink coffee and stare at the wall. Okay, maybe he was mad. My body. My life, though. I took a sip of coffee and spoke to him softly. "I am genuinely full. I am not starving in front of delicious pie. I am trying to get an education I can afford, which means something as simple as trying new foods and stopping when I am full. It's okay. I'm okay."

He nodded but continued to sip his coffee without a word.

I got up to help clear plates as Victoria came over to help me. We loaded the dishwasher while William and Sheridan filled up ice chests brimming full of frozen steaks, duck, chicken, pickled green beans, tomato sauces, eggs, and jelly for each of the kids.

Before the last plate was tidied, I suddenly remembered something burning in my heart.

"Chicks and kittens!" Victoria beckoned me towards a hallway that led to a guest room. Off to the side, past a beautiful four-poster mahogany bed, was the bathroom. There was a battery-operated heater in the back of the tub, and the chicks were huddled near it in fuzzy yellow clumps. "Oh, my goodness."

"Pick one up, Amy. They are old enough."

I tried to repress it, but I squealed in delight at the prospect. Choosing one that was awake, I made an effort to scoop him up, but he bolted from my fingers towards the water spout. The little guy was unbelievably fast.

"Like this." Matt was behind me now. He made a scooping motion with both hands, cornering a chick against the side of the tub. His giant hands were covering it carefully as he handed it to me. I sat down, afraid I would drop it from a standing position. Victoria slipped out the door with a little wave.

"Forgiven then?" I asked. His hand remained on mine.

"Worried. Just thinking about what I can do to help. Never mad, sweetheart." He sighed. "Just remembering our conversation in the back of the truck. Worried about you."

"What I said makes sense, and it is fair."

"It's not the pie, kiddo. It is the bigger picture. We can talk another time."

"Okay." The chick was dominating my attention. He sat down next to me.

"Close your eyes. Good. Now bring it to your ear. I will help you." His hand was on mine, guiding it. "Now listen to its little cheeping sounds. Isn't that cute?"

"A month ago, I could never have imagined you would say that to me or anyone." The chick was softly pecking at my hair.

"And now, what do you think?" He looked tired.

"I think you are a man who will never stop surprising me with the depths of his beautiful soul." He kissed the side of my face, and with his forehead pressed to my temple, stayed close to me, unmoving. A couple of minutes passed comfortably in this way before he spoke.

"Amy, I make enough money for both of us. I can..." He paused finding his words. "I can provide for you. Would you be willing to forfeit your scholarship and quit the bar? You can focus on school. I can give you foundational support, as we discussed. You can sew."

My heart was racing. I leaned over and replaced the chick into the bathtub, regretfully relinquishing it to its siblings. We were both standing now. I took his hands in mine and looked up at him. In his eyes, I could see only love. He looked older suddenly to me. Tired. Wise. And giving.

"Oh, Matt, you are offering something more than I can take. It's too much for you to offer. For me to say yes to. Listen, I trust you, and I need you to trust me. I am going to get through this summer, hell or high water. The condensed summer coursework is a huge challenge. And then comes the real test with fall. I might make it, honey. I need to try."

"I am proud of you. And I understand. You need to promise me to be good."

"I do promise you that."

"And be honest with me at all times."

"I have been and will continue to be."

"Okay, I feel better."

"About me not eating three more bites of pie." I smiled.

"And not finishing your green beans, three tomatoes, and venison." Ignoring his last comment, I reached out, touching his arm lovingly.

"You are a good man. And I am grateful for what you have offered me." I made a motion for him to lean down, and I kissed his cheek. "While we have a minute alone, can I also tell you how much I like your family. All of them. Your parents, your siblings, your sister-in-law, the dogs. Can we see the kittens before we leave?" He smiled.

"Sure, sweetie. Come on. Glad you like them. They like you too, I can tell."

"You think so?"

"Yes, I know it. My mom loves you more than me already." He held my hand as we walked into the kitchen to say our goodbyes.

"Amy." Sheridan came over to me as we were about to leave. "Listen, next week, I am going to make wild violet jelly. I would love to show you. We can go out in the field with baskets and pick bunches together. It comes together very quickly." Matt smiled at me.

"See," he whispered into my hair.

"That sounds wonderful. Thank you." I looked at Matt as she addressed him.

"Matt, can y'all come next weekend?" He held my hand, big fingers running slowly over mine, and turned to his mother.

"Yes, Momma, I will look at our work schedule, her training schedule, and get back to you."

"Goodbye, everyone. Thank you. It was such a pleasure to meet you all."

"Matt, everything is loaded in the back of your truck, son."

"Thanks, Dad. Love y'all. Night."

"Enjoy the kittens. Some of their eyes aren't open yet. And drive safely."

"Oh, wow. Amazing. Thank you all again. Good night."

We walked into the long entry hall. I took my bag off the peg and looked at the black and white faces of his childhood. Muddy little boys running, a rope swing in the barn bending mid-ride, candles being blown on a cake. It was so sweet. I watched him strapping on his shoulder harness over his undershirt, and then reaching for his dress shirt on the peg, he began to button himself.

"What is this called?"

He grinned, "A firearm."

"No, like what kind?"

"A pistol."

"Its name." I frowned.

"It is my friend. Got it three years ago, so maybe I could call it Buddy."

"So irritating. You are so coy." I rolled my eyes to the ceiling.

"It's a Glock 17T. First generation. Semi-automatic. 9mm short recoil action. Range is about fifty yards. It's a great reliable gun. I think I will go with Buddy after all." He chuckled, tying his boots. "Did I hit your question?" He smiled up at me.

I nodded, not knowing what I had actually wanted to ask, except: "Why do you have it?"

"Why wouldn't I?"

"You just don't seem afraid of anything. So, what I mean

to say is, you've been in so many fistfights since we met, and why would you need more?"

"Well, you can't bring your fists to a gunfight. And you never know who's angry enough or crazy enough to take it to the next level. You hope it's not going to happen, but you can at least do something about it, if it's inevitable. Part of being a responsible good person is doing right action. Self-protection, the protection of innocents. And to be clear, I am afraid of a lot of things."

I made a face. "Name something."

"Canoeing with hippos. What else?" He paused, running his fingertips over my shoulder, "World annihilation. Alien invasion. Giant South American bats, I think they are called spectral bats. I don't even care if they are fruit bats. But these, if I recall, are carnivores, so quite likely the blood-sucking kind." He frowned speaking pensively, "I'm talking about a four-foot wingspan. No thanks." His smile revealed him.

"You're joking."

"Yes, of course, I am. I don't believe in doomsday, aliens, or bats." He kissed me, shielding my head from a hook on the wall.

"You don't believe in bats?"

He crinkled his nose and went in again for his kiss. "No. I don't."

I laughed softly, "You are so silly tonight!" He nodded, reaching for my hand.

"I'm happy, Amy. That's what it is. And if I am speaking honestly with you, I am afraid of things. Sure I am. Since I met you, that has honestly skyrocketed. I need you to be safe. Healthy. I need us to maturate our relationship, to grow us. I want to be enough for you. Be what you need. I don't want to disappoint myself or you. Yes, I have real fear. But not bats. I would punch one in the face if I needed to. I can't imagine the scenario where I would. But you can't punch death. Or us dissipating, or something horrible happening to..."

We kissed, unable to carry on with words. We continued our conversation for some minutes, my back against the teal wall of his childhood home. An umbrella hanging from a hook fell to the floor.

"Matthew Abernathy, are you still here in this house, son?" Sheridan called from the living room. Matt reached in his pants and jingled his car keys.

"Got my car keys, Mom. Night." He laughed sweetly, his hand pulling my head to his chest as we walked out onto the front porch.

"There is a voice that doesn't use words. Listen."
—Rumi

"But I am a girl. I am emotionally charged. And I believe I have cried on all three of our dates at one point in time." *—Amy*

CHAPTER TWELVE

"I Know You Now"

Descending the steps hand in hand towards the barn, I looked up at the stars, praying silently. "Thank you, God." I prayed as we moved out over the wooden floorboards of the old porch. "Thank you so much that it went well. Thank you that Matthew is in this spiritual place of caring and affection. God, please give me the strength to take the harder road on my own. To learn to say no to him again and again when it is right. And yes, when it is right. To have my own voice."

We moved from the porch to a side patio filled with fragrant plumeria and bougainvillea that spilled over a deck in their reckless fuchsia way.

"It makes me happy that you grew up here, Matt." He smiled.

"Me too. Looking back, it was just what I needed. When I was a teenager, though, I didn't see it that way. I felt trapped by our substantial property line. By how far back the world was. The girls, the parties, alcohol, and reckless nights...the stuff I considered to be the good stuff. Now, listening to the crickets with you walking along in the dark, crushing a million June bugs under our feet, I would move out here the first chance I got."

"Ew. What? Matt."

"The country is nice, honey." He teased.

"Yes, I know that. The bugs. The last part of what you said." I laughed as I looked down careful now about my steps.

"They won't hurt you."

"I know what they are. Too well, I'm afraid." It was getting darker. He squeezed my hand—little pulses.

"Do tell."

"Well, we were living in Amarillo, Texas, at the time. I was seven years old, and my Girl Scout troop was camping in the Palo Duro Canyon. It was beautiful, Matt. It was days like last week—nights like this one. Perfect weather, wildflowers everywhere. Hills and hills of bluebonnets like playful shadows from clouds. Well, I had been trying to look after my sister while I was going through the activity programs that they had set out for us: namely weaving, archery, painting sticks, building a fire, and making trail mix."

"Oh, man. Well, at least they taught you about building a fire."

"Not really," I was digressing. "It was more about fire safety and how to use a lighter."

He chuckled to himself. "So, you can use a lighter then?"

"Yes, honey, of course." My eyes squinted, remembering his comment to Jason in the basement.

"Good." He seemed amused. "Go on."

"Often, I would look after kids at church, or potlucks, and prayer groups. Always had a kid on my hip and very often my sister. And I was watching Laurel this day during camp. So, I set my sister, who was about four, by a tree to string a snack necklace and went to the stick painting station. When I came back only a few minutes later, eyes on her the whole time, mind you, I found it wasn't Cheerios she had been popping continuously into her mouth," I paused for effect.

"Oh gross." Matt frowned playfully.

"It was horrendous, Matt. I had to make her spit them out and got her water. Trying not to make her feel chastened about the little legs wiggling out of her smile." We both laughed until our voices were lost to the sound of the night insects calling.

"I like the feel of your hand in mine."

"Me too." Suddenly I looked around me, noticing I couldn't see. "It's so dark. I can't see to go on. Maybe I will step on something." I was thinking about more than the distasteful little amber-brown bugs under us—all their short wiggly legs. There could be snakes, turtles, literally anything underfoot, and my imagination was running wild at the prospect.

"It's okay. Keep your hand in mine. Your eyes will adjust."

"Don't you have gum, flashlights, knives, and some sort of multi-tool accessories in your pockets?"

"I do."

"Well, let's get them out, please."

"Let's not. We don't need them. I will see for both of us, and your eyes will adjust. Be patient. Look at the stars. Then look at the horizon." My eyes flashed up and then down to the skyline.

"It's working, actually," I admitted after a moment, somewhat surprised. "How far are we going?"

"It's right here where the path turns to the left." Astonished, I could now see the trail, at least the gray color of it, I nodded.

"It is so far from the house."

"We have six different barns on the property. The closest one we passed earlier, well, it's the one I really love. It's over fifty years old and just beautifully built. My mom didn't want the animals so close to the house—the livestock, I mean—so it became ours; my brothers and I. Oh, we used to make forts in the hay, catch little grass snakes, and bigger black rat snakes in there. A big rope swing hung from the top of the beams that swung out from the loft right out the open door. My mom was inspired by *Charlotte's Web*. After she read it to us one night, she told my dad that next morning, and by that evening, he had managed to find the time to go to the hardware store and get it done. My parents are sweet like that. Anything she wants. She doesn't want a lot. She's a real sweetheart, so she's careful what he knows about in that way. But the second he hears she wants something..." He snapped his fingers. "Coming back to that kid classic, did you ever read that one?"

"Yes, I remember it well. How Fern and her brother Avery used to swing in Wilbur's pen, past the web, out the door."

"Have you read it recently?" he laughed loudly, turning to me.

"No!" I pushed him gently in the dark. "No, no, I just remember the description of that swing so distinctly, and I remember at the time reading it, thinking how wonderful and fun that would be. Is it still there, the rope swing?"

"No, it is stored someplace. But the hardware is still there and strong. When we were teenagers, we fashioned the barn into a gym, if you will. There were weights, a big rack, a punching bag. In the back tack room, we made a woodshop. Spent some time in that barn." Instantly, I remembered a fight from my first week on the job. He was "raised there." He went on, "I still associate the smell of hay and fresh-cut wood with hard work and the taste of blood in my mouth."

I smiled at him in the moderate privacy of the dark. How different he was from me.

"Okay, here we are. This barn is different, though." He opened a lock on the door and turned on the lights. "This is a steel barn smaller than the other four modern ones farther out. This setup is for bovines and pregnant mothers."

He turned a light on the wall. Sweet, almost cartoonish big brown eyes followed us as we walked along the stalls.

"Oh, Matt, look how sweet the little ones are."

"Yeah, they are cute. They taste good too."

I made a face. So inappropriate. "Matt."

"Well, they do. Veal is expensive for a reason. It's very tender."

"Do you have to kill them here?" A sudden terrible thought came to me. "Have you killed a baby cow?"

"No, honey. I have never killed a cow, baby, or otherwise. I would if I needed to, but no, they are sent to a slaughterhouse and meat processing factory."

I made a sad face as I touched a wet nose of a youngster.

"Let's not talk about it. They might hear us," he suggested, wanting to change the subject. "Kittens are this way. You want my flashlight? They are apparently…" he oriented himself looking at the back, "just over here."

He held my hand, towing me past big soft eyes. A cow lowed loudly or peed every so often, and it sounded like someone pouring a pitcher of iced tea on the cement. "Eww."

"Yep, they are animals. That's why we take our shoes off when we come in the house. Mom's rule."

"I adore your mother. All of them," I reminded him.

"You know, Amy, as we left, she told me she has never seen me this happy. And she is so glad we found each other." I smiled.

"Do you remember when we first met?" I covered my mouth with my hand, suppressing my laugher. "You were so mean to me, babe! You told me to go get ice cream!" He stopped walking as we passed the last stall to ceremonially spin me around like we were dancing and then scoop me up and carry me the rest of the way.

"Well, I am so very sorry about that," he whispered in my ear. "And I am so happy you were stubborn and didn't listen to me." He set me gently on my feet. "Over there."

He pointed towards a snug bundle on a horse blanket in the hay pile. I clicked on my flashlight and used my other hand to shield the light from them. A mother tabby lay on her side.

Nursing and kneading her happily, seven winsome kittens lay silent, only their arms and mouths moving.

"Oh, they are so cute!" I sank to my knees near them. "Is she friendly? Is it okay to touch one when they have finished?"

"She is an adopted cat from a shelter. Like I say, my mom is a real sweetheart. And we don't know her well yet, but I believe she is friendly. Mom likes her and handles her." He picked up the orange tabby on the end; it made a soft sucking sound as it was slowly ripped from the nipple.

"Oh no. Don't. We can wait."

He looked at his watch. "Not really. I want you to get good sleep or have more study time." He smiled supportively.

He held the soft lump of fur in his giant hands, turning it over. Its tail was stiff, sticking straight out. "A boy," he handed it to me to hold.

I held it carefully in both my hands. "Oh look! His eyes are halfway open. Poor little guy." I cooed, holding him. He hissed at me, eyes closed, completely defenseless. "Oh, he's stressed. Put him back, honey."

Matt smiled, and taking the kitten, put him a half-inch from where he had been taken. The nipple he had been on was available, the fur around it wet and matted a quarter inch around, but he remained motionless.

"Oh no. We shouldn't have picked him up," I leaned back on my heels, worried.

"He will be okay. Watch." Almost a full minute later, the kitten began to move, following his nose left and right until he latched on again. He resumed his nursing, and his paws began kneading just as before, his arms pumping in and out in blissful feeding contentment. "Let's go, sweetheart. "

I nodded, blowing the young family a little kiss. We started the trek to the truck. "The father is your cat too? Will he stay in the barn as well?"

"I'm not sure the parental details of the kittens. But no, he won't stay. Animals are not like that. Most."

I nodded as we stepped out into the fresh air under the stars. Matt turned off the main lights and relocked the padlock on the door.

"I can't wait to leave the dormitory so I can have an animal. I considered being a veterinarian, but the schooling is beyond me. After more research, I was surprised about the heavy focus on vaccines and neuter/spay. It's less about petting them." I laughed, teasing. "So, I think just owning one would satisfy that need considerably more."

"I understand." Our eyes were adjusting from the light of the barn to the soft glow of thousands of stars. Texas stars. Bigger and brighter than all other states, I mused to myself.

"Sit down with me." He had somehow found a beautiful wooden bench in the darkness. I sat with him, my head on his arm, my hands folded on his lap as I leaned in, looking up. The sky was pitch black, and the stars were twinkling on high.

"There is still so much I want to know about you, Amy. So many, many conversations we still need to have. It will take a lifetime."

I nodded against his shoulder.

He pointed out the constellations to me, starting with the North Star and mentioning them all by name. A country boy, he had undoubtedly spent hours stargazing over the years. "Amy, I know you are beginning your higher education while I am at the end of mine. Do you have an idea of what you want to do yet? It's okay if you don't. I didn't have it as specific at your stage."

"I do, Matt! I had originally wanted to get into social work. I looked into this a couple of years ago very deeply and even volunteered with social workers. Joining them in the office for paperwork and following up on families." I shook my head. "These people are saints, Matt. Like the military, your dad, and other police forces, like doctors and nurses, like so many. I wanted to love it. But I am a girl. I am emotionally charged. And I believe I have cried on all three of our dates at one point in time." He smiled, hugging me.

"You are sensitive because you have a big heart."

I turned to him with shining eyes, "I love how you rephrase things, to see the best in me. You are an amazing person. I am in awe of you."

He paused our conversation to guide my face in the darkness towards him. Finding my lips, he imparted how he felt about my compliments and then pulled away reluctantly.

"You were saying? I am interested in your dreams."

"So, at the end of my internship, if you could call it that, I realized that I am not strong enough to deal with children being hurt and displaced, families being torn apart by drugs or abuse. It is something that doesn't leave you. And I want a family. I want children. I remember thinking you cannot come home to your children, taking ten minutes to cry it out in the driveway before walking through the door every day for years, and then resume the role of a fun, happy mother. Some people can, and God bless them truly. I pray for them all the time." I shook my head. "I don't have the adamantine spirit needed for that kind of work. I am ashamed to say that I don't."

"You shouldn't be ashamed of anything that is honest. I would worry all the time if you chose this line of work. It would break me eventually. Honestly. Please tell me you want to test the softness of cotton fabrics and write about it professionally from beside our fireplace in the living room." I smiled, then laughed loudly at his absurdity.

"You're funny. Close though on some accounts." I felt him turn his head in the dark and could almost imagine the face he was making. "Matt, I have a secret."

"Tell me your secrets. Trust me with them." He kissed me, urging me to speak.

"I am an artist. I love to draw, paint, ceramics—all of it. I think I have a shot at making it into a career, something real. I plan to try it out in the professional world but I would get my teaching license to go with it as a backup. Elementary art."

He hugged me, relieved my secret worked well into his plans. "I didn't know. I would love to see some of your art. Your style. This makes me very happy, Amy. I cannot tell you how happy I am. I will build you a studio myself and buy you every color of paint imaginable."

"Well...thank you in advance." It was hard to know what to say to such a promise. "This upcoming week, would it be okay to draw you sometime?"

"Yes. If I can bring some work. I have to study as well."

"Of course. It's better. You will be still and less pestilent." I felt the threat he posed as his fingers found my knee cap.

"Don't. Don't! Please. Tell me what finance means. I mean, in terms of what you actually want to do with it. The application." It was a distraction, but something of genuine curiosity for me.

"Well, I like math and organization, which led me to finance. I want to work in equity, to work with professionals, to network with investors to gain equity in the private sector. And I want to basically apply this to business investments that diversify investors' portfolios. I started investing in the stock market as a teenager, just playing around. I made mistakes, lots of them, but learned from them, thankfully. I was reckless at first, but I got good at it, miraculously, investing heavily in a budding local tech company when they went public in 1996. That went very, very well. Dell Computers. Have you heard of them?" I nodded. "So, when I started making money at the bar, I found it to be a good opportunity to invest in a varied portfolio. Bull or bear markets? Know anything about that?"

"No," I readily admitted.

"Well, it is fun for me anyway. I could have gone either way, military, police, or investments. I guess like you, I was thinking of the future. So far, it's been fun. I bought a house off of Barton Springs near downtown. Paid it off in just a few short years. Well, six, without touching the bulk of my stock investments. Fixed it up myself. Luke and Samuel helped a lot.

I'm the guy that works on my deck almost every weekend for over a year now. Never actually sit out there." He smiled, his perfect white teeth shining in the dim light. "My schedule forces me to be patient, go slow with school—that's, in part why I'm so old in my last year. But I have a house, so I guess it's worth it."

"I have never even asked where you lived. I wondered a month ago, but I was too shy to speak to you."

"I'm sorry. I can be unapproachable. I know that about myself. And it is some sort of shield, maybe armor would be a better analogy, that I have built for myself. I don't even really know why. All I know is with you; it is down. There's nothing there to protect me. I am completely vulnerable, and my beating heart is exposed. And I don't care about the ramifications of that because—" He stopped telling me, deciding to show me instead.

He was kissing me softly, the moon and stars as our only witness. He started to speak but I pulled back from him.

"Can we be done talking now, I think I would rather kiss." He laughed loudly, his lips leaning back in towards mine. The breeze blew my hair, whipping it wildly as he grabbed it in his hands, combing it back and keeping his hand on my head. I closed my eyes, feeling that oceanic cadence I had described as water balloons splashed around us; that first night, we had discovered the magic between us. We spent another half an hour in heavenly bliss, fingers entwined, lips locked, time lost. The buzzing of his cell interrupted our session under the stars.

"Get it. It's okay." I pulled away.

"No." Matt let it ring, ignoring it. He pulled away when the caller rang a second time. "Hello. Hey, man. Yep. Yes. Sure, go ahead." He covered the phone. "It's JR, need to take this. Walk with me."

I held his hand in the dark as the three-minute conversation came to fruition.

"So," he said, pocketing the phone. "We are good. We have come to terms with all things pertaining to you, schedules, and the music playlist." He laughed. "More Def Leppard, less Madonna."

"Oh, I am glad you guys got resolution," I said as his phone rang again.

"Hello. Yes Sir. I did in fact call you back five days ago. Left a message with Sierra H. Brown. Yep. I work full time and I'm a full-time student. Not avoiding you, just working hard, paying the bills. I can make that date and time. I'll ask her." He put his hand on the phone and turned to me in the dark. "Amy, can you meet the policeman handling our case this week?" I nodded. "Is Wednesday after drill practice, okay? I can pick you up at ten." I nodded again as dread like ice water began pumping through my veins. He finished the phone call, closing the flip phone, and reached for my hand. "Everything is okay, Amy. They just want to ask you some questions, sweetheart. Clarify some things for them. Charlie and I have already gone downtown and made our statements." We were approaching the truck; I could see its shiny reflection in the porch light like a ghost leaning against it. "Do you remember taking to the female officer, I'm forgetting her name, at the hospital?" I shook my head. "No?"

"No."

"Don't worry, Little. Just an initial statement from you. I'll be there." I smiled in the dark, my worry dissipating slightly with his words, as he opened the door and I climbed in the cab of the truck.

He walked around, stopping to get two water bottles out of the back. He handed me one once he was beside me.

"Amy, tonight has been so nice. Thank you."

"You and your family have made this a wonderful memory. So, work. When do we go in this week? I want to draw you and keep my word to your mom." He smiled, turning onto the farm-to-market road.

"So, we have identical schedules now. This will help my anxiety about you working downtown immensely. We work Tuesday and Wednesday, that is if you can stand the sight of me after our meeting with Officer Brady." I turned to him in the pitch dark, but he kept his eyes on the road.

I tried to not think of the meeting at the precinct. "Okay, I'm sure it will work. Is everything in your ice chest going to be okay? We keep forgetting about it?"

We were on the main road now. An hour to Austin, and we would be home. Suddenly, I felt sad we lived in different places. I didn't want or need a break from him. He was intense, but I had grown so happy satiated on his intensity and constant affection. His voice broke my thoughts.

"No, honey. Everything is fine. The cooler is iced, and the meat is all frozen solid. My mother is so sweet. She marinates everything in a basic marinade for all of us. Then she makes special marinades, so we all have our favorites and variety. She does this for every Sunday dinner. And to be honest, it must be so much work. But she's the type of person who shows her love by hard work and service. She's always been that way."

"I can see that. And I can see it makes her very happy to take care of you. The ranch is overwhelming magic. Just like your family. Like you." I giggled thinking of the wonderful dinner, "Matt, I can finally see how you can eat so many calories."

He grinned. "Well, it wasn't easy in the beginning. When I was young, and we made our gym in the barn, as I said, it was hard to eat enough calories to get the bulk needed to transform it. So, my brothers and I started by adding a chicken breast to every meal or a small steak. Then we added an orange Julius. Orange juice and vanilla with raw egg. We put in three raw eggs, and we drank two or three of these a day. Now I just do protein powder. But back then, we didn't know about that, or they didn't have it readily available yet. Not sure. And when we were older, we all set alarms for two in the morning to meet downstairs and eat eight to twelve ounces of cold steak and roasted sweet potatoes and trudge back up to bed. It got easier when I started working downtown. I grill something almost every night, morning rather, whether I get my pancakes or not."

"Wow. You're like an infant. On a very specific feeding schedule."

He laughed. "I guess you are right. Funny comparison, though."

"Not really," I teased. "You throw tantrums and need to eat every two hours on the clock."

"Amy, I will pull this truck over and tickle the hell out of you for an hour. I've got the time. You are the one who needs to study. So, I guess I can be nice."

What? He wouldn't do this. The prospect was terrifying, though. Clearly, he was joking. "Wah, wah, wah." Why was I doing this? Stop, I lectured myself! Don't test him. You have to push a man like this, I argued with myself in my head. He didn't move, but I heard him turn on his blinker, and we changed lanes. "Matt, no! You need to be able to take a joke. I was just joking, please."

"Too late."

"What. Why? I said sorry."

"You didn't, actually."

"Oh, well. It was a joke. I am sorry. Matt, I will call your mother—"

"You don't have a phone." I reached for his too late, and he put it in his shirt pocket. "She gave you her number? That's so cute."

"It is. She wants to discuss the jelly process before she teaches me this weekend. And I am going to bring her some jars from our co-op. Are you okay? Are you feeling better?" I saw an exit coming up.

"I feel fine, sweetie. Worried about you in a few minutes, though." What. I heard the familiar rhythmic tic tic tic tic of the blinker ahead of the exit.

"Matt, don't!" I was firm, my heart beating fast.

He looked over, grinning. "Okay." He turned to me, assessing me, then laughed uproariously. "You look so scared. Now I'm sorry."

"Well, you should be. I can't stand fifteen seconds of being tickled by you. An hour would make me lose my mind."

"Honey, I would never, ever, do that to you."

"Oh, really? Because I recall a cab ride. The longest cab ride of my life today, after the party and hotel date, where I was mercilessly tickled."

"It was four minutes off and on. You squealed incoherently. You never asked me to stop. I would have stopped if you had asked me. Asked me politely." he confirmed, winking at me.

We pulled up to the dorm. "Well, I am going to call her anyway. Not tonight, it's late, but she needs to know about you—the type of son she raised." I looked down at him from my seat as he helped me out.

"Oh, she knows, honey. Say whatever your heart desires, of course. But she knows."

No doubt. He'd always been this way. I could never go back to seeing him as this alien, robot of a man, void of emotion. He was wonderful. Playful. Kind. And I was falling into a deeper state of love and affection every second I was in his presence. I would need to tell him. Not tonight.

"Well, then maybe I don't need to call her and tell her about what she already knows."

"Maybe not." He smiled, kissing me, then looked at his watch. "Well, it's 11:00. Are you going to study tonight or wake up early?" He handed me my bag.

"Wake up early."

"Okay, sweetheart. I wish it were earlier. Sorry. What do you want from here?" he nodded at the icebox.

"Oh, I am fine, Matt. I have a pretty strict infant feeding schedule myself."

"Please. My mom literally wrote your name with black marker on some of these." He opened the chest and looked through.

"Okay. That's really sweet. So yes please. That way, I will have something further to speak with her about when we talk." And I could use the meal prep help. Something I was perpetually forgetting about.

He was still digging through the chest. "I love my mama."

"Just two if that's okay. Whichever ones you think. Kate and I will try them tomorrow."

"Steak, chicken, duck, goat, pork?"

"Oh, wow. So, you choose. It's hard to have an opinion without knowing."

"I understand that. They are all good. This is a hard choice if I am trying to impress you off of only one taste. You and Karen, right? Hmmm."

"Kate."

"Let's go with two rosemary garlic rib-eyes. Please tell me you know how to cook these? Otherwise, I cannot give them to you." He grinned.

"I do! Your mother also believes cooking good steak incorrectly is sinful, and she told me exactly what to do."

"Okay. Then take this homemade butter too."

"Thank you."

We walked up to the dorm entrance. He waited with me for the elevator, talking to me about the bar and upcoming changes to it. It came, and he watched me get into it, along with a few more students. The doors started to close.

"Wait." He leaned forward and blocked them with his hand. Stepping in momentarily, his finger on the do-not-close button, he kissed me goodbye softly on the lips. His tongue rocked me backward slightly. "Goodnight, sweetheart."

Then slowly, he stepped out of the elevator, putting his hands up in apology for causing the brief stop. The doors closed between us, and I could feel the stares of the other students' smoldering gazes on the back of my head. I realized, to my surprise, that I didn't care, my captivated heart beating fast in my chest, eyes fixed ahead on the closed metal doors.

"The root of suffering is attachment." —*Buddha*

"I get in unhealthy cycles sometimes. It starts in my head and then I regulate myself so much. Today was a challenge." —*Amy*

CHAPTER THIRTEEN

"Huff and Puff and Blow 'em All Down"

Monday was dreary and overcast. In the early morning, it rained heavily as a storm front rolled through south Texas. Perfect studying weather.

I woke up at five, then spent the entire morning at my desk, Kate by my side, in stationary silent focus for hours. Finally, turning a page, I popped up from my chair, looking at her. "More coffee, honey?"

"Yes, thank you. I am using coconut sugar from the co-op on Guadalupe now. Can you bring it? Inspired by you to make a change."

"Thank Matt then."

"I won't," she smiled cynically at me.

"Okay. By the way, he brought us steaks for tonight from his family's ranch in the hill country. So, don't order anything. I can make them around your schedule; I am home around five, give or take. Apparently, there is a particular way to cook them. His mom and I talked about it."

"He gets it from her, then. You can cook them however you want." I looked up, hurt in my eyes, trying not to show it.

"Kate, please be nice to him. For his sake or mine. It doesn't matter." We felt inseparable now to me.

I walked to the coffee pot, returning with a little tray piled with nibbles, white daisies, coconut sugar, and two steaming coffees. I set it on a small table between us.

"Are you going to eat anything, or are these all for me?" She picked up a biscotti, setting it on her saucer.

"Not hungry yet. Just coffee, thanks." She was giving me a look.

"You always say that."

"What?"

"That four percent you have. I have twenty percent, and I am your friend, so I will look out for you. He is controlling, and I honestly think it won't last." Silence. I needed a moment to respond.

"I appreciate your concern but not the unfair judgment. The four percent is gone. There is no one else on earth like him. He's the man I am going to marry."

She dropped her spoon on the desk with a loud clatter. I kept my eyes on my book.

"I think you are being reckless."

"I understand how you would feel that way. It feels fast from your perspective, and technically it is, but I have liked him for a long time. Half of that time, I didn't know it myself. And vice versa. He is a wonderful person. He is kind, honest, intelligent, reverent, silly, courageous, romantic, and sweet."

"Amy." She rolled her green eyes at me and turned the page. "I don't like how he has changed you. Your opinions on things. Your coffee is just one of several things of late."

My eyes, unmoving from my chapter, were fixated on the word "this." Unmoving from the text, focused on a solitary word, focused on our conversation. "This," I mused to myself. At one time, he had renamed me "This." Suddenly I was very thankful Kate had not heard about this story. It made me mindful of her point, though. I suddenly jumped up.

"I love you too, though, honey! You are my friend, and you are only looking out for me. And truly, I appreciate your heart. But I got this, and I want this with him more than words can articulate. Please feel as you wish but be happy for me too." My gesture and words changed the tone of her voice.

"Okay, Amy. I can try. A bit."

"A bit. Okay, I will take it. Thank you, Kate. I am grateful." I went back to my book and coffee.

Two hours later, I was on my bike, pumping briskly through the pouring rain from drill to my first class. Taking notes and sitting in the second row, I looked up, surprised to read "Matthew" written on my paper's top header in curly cursive lines. A heart was around it, enclosing his name like a safety bubble from my notes on homeostasis. I had no idea when I had written it. The professor was waiting on no one.

"...appropriate condition such as proper pH, and appropriate concentration of a variety of different chemicals..." I rushed to write this down in shorthand. "Now these particular conditions, I have outlined here..." he nodded to the whiteboard beside him, "...may, however, change from one instant to the next."

I thought of huge hands holding mine in the dark as we walked towards the bovine barn. My fingertips feeling his calluses, softly running over them.

"Now most organisms, a high concentration thereof, can properly maintain all internal conditions..." I thought of the gait of his walk, confident and assured like no one I had ever known. Like his back hurt. And like he could handle any situation. My mind flashed to the faint wave of short brown hair as it met his neck.

"Now that is well within a very tapered set of numbers, almost constantly, despite an outstanding variety of diverse impacting environmental changes manifested through the 'steady state' known to us as homeostasis."

My mind followed him from behind as we walked, his

hand held out behind himself, reaching for me, barely visible in the dark—his broad shoulders angling to bend down and open the lock on the metal door.

"And thank you for your time and attention. Read chapters twelve to sixteen for the next class." I wrote this down near his name and closed my notes.

My second class moved even more slowly. My hands wrapped around a steamy mint tea was the only relief from my wandering mind and profound confusion in math class.

Finally done with the entirety of my classes, I biked down to the university gym and parked my bike next to Stephanie's. I showered quickly, rinsing the biology and algebra from my mind. Then grabbing my towel, I stood in line near the dressing room, silent and broody, waiting to hear my name. I already knew.

"Patterson."

Stephanie walked past the far hall, changed and ready. She looked up and blew me a kiss, pointing to the gym. I smiled. I hadn't had anything yet but coffee, water, and half of a mint tea. It didn't matter.

"Emerson," I stood on the scale.

"112." The assistant coach looked me in the eyes as I turned my head from the scale to face her. I felt a little ping in my nose as emotion hit me, but I didn't show it. "It's okay, of course, Amy. I just don't want to see you get *under* 100 again. You're fine. Enjoy your day." I managed a smile and stepped off the scale. It was not fine. It was not fucking fine, and it didn't matter who said that to me. Oh my God, I was cursing. Cursing in my head. Holding back the tears, I lectured myself, fumbling back to the showers, no bad words. And don't blame Matthew's influence for what you said. Thought. Whatever. I rushed back to the shower stalls, undressing in a flash, my hair still wet from the first one. In the privacy of the shower, my forehead on my forearm as the water splashed over my shoulders, I made my plan. I could work my studies around it, if I focused hard and went now. I looked at my watch.

Five minutes later, I met Stephanie in the gym. "Hey, sexy."

"Hi, honey." Today of all days, I was not wanting her to say something like this. Maybe the party had her feeling more comfortable with me in this way. "Tell me about Trevor, friend."

"Amy, we hooked up at the house party! I'm not sure if we are in a relationship or even if I want that. But he is cool." I smiled. So, she hooked up? She hooked up. She met up? So, they met at the party, but she's not sure if it's something with staying power. Hmmm.

"Well, just give it time and think about what you want. Just be honest with him and with yourself." It seemed honest and general enough to make sense though her words were ambiguous to me.

She smiled. "You give great advice. Love you, girl." She hugged me.

"Steph, how do you keep your weight in check? You are so perfect. You don't seem to lose or gain weight dramatically. If I can confess to you, I am struggling in my classes, my workouts, my sleep, everything minus Matt is stressful to me right now."

"First of all, let's address something good. So Matt is really a cool guy. He's really into you, and he's honestly super cute, if it's okay to say that."

I nodded. How many girls did I see at the door trying to get his attention? I had almost forgotten about that. I had noticed it before on several occasions, but it never made me feel jealous for some reason. Even as we started liking each other in secret before the water balloons, it hadn't made me feel bad in any way. What about now? No. No, I guess it was because his response was always uninterested and reserved. That's what it was. It was him. Even last week, before our relationship was established, I watched a beautiful blonde jump in his arms, complaining of a broken heel. Seemingly unaware of her affections, he had pulled some electrical tape out of his back pocket, and sitting her on his knee, he had flagitiously fixed her shoe, setting her upright and pocketing the tape. I had laughed to myself as I proceeded towards JR in the basement. Boys are such problem solvers. It was kind of endearing. Sadly, at this point, knowing all the weird primal courting rituals associated with humans in a bar, she had likely broken it herself just to talk to him. How strange we all are as human beings, I thought to myself.

"Amy." Steph was staring at me, somewhat concerned. "I asked you about our set. Are you okay?"

"Everything is fine," I quoted Matt's most common phrase.

"Listen, you choose. I will obey. I just need your help a little bit. You have genetics on your side along with your hard work. I only have hard work and bad habits. And honestly, it's not cutting it. I don't care what anyone says."

"Amy, you're okay. The program is flexible. There's no stress unless it's coming from you." She threw her arms around me affectionately.

"Oh, it *is* coming from me. Haha! It is definitely coming from me. It's just the way I am. How I have always been. I appreciate your friendship, and honestly, I need your help."

"Remember when we were afraid to put the weights back because of him. Look at you. So happy and confident. Let's get that going with our workout now." I smiled, her pep talk urging me to work.

"We are going to do the stationary bike for thirty, stair stepper for thirty, and leg sets for another forty-five, and we are done." She's going to kill me, I thought. But I am going for a five-mile run too. Tell her, I urged myself. I bit my lip, reading hesitation on my face; she said, "Okay, you get on the bike, the highest setting, and I will be right back. You have water?"

"Yes."

"Okay, back in two minutes. She disappeared towards the locker room, emerging a few minutes later. "Take these." She handed me two small white pills.

No. Nope. "Steph, what is this?"

"So these are just mild caffeine pills. I take four, but I thought you would be better with two."

"It's just caffeine?"

"Essentially, yes. It's pure caffeine, like having an espresso before our workout. We could do that instead, or you could take these."

I could go for a coffee. I thought of the workout, my need to review notes from today, and simultaneously do laundry in the basement. I thought of Matt. It's just caffeine. I nodded at her, thanking her, and swallowed one of the white pills. I was scared of the jittery feeling associated with too much coffee and pocketed the second one. We started our set—highest setting. Go.

A good fifteen minutes later, I felt a surge of determination and a new energy take over. "Great, you drive, white pill, I'm done," I thought to myself. Proud for finishing the workout without much prodding from Stephanie, I wiped down my machine. She stayed with me for my extra half hour on the rower, feeling inspired herself.

Exhausted, we rinsed off then sat in the sauna for ten minutes before showering a third time and parting on the sidewalk outside. The rain had cleared, but the streets remained wet, fragrant with decomposing leaves and briny damp cement.

As I headed home, I suddenly remembered my plan. Five miles. I could park on Dean Keeton and run through the beautiful neighborhoods just off campus. I turned around fast on a hill and promptly fell off my bike into a hedge on the other side of the sidewalk. I lay there a moment, too stunned and embarrassed to move. I closed my eyes briefly, hoping no one had seen me. When was the last time I had fallen off my bike?

San Antonio, five years ago at twelve years old? I couldn't remember a time since that Fourth of July bike parade.

Then to my horror, a boy from my English lit class peered into the hedge. "Are you alright?"

He had a friendly face. I tried to speak, but words failed me.

"Arg. Ouch." No words then, just pirate sounds.

I finally moved, trying to right myself like an insect with a heavy exoskeleton, who once overturned, struggles almost to the point of death to correct the upheaval. It was not pretty. Finally, when I was on my feet, he pointed to my arm.

"Can I help you?" Blood ran down my arm and dripped off my elbow as I turned my arm over at different angles to try and locate the wound. "It's here." He pointed to the back of my forearm.

It wasn't too bad, but it was bleeding a lot. I looked at my watch. 3:45. I could still make this plan work. I could work on losing eight to ten and still master science tonight. And laundry. And one more set of abs.

"Urg." More sounds from the high seas. I needed to speak in words now. It was time to behave normally. "You don't happen to have water with you? I'm out." I managed, catching my breath.

"Sit down." He pointed to a small stone fence by the University Health Services sign off Dean Keeton Street. Ironic where I fell, I thought. He rinsed and dried my arm on a Kleenex he had in his bag, and then put a bandage gingerly over the wound. "There."

I thanked him profusely for being so kind and efficient with time and then took off towards Speedway at a fast pace.

Locking my bike near a coffee shop near campus, I set a timer on my watch and proceeded on my route at a sprightly pace. Five miles later, on a side street near my bike, I popped my arms behind my head, walking briskly and enjoying the breeze whipping the leaves off the street.

Nearing my bike and looking into a health food store across the street from it, I grabbed my wallet and walked in. Selecting some mineral waters and premade salads with protein, I paid out feeling like I was meeting goals.

I was hungry and exhausted as I mounted my bike, heading home. As I peddled, I realized I hadn't thought of my boyfriend in over half an hour. I thought of his handsome face and smiled to myself, remembering something exceptional and good in my life.

Parking my bike on the rack, I dashed inside the dorm lobby. Dropping the bags of food on the floor of our flat, I went to the shower, not even bothering to refrigerate anything or find Kate. In the sanctuary of the water, I felt better than I had all day. I got out, feeling refreshed, and dried my hair. I put on my navy silk nightgown and bounded out into the living room.

"Kate, are you here?" She popped out of the kitchen.

"I just refrigerated your groceries." She grinned at me as I hugged her.

"It's so good to see you."

"You too," she said, eyeing my hair. "Your hair is so long. What happened?"

"I just blow-dried it. So maybe it's just an inch or two straighter, maybe. How was your day?"

She told me about her philosophy professor who had fallen on a step mid-lecture and had to go to Brackenridge, the hospital nearest us. "Oh, that's so sad. Probably broken?" I sighed, thinking.

"I think so."

"We could make him banana bread or something." She nodded. This of course was one more thing I didn't have time for but was just as necessary as science. "Can I make us dinner now? I am famished. Long workout, long day, little food." Change that to no food. I had told Matt I was reasonable just yesterday, and today it was a lie.

"Sure. Let's make the steaks. I have zucchini noodles

prepped and ready."

"Oh great, that's perfect. I will go check messages and be back in a couple of minutes."

I ran to my phone and turned on the message machine recall feature on my phone. He had called while I was in the shower. His voice was pacifying to my weary soul.

"Amy, how are you doing today? What classes did you attend? I miss you." He paused. "I was on campus for two hours starting at 3:00, and then I came home and sat out on my deck, if you can believe it." Good, I thought. You deserve it. What did you grill? "So, I read several chapters in my text on fixed and derivative markets, then I grilled lamb over rosemary skewers tonight. I hope you like the steak. Call me when you can. Bye, babe." He hung up. I played the message again, listening to the inflection in his voice and missing him so much.

Then I picked up my phone and dialed his number. Voicemail. Shoot, I wasn't prepared to leave a message. I looked at my watch.

"Hey Matt, just got home, long day. I just took a shower, and we are about to cook the steaks. I set them on the counter to come to room temperature, as directed." I paused, wanting to really tell him how my day was. How lost in the course load I was, and how bullied and body-shamed I felt in my own head. The words I said to myself in the shower were really unforgivable. And I had cursed. It had been a day, one I wanted over. "I miss you. I will call you after dinner and tell you my critique. Night."

I went to the kitchen and put on a long white apron. I put the rosemary stalks in a pan with two tablespoons of butter. Was that right? I went to the spice cabinet to grab the salt and pepper. I smashed three cloves of garlic with the back of my knife, diced it, and put the pile in the pan. I added a dash of salt to the butter and a few sprigs of thyme. The butter was bubbling, so I took out the herbs. putting them and the garlic on a side plate, then I put the steaks in the pan on high heat, turning every three minutes. Apparently, this is how you get a crust but keep it medium-well on the inside. After twelve minutes on low heat, I moved the steaks to the far side of the pan. Next, I added the garlic and herbs back to the pan and another tablespoon of butter. I tilted the pan, scooping the foaming aromatic butter over the steaks again and again for two more minutes, then stuck a meat thermometer in the thickest part. When it reached 115 degrees, I placed the steaks on large white plates to rest. Finally, I added the butter and herbs on top. I peeked at my watch. "Kate, dinner is ready in ten."

She came out of the bathroom with a towel twisted on her head. "It smells amazing in here. Like a five-star restaurant." I smiled, pleased with myself.

"It does, actually."

Opening my notes, I reviewed the science and math from earlier today. Not that it made much sense, but I checked my work as thoroughly as possible. I kissed Matt's name in the heart and closed my notebook. Kate was finished cooking the zucchini noodles when I walked into the kitchen. She carefully plated them next to the steaks, and we went out on the patio to watch the sunset and eat.

"This is the best steak I've ever had." She was emphatically nodding her head, her towel about to fall off.

"Well, that is because Sheridan, Matt's mother, has spent years perfecting recipes for her boys. And she was kind enough to share the secret with us so that we could enjoy it." I looked over, hoping I wasn't too lecturing in my tone. She smiled.

"Do whatever she says." Right. Take advice when it's good. Be self-discriminate.

"Thanks, Kate. I appreciate you trying. She is honestly so nice. And she didn't ask me to abandon kittens in a forest. She asked me to try her recipe. I will continue to make judgments for myself. This steak is amazing, though." We talked until long after sunset and reluctantly went in.

I did the dishes, brushed my teeth, and decided to put laundry off until tomorrow. "Night, Kate," I called into the living room.

"Night, honey." I heard her open a book and click on the television as I closed the door.

I picked up my phone, dialed his number, turned off the light, and brought the phone with me, making a little tent under my comforter.

"Hello." His voice was deeper and richer than I remembered.

"Matt."

"Sweetheart!" His voice rose an octave on hearing mine. I smiled into the dark night of my blanket cave.

"So, the steak...it was amazing. Perfectly crusted with foaming warm rosemary, thyme, and garlic-infused butter. It was delicious, honey! I was wondering how you eat so much steak. And now I am wondering why people eat anything else." Laughing on the other end of the phone, he went on to describe his dinner and how you grill lamb. Which apparently can get tough if you are not careful.

"So, how was your day? I could hear in your voice that it was hard."

I turned to wrap myself hidden from the world in my comforter, alone with the phone; I confessed my day to him. He listened. He listened patiently, and after five minutes, I had told him everything about my classes, the pressure I was putting on myself, my elbow, and some of my new plan to drop weight and get ahead. Just not the specifics, which I was still working through myself.

"I'm mad." The summation of my day was concluded perfectly in two simple words. I laughed.

"Me too. Tomorrow is another day. Can I still see you Wednesday and draw your portrait in the late afternoon? I would like to spend some time with you. Not much, of course, we are both busy."

"Yes, after our appointment mid-morning downtown of course. But listen, I am so worried about you. It's just what I thought it was when we talked Sunday." He sighed into the receiver. "What is your main stressor right now?"

"Math and biology." I sighed. "Everything else is just stressful because it takes time away from...math and biology."

"Do the premade health food boxes you bought have calories on them?"

"Yes," I remembered seeing the calorie count on each box as well as the ingredients listed. "But I haven't looked into it too much. It looks like more calories than what I would normally eat, actually. I think this might help, so this is a good thing."

"I can show you how to meal prep, Little. It's about the numbers. The calories and the quality and balance of the ingredients. I can teach you."

"I would like that. I am trying to plan and figure everything out. But I get in unhealthy cycles sometimes. It starts in my head and then I regulate myself so much. Today was a challenge."

"Oh, I imagine. To be definitively clear, If I were there, I would have huffed and puffed and blown away the mean words in your head. And that wet pavement that made you fall. And your biology professor's never-ending notes." It was so weird. This is the exact analogy I had envisioned when my day was happening, and here he was saying it on the phone. We were becoming so emotionally entangled that our thoughts were aligning. I chuckled.

"Thanks, Matt. Everything is fine. At least I have a plan now."

I could almost hear him smiling into the receiver, "Amy, I would love you to come see me Wednesday. I will pick you up. And I will work my studying around it, and then we can see each other at work too. I want you to see where I live, and you can meet Lolliboo."

"Who or what is Lolliboo?" Haha! I loved the creature or person who had this name so much already. I wouldn't need to actually meet it, I already loved it.

"Well, you will have to wait until day after tomorrow, Little. Goodnight, Amy. Sleep well, sweetheart."

"Goodnight, Matt. See you Wednesday. Night night."

"Through love, burning fire is pleasing light."
—*Rumi*

"Girls are different. Sweet. They don't exactly get over that real quick." —*Matt*

CHAPTER FOURTEEN

"A Face that Needs Punching"

Tuesday flew past me in a torrent of tests, classes, and demonic caloric discipline. I woke up at six Wednesday morning to the sound of Kate on the phone. I turned over in my sheets.

"Mmmmm." Why was she up so early?

"Coffee?" She brought me a cup. "Your alarm is going off, honey, so when my aunt called, I answered it."

"Of course. Whether I am getting up or not. Please, Kate. You know you can. I thought it was three a.m. just now."

"What's your day like today?"

"Good. I want to work out here in a bit, read something. Going on a run, then the gym, British Lit, and then off to see Matt. We have an errand downtown, and then he has a class so I will work out or study. Then we are going to his house. So, it's a busy day but in an escalating order of happiness for me." I was already dressed in workout gear and stretching.

"That sounds good. Where does he live?"

"Somewhere off Barton Springs. He has a Lolliboo. Have you ever heard of this? Is it like slang or a bad word for something?" I winced slightly.

"No, I have zero ideas what that is." She was laughing.

"Okay, good. He seems to like it. I want it to be something

nice. I could hear the affection in his voice over the phone when he said its name, so I was hoping it wasn't something off-putting."

"I want to like this guy and his lollipop? What was it?" She gave me a look.

"It's a Lolliboo." I shook my head. She was snarky today. "I will tell you when I am back. He's picking me up at ten."

"Have a good run."

I went into the living room and did wall sits, planks, push-ups, burpees, and abs. I got up from my last set forty minutes later, my head spinning, glistening in sweat. I almost forgot. I went to the fridge. Day one, meal one: a tabbouleh salad. Looked okay. I usually didn't do breakfast, but if I did, it would be this. Meal two would be grilled chicken breast over iceberg lettuce and lemon dressing. This would be tougher but manageable. I shut the fridge not wanting to look at my random buys further. I had no problems with my plan, I was just not in the mood now.

My stress was dissolving away as I put in my earbuds, stepping into the soft early morning sunshine. "Let's go. Time to move." I tried my best at a Steph motivational speech as I sprinted down Speedway and turned left on Guadalupe. The stores were bright, with books and baskets of homemade jewelry already being set up on the main drag sidewalk. It was eye candy after eye candy of people watching and happy campus murmurings.

Less than an hour later, my body shiny from sweat again, I turned the corner on Guadalupe, heading home. My seven-mile jog had my endorphins buzzing through my brain as I opened the door. I jogged breathless into the flat, putting coffee into the machine and pressing the button before dashing into the shower. The hot water instantly resuscitated my weary soul. I looked at my watch. It was seven-thirty. I was so tired that I thought about leaving naked and wet to pour myself a cup, but in the end, I just finished rinsing the suds and exited fast, almost slipping on the shiny white tile. Wrapped in a terrycloth towel and with another on my hair, I poured the coffee into my mug and rushed to dress.

Out the door and on my bike. Ten minutes later, I walked into class, greeting some friends near me, and sat down, opening my biology notes.

Class was long and slow, and my eyes were constantly traversing from the whiteboard filled with notes to my drawings in the margin, mirroring my worries about the police station. Stressed, I worked to push it farther from my mind, concentrating on the detailed information provided on prokaryotic and eukaryotic cells. We had discussed them in terms of cell metabolism last class, and now we were focused on cell composition and communication. Overwhelmed by recent events, I copied notes neatly but remembered nothing of the meaning behind the sentences I wrote. I sighed at my absentmindedness.

Finally, twenty minutes later the class was over. I sprinted home, looking at my watch as I opened the door. I had an hour to spare so I dashed downstairs to the little gym in our dorm and immediately got on the exercise bike.

I thought of how mad he would be if he knew how hard I was pushing myself today. I stuck out my tongue to the wall and looked over next to me as a man got on the available equipment to my left. He had an odd look on his face. He had, without a doubt, seen me stick out my tongue passive-aggressively to the wall. Great. Now I looked like a crazy person. Maybe I was. I looked over at his digital display, a crazy person doing twice the resistance he was doing. At least I had that. He looked over at me, and I looked straight ahead, too embarrassed to move.

Finally, my watch's timer beeped, and I got off and wiped down my machine, quickly entering my dorm room.

I showered quickly and dressed, finding some English literature reading to bring. I looked at my watch. Five minutes to ten. Upon entering the kitchen, I decided to forgo my plan out of haste, instead drinking a large sparkling water and a cup of cold coffee. I looked at my watch, quickly brushed my teeth, and applied mascara. I grabbed my backpack and walked out of the room so I could meet him in the lobby. He would be coming from class, too, and the schedule was tight. I was just walking down when I saw him turning the corner, a large white magnolia blossom in his hand.

"Good to see you again, sweetheart. I picked this on west campus; it was hanging over my truck where I parked on Red River." I kissed his cheek, taking the giant flower.

"It's like perfume. Thank you."

"Shall we?" I held his hand, and we walked out towards the truck.

"Matt, there are little black bugs in it."

"Sorry about that. Aphids. I shook it out after I picked it, but likely there are still a few. Let's set it in the backseat. It will make the truck smell good." I nodded.

"Matt, are you in trouble?" I finally blurted out. I had been worried all day, and with little information, my mind had wandered to dark places.

"No, not really. Maybe just a little bit," he laughed.

"I am so worried. Honey, can you be charged with something?"

"Possibly. I have a lawyer if needed. Our family retains one for the ranch—a good family friend who likes steak. I have spoken to him and had a couple of meetings both in person and over the phone, and I believe everything will work out. Charlie is meeting us here too. We have made private individual statements, and now they are just checking for inconsistencies. My story won't change, don't worry. Charlie is good. What happened, happened. I have the tapes from above the bar, and I hope that will help clear up the situation." He was speaking carefully. "Just answer the questions honestly and briefly."

We drove to the police station downtown and parked in a parking garage adjacent to the building itself. We walked in a short time later and gave our names to the officer behind the desk.

"You can wait over there." She pointed to a sitting area partially filled with people. I walked towards the chairs, but Matt grabbed my hand, pulling me backward to lean against him by the far wall.

"Don't sit." I leaned against him, his arms around me, and opened my book with him reading A *Midsummer Night's Dream* over my shoulder. "I didn't know this book was set in a forest outside of Athens. I always thought it was Florence."

I grinned, my hand falling behind me on his chest. "Ready?" He nodded as I turned the page, our eyes following the accolades of mischievous fairies. We read a few more pages in this way until a woman behind the thick glass called his name.

"Abernathy, Matthew." We looked up from our sixteenth century romance and followed the officer down a narrow hallway to a series of beige offices. "Officer Brady will be with you two in a moment." She closed the door.

"May we sit?"

He smiled. "In here, yes. First give me a quick kiss." He bent down to kiss me and then pulled out the chair, and I sat down as the door opened and Charlie joined us. We stood again and greeted each other.

"Amy, you look so pretty," Charlie kissed my cheek. "Matt." They shook hands as Officer Brady entered the room. I was introduced, and hands were shaken again as everyone took a final seat.

"Thank you all for coming in this afternoon. Amy, I will address you first. I have statements from Charles Brucouski and Matthew Abernathy. Additionally, Amber Bosswood has also given her statement, but she only witnessed the initial twenty minutes of the ordeal before the alley and basement situation. So her initial is all I need from her. Officer Jenna Dodds was sent to Brackenridge ER on…" He paused, looking at his legal pad. "June 5th at 11:17 p.m., to be clear when this occurred. You were able to confirm your name but not to answer any further questions. She took statements from health care professionals as well as collected the GHB sample and left." I nodded, so he continued. "Can you go over with me your account of the evening of June 5th? Start four hours before entering the bar."

"Okay. I went to campus and got home from biology class and the gym in the late afternoon. I showered, and then I ate dinner with my roommate, Kate. And I took a long nap."

"And what did you eat?"

"A grilled chicken breast with pineapple and a salad."

"What did you drink?"

"Water with lemon."

"Did you consume any alcoholic beverages at dinner?"

"No."

"Did you consume any alcoholic beverages or take drugs of any kind before coming into work?"

"Yes." I felt Charlie turn to look at me, but I continued to look at the officer.

"And what did you consume?"

"An aspirin."

"Oh. Okay. Any recreational drugs? Anything else?"

"No."

"Why did you take an aspirin?"

"Biology. Long day. Long workout. Lactic acid." He nodded and smiled.

"What time did you enter the bar?"

"Ten o'clock."

"What were you wearing?"

"Black jeans, black tank top with the bar logo on the front, and a jean jacket. It's hot in the bar once it's crowded, but cool outside once it's early morning." He nodded.

"Amy, what did you do upon entering the bar?"

"I went downstairs to speak with the manager named JR."

"What did you speak about?"

"I am in training, so I have to report to him and see who I am mentoring from and at what station, that sort of thing."

"What did he tell you?"

"To go upstairs and work with Charlie and Amber. Normally only two people are bartending upstairs, but it was a Saturday night, and it would be more crowded, and so that's where he put me. He wanted me to bartend when needed and waitress the tables if and when it was crowded enough to do so." I was starting to feel nervous.

"How did you encounter these individuals?" He put a series of photos on the table. The air caught in my throat, and I felt like I couldn't speak. I could feel Matt's leg moving rapidly up and down as he sat next to me.

"I...was walking..." The excessive black bruising and lacerations on their faces were so distracting suddenly; I couldn't remember what he had asked. I was starting to understand why we were here. Oh my God, Matthew. "I'm sorry, Officer Brady. What did you ask me?"

"How did you come into initial contact with these boys?" He tapped a pen at the desk, but I didn't look down. This was going to be hard.

"As I was walking to the bar towards Amber and Charlie, one of the boys grabbed my hand to see if I would take a shot with them. They were at the first table about thirty feet from the bar. I told him yes but that I would bring them the shots because I was a bartender."

"Which individual was it?" I worked on composing myself and steadying my voice as I looked at the photos on the table. I needed to not cry for Matt. I needed to focus and speak simply and clearly, as he had said earlier. My finger moved lightly over the photographs.

"This one." I tapped a photograph.

"Are you sure?" I wanted to cry at the sight of his face. The bruising was excessive.

"Yes."

"What did he order?"

"Alabama Slammers."

"And what is in that?"

"Amaretto, orange juice, gin, Southern Comfort."

"Who made the drinks?" Charlie raised his hand.

The officer nodded and looked at me. "Did you have one too, Amy?"

"Yes, but mine was grenadine and orange juice." Officer Brady turned to Charlie, who nodded.

"And why was yours different?"

"I chose not to drink."

"Any reason why?" I needed to protect the bar.

"I do not drink—my preference. I have to work all night, for starters. We didn't charge them for mine, to be clear. I talked to Amber while he made the drinks, and when the drinks were ready, he nodded to mine, which was a slightly different color and had a small black dot made with a dry erase marker. I brought them over and this guy met me halfway to the table and put money in my back pocket. I told him that he didn't need to pay for mine and he said, 'Don't worry. And keep the change.'" I paused.

"Go on, please."

"So, I set the drink tray down on the table. This guy," I pointed to a boy, whose left eye was sealed shut in ebony smudges. "This guy looked down and saw the black dot. He looked right at it. So, he asked me about it, and I said—" I paused and took a sip of water. "'It's mine. I don't like Southern Comfort. Mine's a bit different.' Which is the truth. They teased me, I guess a little bit, and I turned my back to address this boy," I pointed to a brown-haired boy whose face seemed unscathed. "I thought it was his birthday, but it turns out this was a bachelor party. His name was Adam, he said, and he was the bachelor." I took another sip.

"Continue, please."

"Sorry. Well, they were giving me a lot of attention, so I asked about her, to you know, remind them to be nice. He said her name was Brittany, so I raised my glass, and everyone took one. And I said, 'To Brittany.' They repeated it, and we took our shots. I gathered the shot glasses, and one of the boys, I do not know which one because my eyes were on the shot glasses, gathering them, said, 'Oh, you work here?' So, the boy that paid me didn't advertise that. They were trying to have fun, and I think he liked the idea of me just taking a shot with them, not associated with the bar."

"Why do you say that?"

"He paid me discretely, he clearly didn't tell the other people in his party, and he ordered and paid away from the table. I don't think he was trying to be bad in any way necessarily. Just cool. I understand."

"What did you do next?"

"Side work. I put the shot glasses in a carrying container for Henry, our barback, to take downstairs to the kitchen. I spoke to Amber, and I made a few drinks. It was becoming more crowded at this point."

"The medical staff at Brackenridge confirmed that you had GHB, high levels in your system. When did you first feel the effects?"

"Fifteen minutes maybe. I felt weird. The lights and the music started to be very pronounced, I guess. I felt like I was floating when I walked. I started bumping into Amber when I was trying to work. I dropped a glass, breaking it, and I normally do not do that. Someone ordered three Long Island Iced Teas—"

"From this group?" He referenced the photographs.

"No. Two tables near them, though, and I carried the drinks on a tray for her. I spilled one as I set the drinks down. I've never done that waitressing before."

"Okay. What happened next?"

"Well, I continued to tell myself that I was just stressed, that I needed to sleep better, eat better. I was thinking of asking JR or Matt if I could leave early. But not wanting to disappoint anyone, I decided to push through. On the way back from the table, one of the boys grabbed my hand to speak to me. I thought they would order more drinks, but he just wanted to talk for a minute. I don't really know which one he was, and I don't remember anything more until Matt came." I took another sip of water.

"Okay, start there."

"By this time, I was back behind the bar with Charlie and Amber. And I remember hearing Charlie saying something like, don't worry, that Matt was coming. And this made me very worried." I looked over at him briefly, and he put his hand lightly on my leg. "I was a little nervous around him the first few weeks we were working together. He didn't seem to like me at all. I was in training and not very fast yet. JR had hired me, and he probably wouldn't have. I wanted to be especially competent around him, and it seemed like at every turn I wasn't...so I didn't want him to see me like this. I didn't know why I was behaving so badly, and I was starting to get scared. It had started off by feeling sort of happy and clumsy. But at this point, I was having a hard time standing, and Charlie had set me down behind the bar. I felt disoriented, dizzy, and very scared. When Matt came, I expected him to be mad at me. He has high expectations for staff, for himself, and I was so confused."

"What did he do?"

"He squatted down next to me and flashed a flashlight in my eyes and spoke to Charlie." Officer Brady made a note in the notebook.

"We will come back to that, guys."

"Fine," I heard Matt's deep voice on my left and flinched at the sound.

"What else do you recall?"

"Only bits and pieces. In the basement a short time later, I was crying and alone on the couch. I was terrified. In a high school psychology class, I had read that neurological problems like schizophrenia can occur in your late teens and early twenties. I became concerned that I had this. It seems illogical now, but at the time, I was petrified that I was having a psychological break. I was so frightened that I was hiding between the couch and the desk with my eyes closed and my hands over my ears when Matt came downstairs."

"I am so sorry this happened to you." I nodded. "And what happened next?"

"I remember hearing Matt's voice, and he didn't sound angry with me, which was surprising. I don't remember what he said initially, but he was crouched down on the floor with me and spoke very softly and kindly. I thought he would have been yelling, but it was the opposite. He picked me up and said I should close my eyes and that he was taking care of it. I asked him if I would die, and he said no, that he was in control now, and nothing bad was going to happen. He carried me outside to the alley and told me to keep my eyes closed, and we got into the taxi."

I paused as the officer finished his writing and looked up. "Go on, sweetheart."

"In the cab, I was still very dizzy and scared. I was crying but trying to stop. We shared a seat. He just put the buckle over both of us, and I sat in his lap. I remember he was rubbing my shoulder. He held my head steady against his chest and sang me a song. And I realized at that moment that even though initially I would have wanted to be with anyone else, that there was no one else I trusted more to help me than him. That he was a good person, and he wasn't going to let me die."

"What did he sing?"

"Why does that matter?"

"I am just curious."

"He sang me a Christmas song. '"Walking in a Winter Wonderland."' I looked over at him. "I just remembered that, Matthew. How nice you were to sing that to me." My mind hummed the lyrics, remembering glistening snow and sleighbells.

Matt's voice being quiet for so long was a welcoming comfort. "Well, I didn't know what else to sing to you. It worked, though, and you stopped whimpering...and crying. You just looked up at me quietly and listened, so I held you and kept singing." He smiled slightly at me. I continued, wanting this to be over.

"He was singing and being nice, petting my hair with his thumb, but he was hurt. He was bleeding from the temple, and it was seeping through his shirt into mine in some places. I tried to wipe it, but he told me he was fine. He was shaking just a little bit like me. I laid my head against his chest and closed my eyes. I don't remember anything else."

"Hum. Sounds like the adrenaline leaving your system, Matt. That must have been a very scary experience for you, Amy." Still looking down at his notes, he continued, "Okay, I appreciate the statement, Miss Emerson. Matthew, did you bring your medical records?"

"Yes," he reached in a bag and pulled them out. He handed them to the officer, who looked through them. "Okay. You got banged up too then." He read through the medical report.

"I did. I told the officer that in my initial. I couldn't work for a couple of weeks. Had to go to my parent's house for a week like a sick dog. Worried my poor mother. I still have healing fractures." He turned to me, still talking to the officer. "It's better." This was for me, but it didn't help how I was feeling. I smiled weakly, remembering his absence and being worried about him. He had never really said anything about it.

"Fractures. Where?" He was looking at the medical report.

"Ribs. Three fingers on my right hand." He read for a few minutes in silence. I touched Matt's jostling leg, careful not to look at the photographs on the table or even him. I needed to get out of this room.

"Okay. Charles. I have a comprehensive statement from you. A couple of things clarify what was discussed when he came up to assess her with the flashlight. She is behind the bar. Drugs in the system."

"I told him what happened. Who it likely was. The guy who put drugs in her drink. And who was grabbing her, trying to get her out of the bar."

"Identify for me."

"Drugs." He pointed at the boy with one visible green eye, the other sealed shut. "Saw him use some himself and put it back in his pocket. Trying to get her out of the bar...these two. And this guy." He pointed to the boy in a red shirt. "The other four may or may not have known anything. These are who I witnessed. I watched them for over three minutes. Made sure I was right and that they were on camera before I came and got her." He turned to me. "Sorry, Amy. I needed time to be right."

"It's okay, Charlie." I felt my stomach tighten.

"You told Officer Sampson you didn't have a tape."

"No." Matt spoke up. "He asked very specifically if we have a tape of the back alley. And I do not. We have one over the front street. And over both of the bars downstairs and upstairs."

"A first year." Officer Brady mumbled under his breath, referring to Sampson, and took a moment to look at me. "I will need to see the tape over the bar. Matt, can you get me that this week?"

"Yes. I—"

I put my hand on his leg, interrupting him. "Matt, don't. We don't need to escalate this—"

"Don't speak for me." His eyes were burning straight ahead, but when he turned to me, they softened considerably. "Don't speak for me. Everything is going to be okay, sweetheart." He turned back to the officer. "I made you a copy." He looked up, somewhat surprised, as Matt reached in his bag.

"I will make my own assessment, mind you, after watching it in a minute. But does this confirm your account of the situation?"

"It does. I've watched it dozens of times. I don't know how they plan to press charges. It's worse than described in my initial statement and whatever could be in theirs. I don't want her to see it." He nodded at me. "Amy, can you step outside, please." I looked at the wall. Officer Brady addressed me.

"Amy, would you like to see this tape, sweetheart?"

"No."

"Then please leave the room. There is a coffee station and sodas to your right." I nodded and looked at him briefly, my fingers resting on Matt's shoulder a moment; I rushed out the door, relieved to be released.

The officer stood slowly, adjusting his holster, picked up the tape, and stood near the television where he fiddled with the equipment. "You know, Matt. I'm on your side."

"Good."

"It was just excessive." I had lingered by the door a moment, their voices carrying slightly in the hallway as I left, curious as to what I wasn't supposed to see. It's not that I had changed my mind exactly, but suddenly something was bothering me about Matt's adamant attitude that I was no longer supposed to be there.

Matt looked at Charlie a moment. "Excessive? Naw. It wasn't, actually. She had such a horrible fucking night in my arms in that cab and later in the hospital. What if they would have gotten her out of the bar through the back alley? What would her night be like in an hour? In three? In ten years? Girls are different. Sweet. They don't exactly get over that real quick."

"They are different all right. Nobody would. I am understanding you and these boys are in serious trouble." I walked to the drink station to make a mint tea and tiptoed back to the sanctuary of the wall, still listening.

"My own mother had a horrible experience as a teenager on a date, and she honestly is still affected by that to this day. It is a part of who she is. And it affected how I was raised and who I am today to an extent." Oh no. I took a sip from the paper cup.

"I'm sorry to hear that. What I am saying to you is your response was excessive. One of these kids had surgery. Has pins in his jaw. Liquid diet for a month or more."

"They are all over eighteen, most my age, these are men, and they should be held fucking accountable."

"And they will be. Mr. Red Shirt has broken ribs and a fractured collar bone. And this guy has a fractured eye socket. It was imprudent." Matt looked down, noticing the ring on Brady's left hand as he fumbled with a clicker.

"Maybe for some people. Do you love her?" Matt nodded at his left hand.

"No. We have been contemplating a separation for a while now. We've got little girls and a boy in middle school, a mortgage." He chuckled. "She's not an Amy. And she's difficult." He put the tape in but didn't push play.

"Well, before you see this. You imagine what you would do different. Eight grown men trying to take her out of the bar. She is still a minor, did you know that? Imagine one of your daughters."

"I know she's a minor. Do you?"

Matt nodded, ignoring the insinuation, and continued. "You say I used excessive force. I had to get these assholes out of the bar and find the drugs to confirm the treatment at the ER. And do it all fast. I told Charlie to call the cops and to have them come to the back alley. Y'all showed up twelve minutes after the call was placed. Twelve fucking minutes on my own. I've thought about it, and I don't know what I would do differently."

"Saturday night downtown. I'm sorry about that timing."

"I'm not." Matt grinned.

"How did you get all of them out at the same time again?"

"I walked up to them and just started talking and introduced myself. And then I asked them which one of them drugged my friend. And when nobody said anything, I grabbed the guy, this one," he pointed to a photograph, "and I wrenched his arm back fast, dislocating his shoulder. I told him that she was not doing well, and I needed to know what drug it was and to give it to me now. And miraculously, he did. Just got lucky. The little vial of Visine that I gave to Officer Dodds at the ER was the GHB. I still needed them out of the bar, so I grabbed this guy's collar. This dude, with the face that looks like it needs punching." Matt pointed vaguely to the boy with one visible green eye.

"Ryan?"

"Yes. The one that drugged her, and you can see him do it on the tape, by the way. The same absurd low-level person who is trying to press charges against me. I grabbed his collar fast and slammed his face on the table. He came up bloody and mad, as you can imagine. Nose broken and all that. Well, you can see for yourself. Then I grabbed the bachelor, who I suspected of being innocent, and said, 'You're fucking coming with me, asshole.' And I rushed him down the staff staircase towards the alley. I counted in my head. One, two, three, and I could hear them all running after me. I mean, these are his closest friends, right? They had to come after him. That's how I got them all in the back alley. It was all I could think to do."

"Quick thinking."

"I had time to look at my watch and ditch my cell on the landing on the way down the stairs. The bachelor likely took a tiny bit of the liquid ecstasy because he was easy to handle. Never fought back. I remember thinking that was weird. It would have taken fifty guys to get him outside." He pointed at Charlie, who smiled at the compliment. "I told him if you weren't involved, sit against the wall. I was never trying to play God, like this guy or his parents pursuing the lawsuit are saying. You know how fast things happen. I had four seconds to say this and toss him to the safety of the brick wall so he could comply."

"Go on, Matt."

"So, they come out surrounding me, thinking they have me, of course, because they are sizable and there are so many of them. And they are all posturing and talking as boys will do. So, I whistled loudly to get them to shut up, and I said to them, 'Anyone who is innocent or doesn't want to fight, sit by the wall in zip ties. Let the cops sort it.' Why the hell they didn't run and scatter in every direction, I don't know. They seemed to think they could win. And that what I said was fair. I looked over as it was starting and saw that Charlie had brought Amy to the basement and was now standing as instructed as a witness. And to be clear, that was the only thing Charlie did, was to obey what I told him to do with her and put anyone I tossed to him on the wall in zip ties." Brady looked at Charlie, who confirmed this statement.

"By the time Officers Rodriguez and Statten arrived, they were all zip-tied by the wall in a neat little row."

"Correct."

"Tell me more about the witnesses to this fight."

"Because these guys are entitled, privileged, and without any ethics, and I knew this was fucking coming, I wanted to have a witness or two. Dave from the La Biblioteca Bar near us was tossing ice in the alley, and Charlie got him to stand as a witness. Here is his contact information." Matt passed over a phone number and email address.

"Any comments about the fight?"

"No." The officer smiled.

"Charlie?"

"This was a fair fight if you can call eight on one fair. In this case, you might be able to. Matt took the weapons. Just fists. And he wouldn't have been hurt much if he hadn't stepped backward on one of them. The kid passed out or fainted or something, not sure. He wasn't supposed to be there, and when Matt stepped back, well, he was on the ground, and they were all on him, kicking him. This is the ribs. But I wasn't too worried; he grabbed one of them fast and used him like a shield, so they were kicking one of their own for a bit. Then he tossed him, knocking one down like a bowling pin, and he was back on his feet."

"So, these two, their bruising is exclusively on the right side."

"Okay." Matt nodded.

"You switched to your left hand then? Or was someone else involved?" Brady seemed amused.

"My right hand was starting to hurt. Just me." Oh, Matt. I took another sip of tea.

"So, to be clear, these two you fought left-handed?"

"Correct."

"Are you left-handed?"

"No."

"Any other comments?"

"No."

"But you pulled two weapons off this one, and who else?"

"This guy had a ten-inch hunting knife." Matt pointed to the picture of the boy in the red shirt. "And this other guy had some sort of a, well...I don't know what it was. Maybe a small blade, but it looked more like a nail file. To be honest, it was weird. And I tossed it in the dumpster with the hunting knife. I told the officer about it in my initial."

"They retrieved them both. It's as you said. Doubt you could file a nail down with what that boy was carrying. Okay, let's see what we have here." He pressed play, pausing it and rewinding it several times to ask questions.

"Did you see that?" Matt pointed to the top of the screen with a pencil eraser. "Rewind. Okay. Right here. Right hand.

Red shirt." I stayed hidden, despite the urge to poke my head around the corner and see what I didn't want to actually see.

"Yes...I do see that."

"That's assault."

"It is." Officer Brady rewound it twice more, watching with keen eyes and taking a note on his legal pad on his desk. The tape finally finished, and the officer sat with his hands tugging on his beard for a few minutes. He sat twirling his pencil, taking a few notes before finally asking Charlie a few more questions. Finally, he stood and shook hands with Charles and then Matt.

"You mentioned on the phone once that you have a lawyer. Meeting again soon. I think you can cancel that appointment."

"No. I can't do that." Matt smiled.

"I am telling you that you are good. Sleep well tonight. You won't need 'em."

"I will. I am countersuing. They drugged my employee. This is a Schedule 1 drug. Clearly, it's illegal, and even though you are pursuing it, I am as well. Possession is a couple of years reduced to months by the system. But this guy." He sat back down and pointed to the picture. "This was a federal offense, what he did. This was inflicting bodily harm and committing crimes of gross negligence by drugging her without her permission, no matter what the intent was. And that is altogether something else, unprovable, and my true motivation for a private suit. She could have had numerous drinks before, she could have overdosed, walked out in front of a car, literally thousands of sad scenarios. And that is just the drug alone as a singularity. She thought she was losing her fucking mind. It was so sad. She finally vomited in the cab as we pulled up to the ER. And I told her I didn't like my shoes, that it was okay. She was so sweet she was trying to apologize, not that it made much sense what she was saying. I tipped the driver, and he was surprised at the gratuity, and I told him, 'No man, there's a lot of blood and vomit back here. There is a carwash on Second Street.' His cab was #223 Austin Ace's if you need to speak to him about our condition. It was a damn mess all night. I stayed six hours with her. Tell me you are pursuing criminal charges. Not just community service. Jail time."

"Yes. We are. Not sure what will effectively happen, but we are. This tape helps a whole lot. You can see him, Ryan, clearly squeeze the drugs in the shot and mix it with his finger. And again, assault charges will be brought up now as well to Red Shirt. Name is Jason Mills."

"Okay, good. I want him dealing with both of us. Can you keep me updated on the assault charges with Mills, and what is Ryan's last name, I keep forgetting?"

"Sampson. I will keep you updated on events. Will she agree with your wishes to litigate? Oh, and by the way, Matthew, to answer your question from earlier, I don't believe I would have done anything different both that night and now legally."

"Thanks, I appreciate that. She will do what I say on this. I will do what she says about other things. We will work it all out." They stood and shook hands.

"I will be waiting here for your silence to break..."
—*Rumi*

"You got lucky. People who love you can see your cracks now." —*Matt*

CHAPTER FIFTEEN

"Succor Me Sweet"

"Are you mad at me? Look at me, Amy." He was behind me at the drink station as I got a refill of hot water for my mint tea. I turned slowly. I had left towards the end of the meeting and had bided enough time alone to be mindful of what I felt and pray about what I didn't understand. I wasn't mad.

"No, I am not exactly mad at you." I shook my head and looked up at him. His soft brown eyes were on mine, looking for a read. He looked like a puppy that had been severely scolded. The hurt in his eyes was exceedingly pitiful and softened my heart even more.

"I know you don't like violence. And I just—"

"I am not mad at you. You are right that I don't like violence, and the photographs were shocking. I wish things had been different that night. That I wouldn't have gone into work at all."

"Amy—"

"I admit it, I saw you differently when you held me and sang to me that night in the taxi. I don't want to think we needed that. The pain of that night. I want to think that we would have always been on this trajectory, but I don't know. You are my Superman, and I am only worried about you. So worried…" I wrapped my arms around him, and I felt his hand slowly coming to rest on my back, touching me carefully.

"Have you even seen a Superman movie?"

"No." It was a distraction, and I wasn't having it. He touched my frown with his fingertips.

"Don't worry, sweetheart. I am going to drop you off. Listen, it's Wednesday and we can do without you tonight. Take tonight off to rest and read, okay? I will call you after work if you want me to." I nodded. I didn't want to go to work.

"Thank you."

"No problem. Come on. Listen, we are right around the corner from that little Tex-Mex place with the cute T-shirts from the foam party. What was is it called again?"

"Little Nina's Yummy Tortillas." I smiled.

"Let's get a corner booth and spend just a little time together. Do a quick lunch. Horchata?" I nodded, taking his arm. We drove up a few blocks to the north of the precinct and followed Lavaca Street until we found some street parking ample enough for his truck under some shady pecan trees.

"Will you hold my hand?" I slipped my hand in his as we walked a block towards the restaurant and up the burnt orange steps. The wide porch reminded me vaguely of his parent's house because of the putty color and girth. The soft breeze and warmth of the sun finding us through the trees made our silence comfortable. My hand found his as my fingers moved over his callouses absentmindedly. The clouds moving overhead were like the feral thoughts in my mind, moving fast over the blue expanse.

We sat on the porch swing, moving slowly with the creaking sound of the chain. He looked at his watch and finally spoke. "They open in ten minutes. I'm always hungry, but I really just want to sit with you a minute. This is nice."

A breeze moved the hanging flower baskets on the porch. My eyes followed their swaying as I moved the flyways from my face and laid my head on his chest, unspeaking. I listened to the steady thumping through his white button-down shirt. The stiff fabric paired with his brawny chest should have been exceedingly uncomfortable, but it wasn't. The familiarity of him was reassuring and comforting.

"Is it hard to be a man?" I asked. His hand appeared on my hair, petting back the strands trying to free themselves from their tie.

"Yes. Sometimes." He paused, looking down at me. "Is it hard to be a girl?" I nodded, feeling my eyes well up, particularly at this moment. I felt overwhelmed and guilty about a situation we had put so far behind us that in my newfound happiness, I had almost forgotten it entirely.

"I am so worried about you—if you will go to jail over what you did. What you did for me, someone you *hated* at the time. Those photographs—" I couldn't hold back my tears any longer. Worry and the images of the excessive bruising from the precinct were pushing them down my cheeks, steady and silent.

"I never hated you." His hand pressed me tighter. "Never." Tears continued to fall. "Never have. Never could." The warm breeze made the wet on my face feel cool and refreshing. I felt like they had been suppressed for hours; they fell so easily, now absorbed on his chest. "No, honey. What will be will be. I would have done the same thing for Amber. And I cannot stand her. Listen, maybe not nearly to the same extent, okay, in all honesty. But you were not present for the latter part of the meeting. It's good news. Officer Brady is under the strong impression that everything is okay. I wasn't worried, as I told you the other night, but I admit it, I feel better. Mostly because he understands the gravity of the situation." I nodded.

"Good. I'm worried about the boys too. They are so young, and to possibly be charged with something. I have been praying for them that they will learn what is right without such a severe consequence. I don't want this to go on and on for them either...I think they are scared enough without—" He put his hand on my shoulder, interrupting me.

"Excuse me, sweetheart. May I quote you from the other night?" I nodded. 'Can we be done talking now? I think I would rather kiss.'" I nodded, tucking my legs up to the side on the swing so I could reach him. "Like this." He spun me around so that I was lying on my back in his arms, just above his lap, his crossed leg supporting me. My arms found a handhold on his shoulders. This position felt oddly familiar. He began to hum "Walking in a Winter Wonderland." And I blinked up at him, reaching for his lips. We kissed away the memories of the last couple of hours until after a few tickles and kisses, I had forgotten any sadness, and slowly the fog lifted from both of us. He turned as a door unlocked and a hand flipped the sign on the screen door from "Closed" to "Come on in, y'all" with a soft slam.

We stood reluctantly and walked inside the old house, both of us marveling at the ingenuity of the interior design.

"Let's go to the back bedroom." We walked along the old floorboards from room to room until we came to the master bedroom, where three tables were set up, the windows open, and the curtains tossing in the breeze. He turned to me, letting me choose.

"This one." We sat down and looked over the menu, discussing it briefly before deciding to order exactly what we had eaten last time. The waitress approached.

"Two sparkling waters, two horchatas, and beef and chicken fajitas, the three-pound family portion of fajitas to be clear. Side of guacamole. Make that three sides. Thank you." I smiled at his appetite.

"Will others be joining your party?"

"No." She looked at Matt.

"And what kind of tortillas would y'all prefer?" He looked at me.

"Corn, please."

"Let's go with both. Thank you." She finished writing and

left towards the kitchen. He looked at me from across the table and sighed. He looked tired.

"Let's list happy things," I suggested softly, my hand in his.

"Okay. You start. I'm not as familiar with this concept."

"Puppies."

"Kitties."

"Small mice." He turned his head slightly to see if I was joking or not. "Small ones." I mouthed to him. He nodded.

"Small snakes."

"Narwhals."

"Is this exclusively animals?"

"No, it is things that make you genuinely happy."

"Beef jerky. Organic and spicy."

"Lemon tea with honey."

"My lips touching yours." I blushed, looking around at the empty room before meeting his gaze.

"My lips touching yours." I parroted, looking up shyly. He smiled broadly, taking off his baseball cap from his knee and running his hand on the brim a few times, accentuating the curvature. "Butterflies. There is a butterfly on the curtain behind you." I grinned as he turned, looking at the orange-winged monarch on the white curtain.

"This moment with you. No one else in this restaurant. I could live on an island happily with you."

"Me too." I blushed.

"I'm getting somewhere?"

"Maybe." I looked down and felt his hand squeeze mine.

"Look, we are about to have sugary cinnamon goodness." He nodded behind me as the waitress set the tray of drinks down on the table.

"This weather." The wind whipped the curtains and blew some leaves in the window as the waitress brought our food. We continued to list happy things, talking and eating until about one, when I looked at my watch.

"Amy, you're not eating. You are just biting your straw.

Here, let me make you one."

"I had a little something earlier. Not hungry and I am honestly just happy to sit with you." He nodded, folding another enormous fajita. "Honey. You have afternoon classes and I have one more. We should go...I had a really nice lunch with you."

"You had a nice drink with me." He laughed. "Half of one. Can you still do art with me this afternoon? My classes are located mid-campus and so I can pick you up around four."

"I would like that. Thank you."

A half an hour later, needing fresh air after our meeting and lunch, I had changed and stretched and was mid-sprint through campus. I thought of him, sitting in his economics lecture, likely jostling his foot as the professor droned on. Suddenly my mind jumped from this happy image of him to the pictures from the police station. It was really hard to think that he had inflicted all of that damage himself. I shook my head trying to rid my mind of the visual as I jogged on. Finally, away from the majority of pedestrian stoplights, I found my pace heading towards Hyde Park. I liked the old homes in this neighborhood and the large shady tree-lined streets. It was weird to think one day, I would live in a house of my own. Maybe I would have azaleas growing, perhaps a pet mouse. It seemed too much to ask to have a dog, but it was exciting to think about, though, exhilarating.

I wondered what Matt's house would look like from the street. I imagined a yard covered in perfect Miami grass; the kind used for golf courses. I pictured no leaves or branches on them, just vertical blades facing the sun like toy soldiers, tall and silent. Perfect boxwoods would be precisely three feet apart under the windows. He would likely trim them on a specific schedule so that they would always be perfect rectangles. I imagined myself walking up the perfect, power-washed steps, a pair of scissors in my hand. Working fast, so as not to be seen, I visualized my hands cutting a rectangle into a triangle under the master bedroom window. Boxwood leaves, tiny and deep green ovals, would fall, sprinkling my sandals like confetti.

The song changed and pulled me from my daydream—such a weird thing to think. I laughed out loud, looking around to see if anyone witnessed me laughing by myself. No one. Good. As I looked around, I didn't recognize the neighborhood anymore. That's okay, I thought; it's still likely Hyde Park. I would probably turn a corner and recognize a genuinely cool neighborhood eatery like Quacks any minute now.

When that didn't happen in several turns, I looked at my watch and decided to retrace my steps. I looked down at my pedometer, showing nothing helpful in terms of cardinal directions. I blinked again, looking at the face: 14,032 steps, about seven miles. I had only intended on three; I was lost, and I still needed to get home. I ran on, the Texas sun blazing down. Trees and cars passed me endlessly. Another twenty minutes later, this was starting to get ridiculous. I saw nothing familiar, nothing to give away my location. I looked down at my hip. 19,871. If I had a phone or saw someone with one, I would need to call a cab at this point. Shoot. Making a left at the next street, I continued on past rows and rows of little houses, hoping to see the main road.

A movement to my right caught my eye. An elderly lady in an oversized floral house dress was shuffling along slowly in her slippers. Large pink hair rollers under what might be a homemade vinyl shower cap were visible on her head. She was muttering to herself, and I noticed she had a worried look on her face. Taking off my earbuds and approaching her from the front as not to frighten her, I introduced myself. Her name was Porche, pronounced like the car, and she lived in the blue house on the left. The problem was she had locked herself out, and she grabbed my hand endearingly to speak with me about it.

"Do you have a cell phone or neighbor we can talk with,

Porche?"

"No phone. No, nothing fancy like those little phones you young people carry today." I smiled. I know, right. Too fancy for me too, friend. I was getting her.

"So maybe a nice neighbor then?" She pointed to a peach-colored house across the street.

"The Romers are good people. They don't own cats."

"I see." I didn't, of course. Not really. I had known many good people who owned cats—my most recent favorite being Matt's mother. But clearly, cats bothered her. Probably something about birds; I looked her over, making a guess. Taking her arm gently, I supported her as we crossed the street. Noticing how she shlepped off the step rather than stepping over it, without any awareness, made me so grateful we met when we did. "Thank you." I focused on God. "Thank you that I got lost and found this sweet woman. Help us get her in her house and me to school. I love You."

"And the thing is, girlie, I have a pie in the oven. And I simply cannot get in the house to take it out."

Oh no! This had changed things. As we approached the door, I stole a glance towards the little blue house. No smoke. But I still needed to handle this fast.

I rang the doorbell. Someone I imagined might be Mrs. Romer answered the door in a bright yellow house dress with a pink flamingo on it. These people were so cute. It was hilarious.

"Mrs. Romer?"

"Yes, how may I help you? Porche, good to see you."

"Mrs. Romer, may we use your phone? We need to get Porche back into her house quickly. She is locked out, and she has something in the oven."

"Oh, dear. Porche, is it pie?"

"Yes, it is, dear. It is a chocolate pie."

"What a shame." This was not the point. A house fire was the point, ladies. They were so darn funny. I couldn't find it in my heart to fuss at them.

"My husband Bill has a spare key if this ever were to happen."

"Great! By the way, does this happen a lot?"

"No, actually only the second time." She handed me the key while they sat down for more coffee. As Mrs. Romer turned, I could see her hair rollers tucked under her scarf as well.

I crossed the street quickly and, to my relief, found no smoke in the hallway, so I immediately went to the kitchen. There was the pie, baked and cooling, oven already off. She must have taken it out and forgotten, then locked herself out. The ladies were on their way across the street, hand in hand, cups out to the sides. I opened the door for them and gave Mrs. Romer back the key.

"Good news, friends. The pie is safe, and so is the house." Porche took my hand in hers.

"You are such a dear. I want to thank you for helping me. I had forgotten about the key with Elly here. Please pick anything from my house to keep as a present." What. No. Looking up at her cheerful face, I could tell that it would be insulting not to. I could use a pencil and paper. Spotting an inexpensive paper notebook by the mail and a pencil, I asked if I could take those items. She smiled, delighted to help me. "Of course, dear."

"Come visit me sometime in my shop on Guadalupe; it is the Buzzy Buzzy Bee. We sell yarn but also fabrics, all organic and local, mind you."

"Okay, perfect, I will. I know that place, actually. I painted a sign for Mary."

"You painted that lovely blue sign on our door? What a wonderful and small world it is. Pie, honey? Please sit with us."

Declining pie politely, I reassured them I would use my new pencil and paper in class in a few minutes. To my delight,

Elly knew where Guadalupe was, and feeling grateful, I was on my way. I looked at my watch. I could go to the gym for most of the time I had initially wanted, then straight to class. I couldn't go back and shower or eat as I had planned, but that was okay. Things had resolved themselves quickly and uneventfully, which was great.

Waving, I set off at a fast pace toward campus. My pencil and paper were gripped awkwardly in my hand as I moved past parked cars and uneven curbs. I was tired. I should have eaten breakfast. Or something with Matt. I hadn't been ready spiritually to fully activate my plan until the door was shut, and I was out in the sunshine this morning, but I was feeling jittery now.

Finally, back on campus in my second home at the gym, I went through leg day with only a moderate amount of fire in me. Considering that I didn't have anything clean to change into, I rinsed my face and then arms in the sink as best I could, and taking two waters from the hydration station's fridge, I strolled to class, still feeling the burn.

Arriving early, I sat down, relieved just to sit, and when my class was over, I could finally be done. I couldn't review my notes, being unprepared in this way, so I started to draw. This could be my new notes binder. It needed decorations, though. I wrote Matt's name with a heart around it and an arrow pinning it in place on the front. Turning the page, I drew the podium and whiteboard, enjoying the challenge of the perspective. I drew my professor standing at the podium with speech bubbles over the head. My mind wandered from my favorite quote from last week, from *Romeo and Juliet*, when I heard a voice behind me.

"Afternoon. Well, almost." He looked at his watch. The TA for the class, Tim, was walking down the steps towards me. "Please tell me I am going to say something intelligent. I need all the luck I can get." He smiled. "I'm filling in today. The professor has a prestigious engagement at UCLA that will interrupt his schedule this week and next."

"Oh, I see, thank you for being available," I looked at my watch, ten minutes until class. Tim lingered on. I didn't want to be engaging with him for so long, so I excused myself to go to the bathroom, recycling my empty water bottle and drinking the second one in route. Was I so enamored by my boyfriend that I felt disloyal in some way to be alone with a man who had politely asked me out more than six weeks ago? I shouldn't be so sensitive. I rinsed my face again and came up from the sink with a nosebleed. Great. I grabbed some tissues and pinched. Maybe now it would be reasonable to hide out in here. I stayed in the bathroom, swapping out toilet paper every minute until noon. At the chimes of the tower bells, I exited, throwing clean tissue in the trash.

Back at my seat, I picked up my pencil and began copying down the board-work set before us. The class had a slow start, as Tim didn't have the eloquent ease of speech or insight of our professor.

Unengaged, I flipped back to my drawing of the room, eager to draw in the beautiful French braid of a girl in front of me when I saw strange writing. Written in the bubble over my drawing of the orator's head, it said, "You should still go out with Tim sometime. It's not too late. He's a nice guy." The cartoon I had drawn of the professor suddenly looked sinister. Eeew. I looked up; he was teaching on, not looking in my direction. Good. I was sweaty, gross, and in love with someone else. He was trying to be funny, I reminded myself. He probably is a nice guy, just as he said. I flipped the front page over, and seeing nothing desecrating Matt's name, found my place and began retaking notes.

After the class was over, I bolted from my seat, my pull-out side table banging loudly as I existed. Oops. I was trying to be fast, not rude. I ran towards home, my notes in my hand. Stopping a moment and sitting by the turtle pond on campus, I re-read them quickly and, sticking my tongue out at Tim's name on my page, picked up my notebook and went home.

In the shower, I used the last of my pineapple body wash to rinse away the day. It was only 3:15 and I was finally done. Today was supposed to be my break day. My easy day. It's okay. Make spiritual gains here, I told myself. Today was not what you thought, but the truth was it was a significantly better day than for someone imprisoned or someone with a dying relative or with terminal illness themselves. I took a moment for these people, trying for a global perspective. I lifted my head from my prayer and immediately felt dizzy. I shifted to see little white spots of movement and color, like tiny swirling bubbles, popping to the left and right of my eyes. When I moved to see them, the feeling was worse. I reached for my towel, not wanting to pass out naked. Careful to keep my eyes straight ahead, I wrapped myself tightly, leaving the water running.

How many times had this happened this week? It was a few, to be sure. I couldn't think. No, wait, it was twice. That's only two. A small number.

I went to the fridge and, grabbing the closest salad box, opened it. Leaning against the cabinetry, I selected something in the form of a cube and ate it with my fingers. Only when I took my second bite did I look down and notice I was eating diced cold chicken. It was good. Opening a drawer and getting a fork, I took another bite like a civilized human being; then hearing my phone ring and remembering the water, I took one more bite before reluctantly setting the box on the counter.

Laurel cheerfully greeted me on the other end of the phone. I told my sister I would call her back later but got the good news that her schooling was going better than expected.

Deciding to achieve a more advanced stage of readiness before eating, I dressed quickly in jeans and a blue floral kimono top. I dried my hair and put on my Converse. I hadn't worn these shoes since our first kiss just shy of a week ago. The silk kimono was short, coming to the waistline of my light blue jeans. If I reached up, you could see a few inches of my stomach. Maybe I should change. I went to the closet to look through other options and heard a knock. He was early. My heart started to hammer against my chest in anticipation as I walked to the door. Holly, from two rooms down, was standing outside with a pot of coffee in her hand.

"Amy, I'm so glad you are here." She burst into the room. I smiled at her ease as she strode in, sitting on the kitchen cabinet, pot in hand. "My roommate, Sarah, was doing a grocery run this morning and forgot all five things I asked her to get for me." She made an exasperated face. "Number one coffee filters and number two sugar."

I smiled. "It just so happens; I have some of both right here." I put the sugar in a baggie and passed her ten filters. "Is this good, Holly, or do you need more of anything?"

"Yes, it's perfect, thanks. Coffee?" She turned her head to the side like a confused puppy that had heard something it could not discern.

I grinned at her perkiness, "Yes, please." I could use some perkiness myself. I was exhausted and I needed to get back to my box on the counter. I pulled out a ceramic cup, and she poured the steaming liquid to the brim; then, turning to leave, she put her hand on my shirt. "I love your outfit. Honestly, that is the cutest thing you have ever worn."

"Thanks, I was about to change."

"Well, don't." She sloshed coffee on the hall flooring. "It is super cute."

"Thanks. See you later." I stayed dressed momentarily, to find my large sketch pad and my new soft lead pencil from Porche. I had lost my soft lead sketching pencil a couple of weeks ago, and I suddenly realized that Porche's pencil was perfect for drawing Matt's handsome face. I put everything in a bag by the door. I looked at my watch: 3:30. I took one more sip of my coffee, then brushed my teeth, erasing its bitterness, and set the alarm for twenty minutes.

Wearily, I lay on the bed and closed my eyes. I woke up fifteen minutes later to the sound of soft talking in the room.

"Awwww. So cute."

"I haven't seen her all day. On days like that, when we don't meet up, it's usually extra time in the gym or the library after to study. It might be a double gym day. It's Wednesday, so we were supposed to meet at noon. She must have forgotten." Kate had let Matt in. My eyes were still closed as my consciousness slowly became aware of him. Something inside of me began turning on the lights at the sound of his voice.

"Look how her hands are clasped in front of her face. Her little Converse shoes. She's so pretty. Should we let her sleep?"

"No, she would be mad to miss time with you."

Thanks, Kate. Exactly right. Wake up. I couldn't open my eyes.

"Amy." Matt was sitting beside me on the bed, his hand on my shoulder. He shook me softly. My eyes were closed, but my mind was awake. Open your eyes, I commanded. Nothing. No. I want to see him. Exhausted, my body would not respond. The lights began turning off again. One by one, more darkness came over me. No, no. No. No. No. No. I want to talk to him. My body would not respond to him or me. I felt him shake me harder, my body rocking back and forth, hair spilling in my face.

"Call an ambulance, Kate. Now." I felt his hand on my neck, finding my carotid artery, his head turning, his arm shifting to look at his watch. "Amy, what is this? I love you so much. We are going to fix this." Flashlight in my eyes.

Wake up. Is this real, or am I dreaming? I honestly couldn't tell. Why can't I wake up? Wake up. I ordered myself to move. I tried to move again. Move! Nothing. I lay powerless on the bed. I screamed in my silent head, suddenly fearful. I heard myself make a sound trying to speak. It was like a small gasp. Matt's ear was by my lips, listening for breathing, his hand on my heart.

"Is she breathing?" Kate's voice sounded strange to me.

Wake up. You are scaring them. Do it now, I commanded myself. Nothing. The doors suddenly slammed in my ears, and I was alone in the darkness. They were gone. All gone. Lost, I guessed, like me now. They must have been talking, but I could no longer hear or feel them. It was quiet. Still and solitary in a sea of vast nothingness. The seconds ticked on—a great nothingness and isolation like being underwater. Deafening quiet blanketed my mind, my spirit. No voices. No clock on the wall. No hum of the air conditioning unit. Nothing at all. I wanted to see him. I wanted to feel him. I was scared, and he alone would make it better. I tried to move, and my hand flinched. Matt's hand was on mine instantly.

"Amy!" His voice was loud. "Is she a diabetic or has a history of epilepsy of any kind that you know of?"

"No."

"Anything unusual to warrant this?"

"She's been staying up late, working out a lot, same Amy stuff. Nothing too different than normal. She was doing planks at 2:00 early this morning, reading over her biology notes when I went to bed. We woke up, and she did a workout, studied, then a run. Normal stuff. I don't know what this is."

"Her normal is too much. Clearly. Oh my God. Her pulse is so slow, fifty-five." I felt him look back at his watch, his hand dropping from his neck and mine. He was kneeling by the bed from the proximity of his voice. Wake up! I promised myself the happiness of seeing him if I would just comply. My eyes fluttered, willing myself to make them feel better. I want to see him. I want to see him. Open your eyes then!

I opened my eyes, taking a soft gasping breath of air, relieved that I wasn't dead. Panicked, I took another shaky breath, glad not to be in dreamland anymore, unable to control my own mind and body.

"Sweetheart!" He was hugging me. "Oh, honey." He pulled

back to evaluate me. I sat up quickly, proving to them that I was okay and that I could move more than my eyes and fingertips.

Dizzily, I blinked my eyes. "Kate, I'm fine." She was standing in the doorway, a contorted look of concern on her face. "Matt, I took a nap." I looked up at him.

"No, honey." He shook his head. "Do you hurt anywhere?"

"I don't know. I mean no."

"Hum."

There was a loud knock on the door as three medics swiftly entered our living room. Matt stood up and moved to the window, giving them space. One medic lingered in the doorway and spoke to Kate as the other two looked in my eyes for dilation as Matt had and began checking my blood pressure. A cold chest piece of the stethoscope was pushing my shirt aside. They asked me various questions like my name, a brief on my medical history, and other questions about my diet, hydration, and exercise level.

Matt walked out to the balcony, phone in hand. I could see him from the window. Phone to his ear, pacing back and forth. He hung up and made a second phone call, looking out at the horizon. I watched his huge hand come up to run his fingers through his hair. Still pacing, he stopped and picked up my sauna vest, drying in the sun on the rail. I saw him peer over the balcony and solemnly evaluate the overhang of the pebble-covered roof below blocking the street. He fingered it lightly, feeling its dampness, then pushed it over the balcony, his murmured voice never ceasing its cadence.

Convinced I was not a diabetic or an epileptic and that only my exertion mixed with minimal calories and hydration were to blame, the medics began packing up. I thanked them as they left, feeling embarrassed to have scared everyone and wasted their time. They politely waved, stopping in the living room to brief Matt. His large hand on the doorknob closed it behind him for more privacy.

I was scared to stand up and scared to close my eyes. Glancing over at the nightstand and seeing a Gerber daisy, I picked it up. I twirled it in my hands, watching the fuchsia petals blur. The living room was quiet now. Had he left? Probably so mad at me he couldn't speak. That was fine because I didn't have the energy to have our first fight. The door opened, and Kate came in carrying a tray. Apple slices and almond butter.

"Your favorite food. Eat please. Or I think he's going to cry."

"Matt is still here?"

"Yes. He's in what I like to call Matt Mode."

"Oh, great." I knew what she meant. And I guess it needed a formal name.

"Yep. Warning in advance, I agree with him. He found your pedometer from your run. And the box on the counter. He opened them and counted them and compared that to the receipt in the trash. He saw your gym clothes drying in the sun from where you washed them for tomorrow. So, he knows you ran fourteen miles, went to the gym, and ate forty-five calories of chicken."

"Oh, great. No. So, Kate, that's not how I intended the day to go. I got lost and ran much farther than I intended, there wasn't time to go back home to eat, and I wanted to eat only from the boxes, so I didn't—"

"Eat. Now. And drink all of this." She handed me a water bottle, and I drank it all, giving it back to her as evidence for the man pacing around in the living room on the phone. Then I started eating the apples and reading the back of a magazine, but I couldn't follow the words.

I was in trouble, and I was too tired to defend myself: my body and my life. I honestly hadn't done any of this on purpose. Five minutes later, Kate came back in. She took my tray and gave me a second bottle of water. "He wants to know if your pee is yellow."

Reluctantly I paused my reading. "I don't know."

"Okay, so he wants you to drink until you have to pee, and then he wants to know what color it is." She handed me another bottle.

"What's he doing, Kate?" She glanced over at me, a bag in her hand, and went to the bathroom.

"He's controlling your life right now. And I am fine with it." She looked up, and I could see she had been crying.

"Hey. Kate, I am so sorry. I have a really good reason as to why today was too much. I helped an older lady who was locked out of her house, a long simple story, really. And I got lost. Since these two things took so long, I went really hard at the gym—the highest levels. I had planned to be there longer and less intense. I didn't want to bring weird cold boxes of unrefrigerated salads to school, so I had planned on coming back, between my run and the gym. But instead, I got lost and meet Porche; that stopped me from coming back and meeting you. I am so sorry. I just remembered we were supposed to meet at noon."

"It's okay."

It wasn't, I could tell. She went into the closet and emerged with worried eyes and an attempt at a smile. Suddenly, she dropped the bag and threw her arms around me in a forgiving embrace, her face on my shoulder. She was crying but not making a sound.

"Kate, It's fine. I have been doing this for a long time. I know how to be safe. University level athletics are much harder than I realized, but it's okay. I am doing what everyone is doing. It's okay."

"I don't think it is," she sniffed, blowing her nose and dabbing at her eyes. "I don't think you are doing what everyone else is doing." She picked up the bag and rushed back to the bathroom with another one in tow.

I went back to my magazine. If she were looking for diet pills or even caffeine pills, she wouldn't find them. She handed me another water; "Don't forget to look at the color." She closed the door of our bedroom.

Silence again. He must have gone by now. I imagined a legal pad worth of notes, written in all caps, on how I was to proceed. It would detail and dictate everything from medical advice to workouts in a facility and home, to specific meal plans that matched his ideal for me. Something I had honestly tried and failed to do for myself. My chin quivered in reflection on this failure.

Ten minutes later, finally feeling like I could trust closing my eyes, I prayed. "Thank you, God, for the hints in my life that something needs to change. Let me own this mistake. It was mine. This was not the university; this was me. I messed up. Thank you for letting me learn a gentle lesson. I could have passed out and hit my head on the tile in the bathroom. Naked." I shuttered at the embarrassing prospect.

I continued, water welling in my eyes, "I appreciate your grace more than you know. I don't want to be mad at him. I know that whatever he wrote down for me is logical and loving. Whatever he will say later will likely be good advice. Let me have eyes to read it, with an open heart to hear it." I paused, feeling the profound peace of a conversation with God. "I always thought I could do this. Everyone else makes it look easy. Matt says I am small even compared to my teammates, but I see only inadequacies. Help me find perspective. It is all too much. I don't want to give up my job." I sniffed. "I don't want to give up my scholarship. It was such an honor to get." A tear rolled down my cheek, where it lingered, then fell from my chin. I used the back of my hand to wipe it slowly, then drank the third bottle of water.

I did have to pee now. I stood slowly, evaluating myself as I moved. I felt fine. Normal. I went to the restroom, feeling a familiar headache coming on. I took an aspirin, popping the white pill in my mouth, and closed the bathroom door. Deep yellow. I washed my hands, my face, brushed my teeth and hair, and then grabbed my biology book and went back to bed feeling better. I turned to my side, pulling my knees in, my hair spilling off the low bed near the floor. The chapter reviews went slowly. I read through them twice, almost finished.

A soft knock on the door made me look up. Matt came in, absorbing the attention of the entire room as my flower fell to the floor, and the curtain to the open window comically blew in his direction as he entered. The command he had on me was no less. My heart was starting to beat hard in my chest. He hadn't left. Of course not. I closed my book and turned to look at him. He stood in the middle of the room, not coming farther.

"Hi." My prayer had worked on my stubborn heart. Say something. Good or bad, I was ready to handle it. He was unmoving, unspeaking. "So, you have been watching *In the Heat of the Night* without me. Playing detective about my day." His nostrils flared slightly as he smirked at my comment, his face fighting to stay mad.

"I will never watch that show unless it is with you. And even then, I'm not watching it. I'm watching you watch it." I smiled at him. He looked at me with hurt eyes, but a slow handsome smile replied to mine.

Finally, ready to say it out loud, I spoke softly. "Oh, Matt, I'm so sorry. The schedule today...it's hard to explain, but I had intended on five miles. It was not the university's fault, my parents or any other influence, this was all me, and I own the responsibility. If I am honest, I thought about you and the type of manicured, Type A yard you might have. Something with hyper-trimmed boxwoods, anyways, when I finally looked up, I was so lost. So lost. I ran for miles and miles unintentionally. I should have stopped and taken my vest off. I should have done so many things different..."

"Amy, Kate filled me in on your day, any part that I didn't piece together myself. You were helping a little old lady, very like you. And you got lost, very concerning to me. Listen, I have suspected for a while now that you are not okay. I have gotten little hints on occasion. And at the party, touching your abs and your hip bones. It all became definitive, and I began to see it clearly. You are right there. Weeks away from clumps of your hair falling out. From internal damage. Okay. You don't see it, but I do."

No. I was not there. He was wrong. Everyone on my team worked out like me and ate like me. In high school, it was the same. We ate cleanly. We worked out hard.

"When we walk to your car at night, sometimes you space out like you can't concentrate." I made a face.

"There might be other reasons for that."

He continued, unhearing, "You never want to eat anything with the rest of us. Because you don't eat, it is all so regulated. So managed and avoided."

"No, I..."

"You are lethargic at the bar like you have no energy."

"I am maybe just not that great at it," I suggested.

"You are great at it. And you are faster now. But I have seen you exhausted early in the night some nights. It's not the bar. It's not the university; it is you. It is your day, it's your lifestyle and habits. It is too much, honey. Football season hasn't even begun yet. The two summer sampler games are over, but there's going to be so much more pressure this fall. So much more with classes." He moved closer to me and got on his knees "No, no. Stay seated," His hand moved me back to the headboard.

"It is okay, honey."

"No. You need help. You need my help. We need to reset you." He tapped my head gently from my temple, little taps, down my head to the base of my skull. "I am going to drive now. And I want you to trust me. I want to fix you. I don't know how to...to care for you any different."

"I didn't do this on purpose. And I am not broken."

"I know that. You got lucky. People who love you can see your cracks now. And it's okay." He paused a moment to kiss my forehead, his hand on my shoulder. "I am a man who can fix pretty little things," his honest eyes twinkled at me. And my heart began to beat faster in response. I loved him. It was as clear as day to me now. We were there. He loved me, too; I knew he did. Had he actually said it? I couldn't remember.

Exhausted, I nodded slowly and with such gratitude that I reached for him to come closer. No words were needed now. Leaning down, his hand cradling my head, he kissed me sweetly, slowly, and full of love and affection.

"Come with me. I am going to take care of you," he whispered. I nodded and felt my nose tingle with emotion, but I managed not to cry. I was just happy.

He lifted me off the bed and carried me out the door and down the long corridor towards the elevator. Once inside, he raised me higher to kiss him as we descended, my arms latched behind his neck.

On the mezzanine, the elevator opened, and two freshmen got in. Matt stepped back, making room for them. One of the girls looked over in our direction.

"She is not allowed to touch the floor," he explained like it made any logical sense. She smiled at her friend and faced forward again. On the ground floor, they stepped out and looked back. Matt stepped out, careening around students and luggage carts. "Excuse me, thanks." Students stepped aside for him.

Leaving the lobby, he walked towards the loading zone, where he had parked his truck. He looked at the windshield.

"No ticket. Amazing. Parking was impossible this afternoon." He opened the door with one hand and put me in the middle seat and buckled it.

"Where are we going, Matt?"

"To Smoothie King and then to see Lolliboo."

"Love is the whole thing. We are only the pieces."
—*Rumi*

"Wonderful. I needed that so badly." —*Matt*

CHAPTER SIXTEEN

"Boxwoods and Finished Decks"

He drove north down Lamar, one hand on the wheel and one arm around me. My head was lying on his chest, my weary body leaning in. He parked with the front and back right tires popped up on the curb off the narrow street in front of a row of little shops. He opened his door and, looking at me suspended in my seatbelt, laughed. "Like a slide. I'll catch you." I cautiously took off my seatbelt, and the sharp angle worked with gravity to pull me toward him. I giggled softly, as science did as my heart commanded—so much fun.

He shifted to let my legs wrap around him on the seat to talk to me. "You have essentially had 175 calories today," he looked at his watch, "and it is now 4:36. I am not sure what you burned, but the math is not good."

"I have gone on fasts before. So, in a way, this is okay."

"No! It is not okay!" His voice boomed.

"Yes, but—"

"You burned too many calories to eat like this. And the day before too no doubt. Fasting is different. It's broth calories usually, good hydration, and low exertion. And Kate and I figured out you eat only one meal with her. Likely, all you eat a day. So yesterday, she thinks you consumed seven hundred calories because you didn't finish your plate. You take aspirin when it all hurts, by the look of the big bottle in your cabinet. You guys bought that a month ago, and she has only used two. I counted them. You need to do what I say. I am the driver. You are the cute passenger. Yes?" If I didn't listen to the coach or even myself, I would need to listen to Matt.

"Yes. Alright, Matt." He kissed me, then turned around.

"Piggyback ride so I can order and pay. You don't touch the ground."

"As you wish it, honey." I was in the mood to listen.

"I haven't seen that movie in years, have it at my house, though."

"What movie?"

"Oh, I thought you were referencing the best movie of all time. Haha. You almost quoted it just now. We can watch it later tonight if you want. But I want you to get good sleep. We can stop at the fire swamp."

He continued to quote incessantly from *The Princess Bride* as he walked in, stooping at the doorframe momentarily as we entered. Looking at the illuminated display board, Matt ordered two large smoothies, both twinned with whey protein powders, vitamin mixes, ginger shots, and extra bananas.

"This is a lot to manage with the drinks." He paid out and tipped the staff. "I will be right back. I am going to return this monkey on my back to her seat so that I can carry these."

"Oh, I'll help you outside, man." The assistant manager was an amiable representation of Austin.

Matt climbed up on the high end of the truck and I squealed loudly as he fought gravity to buckle me in, digging his fingers gently into my ribcage. My thrashing and laughing had caused my sides to hurt, and I had to catch my breath. Exhausted, I tried to run my fingers through my wild mane, trying to tame my feral hair, my heart feeling lighter. He stepped down and closed the door.

"Monkeys." He was still laughing as he shook his head. The

manager smiled and passed him the smoothies. "Thanks, man, have a good afternoon. Is there a place down this road to turn this truck around or a side alley somewhere?"

"No, I wouldn't attempt to turn this truck around. There is a side alley, just as you said, in three blocks. And to the right is Lamar."

"Perfect, thanks."

Matt got in and picked up a permanent marker from the well in the center console. He made a little line one-third down into the giant smoothie.

"If we hit traffic, then I will change this line. But by the time we get to my house, you need to be down to that line. Okay? It is a big smoothie. Talk all you want, but be below the line, please, when we pull up in fifteen minutes."

"Okay, Matt."

"I am bossy."

"You are," I confirmed. He made a petulant face in response. "But if things were reversed in some way and you needed me," I lightly touched his hand, "if you were addicted or trapped by something or you needed me in any way, I would be bossy to you too." He smiled gratefully.

"Thanks, Amy. I believe you would have a strong effect on me if I needed you in that way."

I took a big sip. It was good, and not much of an aftertaste followed. We popped off the curb with a bump, finding our route towards Barton Springs.

"Matt, I need to sleep before we go to work tonight. Just a little nap, not too long. Sometimes I do an hour, sometimes three hours, but usually on nights when I study after work. Kate said she packed my bag. I assumed she put in my T-shirt, but JR likely has extras in a box downstairs."

"No, honey. No. no. no. I am kidnapping you to make you rest. You need a physical, spiritual, mental reset. You are not working this week. I am your boss. I have to work Friday because Johnny has a wedding. It's a small wedding, and though it is shocking to me, this is a close friend of his, and he would be missed. So, I will leave you alone Friday, but you will be safe in the good company of Lolli."

He pulled up to a beautiful modern house on a hill overlooking the Barton Creek Greenbelt's limestone bluffs. Early evening sun reflected soft orange and golden hues against the white cliffs. I looked in awe at the house of glass on the hill nestled in the trees.

"Oh, Matt, it is so beautiful here." The grass was mowed short, to my amusement, but leaves from several sprawling live oak trees were scattered on the grass. There were no boxwood hedges to snark at, and I bit my lip in moderate shame as I moved to get out of the truck.

"Wait, babe." And suddenly, he was below me looking up. "Let me see your cup." He held it to the orange glow of the low evening sun. "Good job." He handed it back to me. "Keep working on it. I will make us dinner around seven. Unless you are hungry now?"

"No, no. This is a lot."

"You need to drink more water at the house. And you need to eat dinner, though, to be clear. It will be a reasonable portion. You will not leave the table until you eat. Please nod."

Was he serious? I didn't really want to know. I nodded, and he carried me through the walkway towards the front door. He set me on my toes momentarily to reach for his keys, then opened the door.

"Don't be afraid. Don't be afraid. It's okay. She's friendly."

"She's so. She's absolutely huge. I haven't seen anything like—" Matt took a knee, making his body a chair for me.

"Sweetheart, meet Lolliboo."

A giant gray head rested in my lap, sniffing my shirt and her nub of a tail wagging so hard the whole of her body wiggled in delight. Her enormous head felt like a lead weight. The short silvery hair was soft, and her ears were cut so that they stood up straight, making her look fierce. Her bright blue eyes looked right into mine, wanting to understand me: my intentions, my associations, and my affections. I slowly rested my hand on her massive head.

"It's okay. I'm with him," I whispered. My fingers ran over scars, and I raised my hand to see four white raised one-inch scars on the top and running down the left side of her head. Her jaws were utterly enormous. "Matt, she is so special. Her eyes are almost human. And not at all because of the unusual blue color. It's that she is searching mine when she looks at me. Oh, look how she makes eye contact. Like right now. I think she wants to be my friend." I petted her softly on her cut ears. "Why are her ears like that? What kind of breed is this? I have never seen anything like her size, her charm, her all-knowing eyes." He smiled, pleased that I initially assessed her the way he had years back.

"She was a rescue that I found four years ago, and just fell in love with instantly. Ears were cut like that when I got her. Tail too. A weakness in the bread, and it's usually done just after birth. A friend of mine had gotten married and found himself in the doghouse only a few short months later. He really messed up." He laughed. "Anyways, he was trying to make right and ended up getting his wife a kitten from the animal shelter near here, the one located off of South Congress." I nodded, and he added, "I bet you know every animal shelter in Austin." I smiled, answering him with my eyes. "Anyways, Chris, he told me about this pit bull mastiff mix less than a year old that he thought I would like. I had just gotten this house two years earlier, and I vaguely began to realize that I wanted a guard dog, so I decided to see it. It didn't occur to me at the time that I was getting a best friend as well. They called her Lolli, and after I got to know her, I affectionally added the "boo." He took her huge head in his hands. "Such a good girl."

"She is just wonderful." My fingers ran lightly over her fur. I was getting used to her powerful head and the soft nudges from it, prompting me to touch her.

He sighed, "Well, you touched her scars. Sad isn't it. Some crazy person beat her with a chain. Less than a year old. She was still healing, covered in bandages when I got her. Look here," he pointed to her shoulders. "She's got them on her back as well." I touched my fingers on her sides to one-inch-long raised curved lines flanking her spine where hair didn't grow. "Ignored her mostly in the beginning. I would watch TV and hold my hand out with steak, and she would take a while, but she'd come to get it from me. Spent a lot of time watching baseball with my hand held out."

"That is so awful." It was hard to look away from them now. It was simply horrifying, "oh, I can't imagine that. Why in the world would—"

"There is no reason." I got up so he could stand.

"I can walk inside, I am assuming?"

"At halfway." He pointed to my cup and picked me up, nestling me in a comfortable armchair in the living room. "I'm going to let the dog out." He walked over to the backyard and opened the door.

I looked around at the high white ceilings and exposed dark beams above—the modern white walls. And instantly, I remembered the chicken house that Sheridan loved so much. I could see Matt's contribution in my mind now. Turning, I saw to my right a modern open concept kitchen with stainless steel appliances and a breakfast bar. On my left was another sitting area connected to where I sat by a giant freestanding fireplace with visibility and seating from both sides of the great room. You could almost walk into it; it was so large. Logs were stacked inside in two parallel stacks resting in a square, ready to light. It was still July, and I smiled, remembering the hotel. Everything was so clean and neat. It was hard to imagine that he had not just moved in recently. I blinked, trying not to envision flattened cardboard boxes by the door.

Matt was back, flipping a switch on the wall, and instantly, several sources of indirectly lightning illuminated both the living room and kitchen. Music in surround-sound speakers began to play Jason Boland at a low, comforting decibel. Matt's voice spoke over my favorite lyric, and I looked up. "Amy, I need to get your bags out of the car." He said something indiscernible to the dog and walked outside.

Lolliboo came over and laid her giant head on my lap. Her eyes shifted from where she heard Matt in the front yard and then to me, her new friend. I lay my hand gently near her face, letting her smell me. Then I carefully touched her head. She seemed to enjoy my touch and nuzzled me, encouraging me to pet her again. Her bright blue eyes were fixated, alert on the door. She stayed with me but watched Matt longingly. "She wants to go to you."

He walked towards a back hallway, two duffle bags in hand, "I told her to stay with you. She's very intelligent. She is extremely well trained, my uncle Jackson worked with her for over a year, but she is naturally smart. She seems to know what I'm talking about when I talk finance to myself out loud or read a book excerpt to her. She turns her head from side to side when I talk about the current bull market and how monetary cycles that are in transition can cause potential intense fluctuations and volatility even if proven initially to be perfectly stable." I turned my head from side to side.

"It's profound understanding or possibly confusion. Good one, Lolli. I personally am going with confusion." He laughed, coming over to kiss me.

"It's boring to most people. It's okay. I've always liked numbers. Loved math my whole life." I made a face at such a prospect.

"You're reminding me about tomorrow."

"So tomorrow, I am going to my classes and yours. I will take notes for you and understand where to start to help build up your foundation. You are going to read, rest, draw, get sun on the deck. Do nothing. Do what you want. Just don't leave."

"What? Matt…" I looked away. I didn't want to have him see me cry every single day we were together. He was so thoughtful—this was more than what could be possibly expected, even from official "Matt Mode."

"Got your schedule from Kate. There is only one class that doesn't work perfectly. It's your British Lit class. I am going to arrive thirty minutes late. But I will ask someone near me for their notes and copy double time. When I get home in the afternoon, I will go over it with you or give them to you to look over as needed. Saturday, we will go to the ranch if you want. Is it okay to spend the night out there? We can go home Sunday."

I felt overwhelmed. Thinking of our night at the cafe, ordering pancakes, and talking for hours, I realized at this moment that I had assessed him exactly right. I felt so adored, so protected—so irritated. I was irritated mostly, that he was putting himself out over me. Inconveniencing himself over something I should have been able to control and fix on my own. I turned my head back towards the fireplace as a tear fell. I wiped it away quickly before he could see.

"I don't know what to say. Thank you so much."

He smiled. "No problem."

He walked to the refrigerator and pulled out three steaks, saturated in marinate and sealed in plastic, and set them in the sink to come to temperature. He stabbed three sweet potatoes lightly on the front and back, wrapped them in foil, and put them in the oven to bake.

"Sweetheart, I am going to go on a quick run. Normally I would bring Lolli with me, but I think she wants to stay with you." I looked at her, knowing he was wrong—probably being polite. He kissed my forehead and smiled. "Why don't you give yourself a little tour. I want you to feel comfortable here, and I have nothing to hide from you. Open any cabinet or drawer you like. Satiate any curiosity you have. When I get back, I will show you around if needed, and we can eat." He picked up our smoothie remains and dropped them in the trash.

"Thanks again. It was good."

"You did okay on it. Three quarters, it looks like." He disappeared into the bedroom, coming out momentarily in jogging sweats, a Ramones T-shirt, and gray trainers. "Your books are here." He pointed to a side table in the living room. "And this is a comfortable chair to read in. And here, more water." He handed me a bottle, then reached over to turn on a lamp beside a West Elm lounger. "I'll be back soon. I'm locking the door."

"Have a good run. Are you going on the green belt?"

"Yes."

"I am so jealous you live so close to this green space; it is so beautiful. It's not possible for me to go?" He shook his head.

"It's not possible."

"Maybe we can go together tomorrow or the next day?"

"Maybe. I would like that. We will see how things go, okay? Your compliance and whatnot." He paused, smiling. "We can take a little walk there together this week. Bye, girls." I heard him put the key in the lock and turn it. I looked out briefly at him, stretching and adjusting his earbuds; then, grabbing my water, I turned to walk down the corridor.

The corridor on the left of the front door had a vintage umbrella stand with an interesting metal top, used as a hat rack. Large paintings on both sides of the passageway flanked the hallway with color. One black umbrella rolled tightly was at the base, and two baseball caps hung above. The army green one read, "Brown Barn Tactical Gear," I flipped the brim of the second one, "Sampson's Bait Shop Port Aransas."

I enjoyed walking around his house. Hundreds, perhaps thousands of little bits of information were being filled in about him just in this hallway alone. I walked on across the large Saltillo tile of the entryway hall.

Sizeable clear acrylic frames housed beautifully painted landscapes behind glass. They were impressive. I did a quick look around; nine of them total, four on the interior wall and five on the longer outer wall on the same side as the door. They were colorful and playful. Quick gesture sketches of gray farm scenes, then in a frenzy, the artist had applied the colors of the golden fields: blue and purple skies, red poppies, and green trees. I wondered if the artist had ever even picked up the brush. Jimmy Delaney, the signature at the bottom, was barely legible. Small thin lines were going in different directions, accurately depicting the bundled hay's beauty and controlled chaos in the fields.

I looked at my watch. How long would he be gone? And would it be weird if I had only moved a few feet in his absence? I smiled to myself. He wouldn't care as long as I was happy.

Reluctantly leaving the hallway, I opened the door at the end to find a complete home gym in the garage. It smelled like new rubber and salty metal. There were two different racks on the left—colorful round weights on the bars and benches underneath. A sticker was visible on the main support bar. I walked over to it; "I Love Porn," I read aloud. The word seemed oddly familiar, yet I couldn't place where I had heard it before. Austin, Texas: It could be many things; however, being the live music capital of the world, Austin had ample venues and musicians. Clearly a band. Probably indie. An easy guess, I smiled to myself. The rack on the far side had various pulleys and attachments. On the right, a setup to house free weights; starting at twenty-five pounds and ranging to ninety-five, all were in perfect order near a stationary assault bike and rower.

A large industrial fan was in the far right-hand corner of the room near the door. I was immediately curious. Skipping over to it, I turned it on. A droning buzz that grew louder like a jet propeller filled the room. I squealed in delight, finding the highest setting and running in front of the fan. My hair tossed behind me, rippling out like a flag waving on a windy lake. I opened my fingers and ran around the open space of the room, darting right and left, letting the air push and pull me. I ran around for several minutes, singing into the fan, eyes closed, and allowing it to push me backward. As it forced me back, I twirled around and around myself, my hair wrapping around me. Eager to find out more, I turned off the fan and, clearing my ears like I had been underwater, closed the door to the gym.

Lolli met me in the hallway, and we walked together back towards the open kitchen and the massive living room. The flooring was off-white and modern, like a resin. I hadn't noticed it earlier. It reminded me of garages in expensive dealerships. It was so clean. I took off my shoes immediately after seeing it and set them by the umbrella stand near the front door, and ran back to the living room, sampling every chair for a few seconds, skidding around on my socks like a bee investigating fields of wildflowers. There were at least twelve chairs in this great room, all expensive-looking and well made. I liked the black and gray loungers near the fireplace best. But the olive ones with white pillows near the wall were perfect for lounging on. I was starting to get excited about my forced vacation here this week.

Skidding into the kitchen and finding an oven mitt, I gingerly turned the potatoes in the oven. Then going to the freezer, I closed my eyes. Tons of steak or a severed head? Why would I even think this? I wouldn't. I mean, I didn't. Clearly, I didn't think something bad would be there. I opened it—fifty frozen steaks vacuum sealed by Sheridan waited to be thawed. I knew it. I closed it and moved past the kitchen to where Matt had disappeared with my bags. I skated along, Lolliboo at my side.

The hallway had more paintings. These were smaller and black and white only. They had similar dashes and lines to form an abstract mountain on the first, an old-fashioned phone on another, and a 1950s style chair on the final composition. I looked at the name, the signature was illegible, but it was a different artist. He had a real stylized aesthetic with art, I concluded. It made me happy to think that he loved art like me, independent of my dreams.

Coming to the end of the hall, I opened the door, and I turned on the light to the most beautiful bedroom I had ever seen. It was large, with a modern fireplace at the left of a low California king bed. The plush bedspread was a gray silk comforter with large geometric gray euro sham pillows. Resting up against these large square ones were hunter-green velvet bolster pillows. A giant potted agave plant was in the far corner by a chair. It had several large green pointy arms facing the ceiling like an octopus in prayer. I smiled at it and, walking over, saw that it had been recently watered. A tiny shiny copper watering pot sat by the windowsill, next to a small white orchid with a crack in the pot. Someone had carefully glued the pieces together. "He fixes pretty little things," I whispered to the flower, amazed. Filled bookshelves fanned the sitting area on either side of the fireplace. I paused a moment, head tilted sideways, reading the titles, my finger running over the stacks of spines as I moved. He was exceptionally well-read. A door leading to a beautiful balcony with twinkling lights of the city at dusk was just beyond this.

Looking around the room, I thought about what he had said to me and the honesty behind it. I thought about my intention—to simply know more about him. It was okay; he said I could. I went to the dresser on the far side of the bed and, hesitating slightly, suddenly thrust open the middle drawer. Folded T-shirts. I closed it and opened the top one on the other side: folded boxer shorts and briefs. I closed it quickly. I didn't need to open anything else to know it was folded and in order.

Finding the bathroom just off to the side, I slid open a hanging barn door to reveal the largest shower I had ever seen. "What?" I stammered out loud, amazed at its size and beauty. An entire family could shower here or perhaps two cows, five dogs, and a groomer; ridiculous improbable and inappropriate situations filled my head, and I quickly worked to dismiss them. The shower was merely big, and that would be enough assessing, I lectured myself. Two large shower heads were hanging from the ceiling and more spouts from a silver bar on the wall. The green subway tile was beautiful. It looked expensive and like it had just been grouted.

What next? Seeing the closet, I flipped on the light to note a rather large deer head mounted over a towering black wall safe like the one at Azure. He had bought them both, I guessed. Rows of neatly hanging clothes fanned the deer and safe on both sides. On the deer's antlers were a few paper wristbands from club entries and various music venues around Austin. I stepped on a metal crate that I pulled from the wall and inverted. He was tall but it was likely needed to reach the top shelf filled with black boxes. At this new height, I was able to read one of the white bands, "The Arc Angels at the Backyard." A great band and at a cool venue. Hmmm. None of them looked too recent, but it was still nice to see that he enjoyed things. Oh, Matt. You have fun sometimes. Good. I only ever see you working.

I reached to turn off the light and, feeling a hand on mine, screamed as everything went black. The hand pulled me into the dark closet and shut the door, creating instant pitch black. I wobbled slightly on the crate but was instantly balanced by hands shooting out to find my waist, and then they were gone. Alone but inches apart in the pitch, I reached out in front of me blindly, my heart beating fast to feel the adamantine bare chest of Superman.

It was smooth and broad, hard as stone, and wet with sweat. My fingertips slid down his large pectoral muscles that soon gave way to the smaller deep waves' sculpted density. The extensive grooves of his transverse abdominis spanning his core seemed almost like platelets, like armor. I picked up my hand, finding his beating heart and feeling his accelerated breathing in his chest. He rested his hand on mine, pushing my fingertips to his skin, pulling them down slowly with me, sliding over the sweat, bump bump bump bump, and then off to the side of his obliques as our hands dropped to our sides.

Our mouths slowly, carefully found each other in the sable darkness. Barely touching our lips, labored breathing became sensual kisses that gave way to something with an urgency and a blazing need that I could now recognize in my body and his. My heart was beating so fast; he must be able to feel it a few inches away. He broke away to kiss the side of my face and gently touch my hair, still breathing hard from his run. He found me again, pushing his tongue into my mouth, a huge hand on my face. The darkness intensified our kisses and touch. Suddenly, he kissed me, spun me in a quick circle, and hitting the light on his way out, and was gone before I could see him.

What just happened? I stood in the closet, facing the blue dress shirt section, and breathing hard. The six dark blue ones were separated from the ten light blue ones. I fluttered my eyes, trying to control and calm my heart rate as well as my racing mind. What just happened? He shouldn't have done that, I breathed. Oh, but he should have. I looked down at my white ankle socks on the crate. I had liked it. I took two long, slow breaths in through the nose, out through the mouth. And again: in through the nose and out through the mouth. I pulled my hair into a hairband and, turning off the light, walked out of the closet, closing it.

I left the bathroom dark, closed the doors, and turned out the lights here and in the bedroom. The house was silent, except for the faint sound of water in pipes from somewhere far away in the house. I couldn't tell where it was coming from. "Lolli," I called to her, and she was by my side in an instant. I petted her head gently as I looked into her big blue eyes.

"He's home, isn't he?" She wagged her tail. "Please tell me he's home. Because I am in love with the man from the closet,"

I teased. She looked at me wisely. "I know what you are thinking. And you are right. You are exactly right. Whatever you are thinking, I know you are right about it."

I patted her one more time, then washed my hands and took the butter out of the fridge. Finding some thyme sprigs amongst other herbs in a water vessel, I washed a few and put them on a plate. Awkwardly, balancing tongs, I took the potatoes out of the oven and placed them to cool on plates.

"Well, well, well. Look at you, finding your way around." Matt had showered in an unexplored back bathroom and was drying his hair with a towel. He was dressed in clean cotton lounge pants and a black T-shirt.

"Hi. How was your run?"

"Wonderful. I needed that so badly."

"The run. Oh, I know what you mean. Today I—"

"Not the run." He walked past me to the fridge, a sly smile on his face, eyes on mine. I looked down.

"Oh, I'm glad that was you. Because that guy was so..." I feigned some sense of relief. He stopped mid-step, eyes on me, evaluating if I was joking or not, waiting for what I would say next. He remained silent, waiting on me. "That guy was so hot. Cuter than you. By this much," I made a little pinch with my fingers and bolted from the kitchen.

He ran after me, grabbing me by the waist and spinning me around, and then gently tackled me to the plush rug grounding the main sitting area by the fireplace. "You tell the worst jokes, Little. Honestly, I like it, though. I like punishing you." His fingers dug into my rib cage, counting my ribs. "One." His fingers made slow circles in between them. "Two." He moved upwards on my sides. "Three." I could barely speak. It was too much.

"Okay, okay," I managed, short rapid taps on his arm.

"Did you just tap out?" He looked impressed.

"Yes. My cousins. You have to stop if someone does that." He smiled. "You do. So, I did."

We remained lying on the floor, the coffee table behind him, comfortable lavish chairs all around us. We lay on our sides, propped up on our elbows, looking at each other. He spoke first. "Amy, there are a million beautiful places I could tell you this. I was going to drive you to Mount Bonnell some evening. And I apologize that lying on the floor now; I cannot wait another second. My self-control is gone. You continuously change me, simultaneously making me weaker and yet stronger than I have ever been. And in the vein of being the happiest I have ever been in my life, living in an ineffable relationship with you..." He scooted to me, cradling me in his arms. "Amy Katherine Emerson, I love you." His smile was causing his eyes to dance and sparkle in the soft light.

Awww, Matt, me too. I smiled, astonished at his words. My heart was beating out of my chest, moved by his honesty behind them. My blue-green eyes, suddenly deluged in water, were making him blurry like there was thick beveled glass between us. "Matthew Waylon Abernathy, I love you too."

His face looked me over rapidly, my soaked eyes to my lips and back to my eyes. I was trembling slightly, moving my left foot back and forth along the plush flooring, trying to hide it. "You do?" he mouthed to me, not daring to ask me out loud. I relaxed my agitated foot, keeping my eyes on him, unspeaking. Water spilled over from the corners of them, falling to my temples on their way to the carpet. Slowly nodding, a slight smile was upturning the corners of my mouth.

"I do. I love you."

He lowered his head down to settle into the side of my body as he pulled my arms around him. We lay silent like this on the floor for some period—time passing so comfortably and happily that I couldn't tell if it was one minute or ten.

Finally, he lifted his head, and finding my lips, kissed me sweetly.

"Amy." He didn't say more. We kissed for a long-time, hands on faces, fingertips slowly running over facial features, before he spoke again. His finger trailed from my temple to my jawbone before he lifted it, as if he had figured me out. "Ah, Amy, I have been waiting for you for so long. I can't tell you how happy I am that you feel the same."

"I feel so much love in my heart. And there are all these physical manifestations when I look at you. Something like butterflies in my stomach...little trembles in my body. You?"

"Well, as I said, I have felt this way for a long time. In the beginning it was something like searing intense heat. Just this intense energy. Like I always know where you are in the room. I don't see you. I *feel* you. And that attraction has turned to adoration and love." I smiled, relieved he felt something like me. He shook his head slightly, smiling down at me. "My heart is full and happy. I love you..." He kissed me sweetly, slowly; then suddenly, he pulled back from me, looking at his watch. "Oh, man. I need to feed you and put you to bed." I laughed at how odd and abrupt his comment was. He returned my smile. "You don't know it yet, but you are on a very strict eating and sleeping schedule—my baby for the rest of the week. We will see about the following week. Depends on how you do."

It would be fine, I thought. A few days reset, and I should be good. I was feeling amazing at this moment. Better than I had since arriving in Austin in May. The last few years, more accurately. Okay, more like my whole life. I grinned, hiding my face in my hands.

"Why are you hiding, Little?" Grinning broadly, he lifted me from the carpet, walking over a few feet, to set me on the breakfast stool in the kitchen. It was tall and very comfortable for what I had expected from a wooden stool.

"Just overwhelmed and happy." I couldn't hide my dopy smile. "I like this stool." I tried changing the subject. He smiled over his shoulder.

"Would you like a glass of champagne? Or should we be responsible? You are my seventeen-year-old slumber party guest..." His voice trailed off. "I feel a little predatory." He turned to me for my thoughts on this.

I just shook my head and smiled at him.

"No, right. We are in love. Right, honey? We love each other, and this is the anniversary of our first date from our pancake date night."

"We are moving so fast."

"We are. But not nearly fast enough, as well." He smiled and I grinned, looking down. It felt right to me too. "Do you have to pee?" I frowned at the resin floor. "Go pee, please, and if it is clear, you can have a little glass. You were so dehydrated earlier, but I think we corrected that." He winked at me.

"Okay, Matt." As I was leaving to the back bedroom, he spoke. "Have you had it before? Do you like something drier or sweeter?" I shook my head in unknown indecision. "Oh, that's right." He winked at me. "Probably sweeter. Maybe Prosecco. Maybe this one." He picked up a black bottle with words written in Italian. "No. But this...this is a very good bottle." He was talking to himself now. The second cabinet was so high he used a step ladder to reach in and grab it.

Watching him a moment, I turned and disappeared into the restroom. Afterward, I found my bag on the bedroom floor and discovered my brush and makeup bag. Feeling refreshed, I returned to the kitchen, my tangled hair now straight and shining.

The smell of steaks hitting the hot butter filled the room. Lolliboo lay on the edge of the living room as if she hadn't noticed the savory aroma.

"Are we good? What color was it?" I shook my head at him. "You won't tell me the color of your pee?" He smiled at me. "You are so shy. I am around such vulgar girls downtown sometimes; I forgot how attractive it is for someone to be feminine in this way. But this is a health question. We did have a lot of vitamins in the smoothie." He began again. "Okay, so is it less yellow than your favorite color?" I grinned, my eyes shifting to the cabinetry, then nodded, and he handed me my glass.

"Thank you."

"You look beautiful. What did you do?"

"Just grooming," I brushed off his compliment. Still grinning, I climbed up on the high stool, and leaning over the counter, we raised our glasses

"To falling in love. The intimacy we have now is more than I have ever had in my entire life. And I am sure I am speaking for both of us here." I nodded and he continued, "I am so grateful for you...that we met." He smiled, his glass dropping slightly. Clearly remembering something endearing, he raised it to meet mine again. "To devotion, the beauty and challenge of creating us over a lifetime, to the fun and magic awaiting us moving forward." He winked at me. "I love you," he reminded as our glasses touched. "And tomorrow I am going to begin my reverent attempt to show you precisely what that means."

Acknowledgments

To my wonderful family: all of whom created a beautiful
chaos so brilliantly exciting and overwhelming that without
you, I truly would've published this book a year earlier.
So thank you for being THAT kind of fun!

A special note for my wonderful husband —
I married so well and I love you endlessly.

To my best friend Ina, whose supportive, beautiful soul
helped push me forward from being a mom into a writer.
Thank you for that inspiration. I love you.

And to "Superman" — fly high darling.

About Atmosphere Press

Atmosphere Press is an independent, full-service publisher for excellent books in all genres and for all audiences. Learn more about what we do at atmospherepress.com.

We encourage you to check out some of Atmosphere's latest releases, which are available at Amazon.com and via order from your local bookstore:

Twisted Silver Spoons, a novel by Karen M. Wicks

Queen of Crows, a novel by S.L. Wilton

The Summer Festival is Murder, a novel by Jill M. Lyon

The Past We Step Into, stories by Richard Scharine

Swimming with the Angels, a novel by Colin Kersey

Island of Dead Gods, a novel by Verena Mahlow

Cloakers, a novel by Alexandra Lapointe

Twins Daze, a novel by Jerry Petersen

Embargo on Hope, a novel by Justin Doyle

Abaddon Illusion, a novel by Lindsey Bakken

Blackland: A Utopian Novel, by Richard A. Jones

The Jesus Nut, a novel by John Prather

The Embers of Tradition, a novel by Chukwudum Okeke

Saints and Martyrs: A Novel, by Aaron Roe

When I Am Ashes, a novel by Amber Rose

The Recoleta Stories, by Bryon Esmond Butler

About the Author

Amy Katherine is an accomplished artist and writer, who has spent the last seven years living in Europe. A fine arts graduate from Austin, Texas, she has been privileged to use her degree to both produce and teach art. She is mother to two amazing and rowdy children that sound like ten children when they are parkouring through the living room. Her latest aspiration is to take an afternoon nap, but the dogs keep barking and those kids keep running and she doesn't want to miss any of it.